EVERY STAR IN THE SKY

Also by Danielle Singleton:

Safe & Sound
Do No Harm (Joseph #1)
The Enemy Within (Joseph #2)
The Containment Zone
Price of Life
Secrets of the Deep

Connect with the author online:

www.daniellesingleton.com
@auntdanwrites
www.facebook.com/singletondanielle

Every Star in the Sky

Danielle Singleton

This book is a work of fiction and any resemblance to persons, living or dead, or places, events, or locales is purely coincidental. The characters are productions of the author's imagination and used fictitiously.

ISBN: 9781005168797

Original cover image by Grigorkevich Ekaterina. Used under license via Shutterstock.

*****

To Will:
For Making Me Believe In Fairy Tales

"There is only one happiness in this life: to love and
be loved."
~George Sand

ACKNOWLEDGMENTS

This book was a long time in the making – so much so that I almost feel like a different author than the one who wrote my previous six books. I've gone through a couple different "day jobs", gotten married, moved homes, and had a baby. Oh yeah, and lived through a global pandemic. But the constant Rock of Jesus remains, and He deserves all glory and praise.

A huge thank you also to my wonderful husband, Will, for always believing in me and encouraging me to keep writing. To Allie, my baby girl, for your smiles and laughter and motivation to build a better world for you.

Thank you to my family and friends, both old and new, for your support and companionship. To my Reading Committee, for helping turn my jumbled thoughts into a coherent novel. And to my fans who supported me during my writing hiatus and hopefully return to read and enjoy this book. A special thanks as well to Benjamin J.S. North, via Severin Wiggenhorn, for the "sometimes I wonder" quote in Chapter 81.

To Caymus, my "second born" – thank you for showing me what it is to embrace every day and love out loud. And, as always, to Gus – my baby. My ride-or-die O.G. and still the best book editor around. Gracias, mijo.

I hope y'all enjoy the story.

Every Star in the Sky

*****

"Once in a while, right in the
middle of an ordinary life, love
gives us a fairy tale."

Anonymous

ONE

London, England
2019

All of London was abuzz with excitement and intrigue. The UK hadn't seen a scandal like this since, well, since maybe never.

"I heard he's going to resign," declared Phil Davies, the eager young reporter who broke the story now dominating headlines. He was standing in the security line outside 10 Downing Street, waiting to gain entry for the beleaguered prime minister's press conference.

"Resignation is the least of his concerns," his boss replied. "Rumor has it, he's facing jail time."

"Seriously?"

The older man nodded. "Misappropriation of funds is stealing. Lying under oath is perjury. I'm shocked that the Queen hasn't fired him yet."

"I can't wait to hear what kind of bollocks story he's come up with to justify it all."

****

Three stories up, inside the rowhouse that served as his office and residence, Prime Minister Richard Arrington sat at his large mahogany desk and stared at the white notecards in front of him. Five little pieces of paper with bullet points in his scribbled handwriting – red ink for points of emphasis; blue ink for moments of emotion; green lines for a pause in speech. *The same writing system I've used since I was a student*, he thought, *when all this trouble started.* He shuffled the notecards in his hands. *Five pieces of paper to save my career.*

None of his speechwriters had seen the material. Only his chief of staff and his longtime assistant, who had been

1

Richard's two confidants the past several months, had any inkling of what he was going to say.

The fifty-six-year-old closed his eyes, ran his hand through his salt and pepper hair, and rubbed the base of his neck. He couldn't remember the last time he slept, and he had lost over a stone in weight since the whole cover-up started.

I didn't mean for it to be a cover-up, he thought. Richard could hear the shouts and chants from protesters on the streets outside.

'Hey hey ho ho, Arrington has got to go.'

Richard sighed and looked down at his desk. In front of the notecards sat the source of Richard's problems. *It all began with you*, he thought, and glared for a moment before closing his eyes and smiling. Because, truth be told, Richard didn't care about the protestors. Or the newspaper headlines. Or the possibility of having to resign from the job he worked his whole life to obtain.

Richard didn't care about any of that. Richard Arrington only cared about Rebecca.

TWO

"They're ready for you, sir," said Tricia Howell, Richard's longtime assistant. Tricia was semi-retired and usually worked part-time for a few hours in the afternoons, but she had been at 10 Downing Street around-the-clock since *The Times* story broke.

"Did you gather everything together?" Richard asked.

"Yes sir. It's all right here," Tricia replied, holding up a brown leather briefcase.

The prime minister nodded his head. "Good." *The proof,* he thought. *Proof that it wasn't all a lie.*

In the lead-up to today's speech, Richard got Tricia to gather every record, receipt, ticket, and document in existence to show that no public funds were used for 'Operation Starlight'.

Sympathy will only get me so far before my enemies bring out the guillotine, he thought. *I did my job and I did it well, with no misuse of funds and no abuse of power. They can't remove me from office on account of also having a life.*

"It's all ready to go," Tricia confirmed. "Oh, and this letter arrived for you from Buckingham Palace."

Richard nodded. "I'll be right there."

Tricia stepped out of his office but left the door open, knowing that her boss would continue to hide from the reporters if given the chance. The prime minister couldn't help but smile at the maneuver. *She knows me too well.* Tricia first started working for Richard when he was a twenty-three-year-old analyst, fresh out of business school. The firm assigned her to his desk because she was older, married, and wouldn't fall for the handsome young man like the other secretaries would.

Little did they know, Richard thought, *I wasn't available then anyway*. He looked down at his desk and the source of his troubles: a small, black velvet box with a ruby and diamond engagement ring inside. It was his grandmother's

3

ring – his feisty, passionate, Spanish grandmother who helped raise him before he was sent off to boarding school.

"La Felicidad," his abuela loved to say, "es sostener a alguien en tus brazos y saber que sostienes el mundo entero."

Happiness, Richard thought, *is holding someone in your arms and knowing you hold the whole world.*

"Sir?"

Tricia's voice broke through Richard's memories.

"It's time, sir."

Richard nodded and sighed. He stood up from his desk and lifted his suit jacket off the back of his chair, swinging it around his shoulders and sliding his arms through the same way he'd done since he was a boy. After buttoning the top button, the prime minister reached down and picked up the box holding his grandmother's ring. He snapped it shut and put the box in his pants pocket.

"You're right," he told his assistant. "It is time."

As he walked down the stairs toward the front door, Richard's thoughts wandered to the first time he visited the hallowed halls of Number 10 Downing Street. A few months after graduation, his firm was hired by Prime Minister Thatcher's office to provide financial guidance on her economic reforms. Richard was brought along to the meetings to help ease the minds of the old-school Whitehall advisors. *After all*, Richard remembered with a laugh, *our ideas couldn't be too dangerous if the son of a peer was proposing them, right?*

Richard couldn't recall much about his company's recommendations, but he did remember meeting Margaret Thatcher. And the question she asked him.

"Well well, my boy. You're a handsome one. Have you got a special lady in your life?"

Barely three months removed from his business school graduation, Richard's heart had plummeted to the floor. "No ma'am, there's no one."

****

Outside of Number 10, the national and international press corps were assembled in the stone-paved street, not-so-patiently waiting for the current prime minister to appear and respond to allegations that he misappropriated government funds, lied to Parliament, derelicted his duties, and deceived Queen and Country.

Richard walked through the front door of his home and office and into the daylight. He blinked as hundreds of cameras flashed in his eyes. Stepping forward to the edge of the stoop, Richard raised his hand to silence the crowd. He took a deep breath and removed the notecards from his jacket pocket. Richard squeezed the ring box in his pocket one more time for strength and good luck, and began to speak.

"I would say thank you for coming today, but I don't suppose there's a need. You've been camped here for a week now."

Under normal circumstances, the reporters would have chuckled and the ice would've been broken for the rest of Richard's speech. But these were not normal circumstances, and this crowd was in no mood for laughter.

"I'll make a brief statement," he said, "and I will not be taking any questions. Nor will my staff." Richard paused. "I will begin with the most important information: I have neither stolen nor misappropriated any public funds. I have not lied under oath. And Her Majesty has been fully informed of the entire truth from the beginning."

Cameras clicked and clacked, and murmurs rose through the group of reporters.

"So it's all a lie?" someone shouted. "The whole story is bollocks?"

Richard opened his mouth to respond, then stopped. He let out a deep breath and ran his hand through his hair.

"*The Times'* story accused me of many things. Lying. Stealing. Cover-ups. Those things," he conceded, "are all true."

The crowd rumbled again. "C'mon, mate. Give us the truth!"

"The truth?" Richard asked. "All right. Well, settle in. Because the truth is thirty-five years in the making."

THREE

Boston, Massachusetts
1984

The first day of class at Harvard is similar to the first day at any school. Nerves, excitement, curiosity, dread. Nerves about the unexpected; excitement about a new beginning; curiosity about classmates, professors, and campus life; and dread over the coming onslaught of work.

But the first day of class at Harvard also has something else. A feeling that was flooding through Rebecca Lewis' veins as she entered Room 102 and looked around. Seven rows of tiered desks formed a semi-circle, all facing a chest-high brown lectern and a chalk board that covered one entire wall of the room. In the back corner of 102, Rebecca saw what she was looking for: a large poster board displaying the seating chart.

Elbowing her way through the crowd of men, the slender, twenty-two-year-old with short, jet black hair couldn't help but ask herself: *do I really belong here?*

For amidst her nerves, excitement, curiosity, and dread, there was also an acute sense that she was at Harvard, The Harvard, and that the classmates jostling for position around the seating chart would one day be jostling for leadership positions in corporate boardrooms, hedge funds, and world governments. She would have all her classes with this same group for the first year, so making a good impression today was even more important.

There had to be some kind of mix-up at the Admissions Office, Rebecca thought as she found her desk and sat down. The shoulder pads in her starched gray suit jacket smushed up around her neck, and she stood to unbutton the jacket before sitting down again in her chair. Number 52 – third row from the front, stage right. *These people are going to change the world. They can't seriously think that Rebecca Lewis from Sandersville, Georgia can too.*

A tall, handsome man with a head full of brown hair and wearing the requisite male business school attire – slacks, light blue oxford shirt, navy blue blazer – sat down at the desk to Rebecca's left and only served to confirm her thoughts. *Now he looks the part*, she mused as the young man placed a notepad and several pens on the desk in front of him. The pens were different colors, Rebecca noticed, and she wondered if he had some sort of color-coded note-taking system.

"Good morning, I'm Richard," said the pen man, turning in his chair and extending his right hand in greeting. The gesture – and the British accent accompanying it – caught Rebecca off-guard.

"Oh, umm, hi," she replied, fumbling with a notebook in her briefcase before turning to shake hands with her new classmate.

"And you are?" Richard asked, amused by her frazzled state.

"Huh? Oh, I'm Rebecca," she answered before returning her attention to the contents of her briefcase. Soon her desk was organized with a notepad, two pencils, a pencil sharpener, an extra eraser, and a watch that she slid off her wrist and placed in the corner where she could see it.

Feeling someone's eyes on her, Rebecca turned and saw her classmate leaning back in his chair with his arms crossed and a smile on his face.

"What?"

"Nothing, nothing," he replied, "you're just very . . . organized."

"You're one to talk, Mr. Color-Coded Pens."

He laughed. "Touché, mon amie."

"What?"

"I conceded the point to you. It means 'well played, my friend.' It's French."

Rebecca didn't share the amusement. "Yeah, well, this is America. We speak English. I'd think you should know that language pretty well."

Again Richard smiled, and this time Rebecca noticed the sparkle that lit his blue-gray eyes.

Stop it, Becky, she told herself.

Determined to prove her father wrong and not be sidetracked by romance, Rebecca refused to return the – *admittedly gorgeous* – man's smile.

"Look, Robert – "

"Richard."

"I'm Rebecca."

"So you said. And I'm Richard, not Robert."

"Oh, well, look Richard – "

A door slammed open at the side of the classroom and Rebecca was interrupted by the entrance of their professor. Short and chubby, the man had patchy bald hair and a wardrobe that looked like it belonged at Berkeley's undergrad, not Harvard's business school.

Rebecca felt a knot in her stomach and adjusted her school supplies one more time to prepare. *Here we go*, she thought.

FOUR

While his classmate turned her attention to the professor, Richard Arrington continued to watch the black-haired beauty sitting beside him. He knew that the teacher's monologue was important – making the most of opportunities and to whom much is given blah blah blah – but The Right Honourable The Viscount Arrington, heir to the Marquess of Dublinshire, had been hearing that same first day speech for the last eight years. First at Eton College, where he lived and learned for five years amongst other sons of privilege. Then at the world-famous Cambridge University for three years where he majored in finance, football, and girls.

Harvard Business School was an "appropriate albeit unconventional" next step for the future Marquess – Richard shook his head remembering his father's words when he told the House of Lords member that he planned to attend graduate school in the United States. "I won't stop you from going," his father said, "but I would much prefer you apprentice here in England. You can learn the markets and how to manage the estate just as well, if not better, from London than from Boston."

Richard had nodded his head, his shaggy hair flopping enough to irritate his dad, and then packed up his belongings for two years in America. His father was right about markets and estate management, but he was wrong about what his son wanted to do with his life. Gentlemanly leisure and the House of Lords were not in Richard's plans. He wanted more.

When the class bell rang an hour later, Richard gathered up his notepad and pens and looked around for Rebecca. The pretty young woman with the serious face and beautiful blue eyes was already gone, having bolted as soon as the class ended. Richard shrugged his shoulders. *At least I know I'll see her again soon*, he thought. *We have every class together*.

The twenty-one-year-old walked out of Aldrich Hall, where most first-year classes were taught, and headed toward the student center, called Spangler, to grab a cup of tea. He had about thirty minutes before his next class and needed a boost of caffeine to get through the day.

Richard Arrington was pleasantly surprised by the warm weather in Boston, having expected New England to be more like, well, England. He knew the cold weather was coming, but in early September he took off his blazer and rolled up his shirt sleeves to enjoy the sunshine. The leaves and grass were still green on the business school's campus in the Allston neighborhood of Boston. Red brick Georgian Revival buildings encircled a large grassy quad full of students studying and playing frisbee. The tree-lined path where Richard was walking connected the various buildings – thirty in all – where he would spend the next two years. Behind the quad, Richard knew, was the Charles River. And across from that stood the main campus where the undergraduates lived and learned.

When Richard arrived in the student center, he found he wasn't the only person needing a pick-me-up between classes. It seemed as if the entire student body was in Spangler. Richard weaved through the crowd to the small drink station near the food court.

"Coffee, coffee, decaf coffee, iced tea . . . where's the hot tea?" he asked aloud.

A familiar Southern accent spoke out behind him. "This is America, remember?"

Arrington turned to see Rebecca, his classmate, standing with her arms folded and a smirk on her face.

"We don't drink hot tea," she concluded.

A frustrated Richard worked to suppress his feelings and keep his cool in front of the pretty girl. "Hi Rebecca. I guess I need to learn to drink coffee, don't I?" He filled a cup, winked at her, and walked toward the checkout line.

"See ya soon, Becks," he called out over his shoulder.

FIVE

Rebecca looked for Richard at the beginning of their next class, but he was seated halfway across the room. This professor, unlike their last, had put everyone in alphabetical order. After taking her seat and arranging her class materials – notepad, two pencils, pencil sharpener, extra eraser, and her watch – Rebecca glanced over at Richard and saw that he also repeated his routine from their first class, with a notepad and color-coded pens. She smiled but turned away when he looked at her. Rebecca's stomach did a somersault and unleashed a flood of butterflies that urged her to look Richard's way once again.

Miss Lewis focused instead on the papers on her desk, refusing to turn her head to the left at all for the rest of the class. Even when someone else was talking on that side of the room, she still looked straight ahead. *Don't encourage him, Becky,* she kept telling herself. *Don't prove Daddy right on the first day of class.*

Her father, a doctor in her small hometown of Sandersville, Georgia, was a proud and stubborn man. A man who believed that a woman's place was in the home. Despite his beliefs, which were shared by many in rural Georgia at the time, Dr. Jefferson Lewis paid for all five of his children to go to college, including his one daughter. Rebecca's brothers all attended the University of Georgia like their dad, but Rebecca longed for an escape. For city lights and being more than a wife and a mother. So, she headed off to Barnard College in New York City, still separate from Columbia at the time but offering a world-class education nonetheless.

"You'll never find a husband at an all-girls college," her father had declared on the day she packed her bags to leave. Four years later, when it was time to drive up to Boston, Dr. Lewis gave her the same speech again.

"I told you, darlin', that you wouldn't find a husband at an all-girls college. Maybe you'll find one at Harvard and finally end all this schoolin' nonsense. Women need to be educated so they can turn around and educate their children. That's why I sent you to college . . . I don't wanna have stupid grandchildren. I didn't send you to New York for you to put on men's clothes and get a man's haircut and think you belong anywhere 'cept in the home."

Rebecca had sighed, picked up her bags off the floor, and said "I love you too, Daddy". The same response she always gave to one of his lectures. He assumed it meant she agreed with him; in reality, it was her way of getting out of the situation as fast as possible. *And I don't have a man's haircut*, she thought. *Princess Diana has this same hairstyle, and everyone thinks she looks fabulous.*

The class bell rang, and Rebecca realized that she daydreamed through the entire lecture. *Shit. We could have an assignment to do and I'd have no idea.*

A familiar British accent broke into her thoughts.

"You can borrow my class notes if you'd like," Richard offered.

"What?"

"It looked like your mind was somewhere else. I'm happy to lend you my notes to make a copy."

Despite her determination to avoid Richard and her growing attraction to him, Rebecca couldn't resist his offer. "Thank you so much," she replied. "That'd be a huge help."

"In fact," he said, "why don't we go over it all during dinner tonight? I hear there's a great hamburger spot across the river in Harvard Square."

Rebecca shook her head. "I'm sorry, I told myself I wouldn't date anyone in my section. It would be too weird after we broke up."

"We haven't even had a first date and you already jumped ahead to the breakup?"

"I don't want to do dinner, okay? I mean, I've known you all of what, three hours?"

"That's the point of a date," Richard pressed. "To get to know someone better. Besides," he added with a grin, "I've known you my whole life. We must've met in Heaven, and I've been looking for you again ever since."

Rebecca's lips started to quiver, and a sparkle entered her eyes. She snorted, and her hand flew up over her mouth to contain her laughter.

"Why is that funny? I'm serious."

Rebecca pursed her lips together and lowered her hand from her mouth. "Come on . . . it's a little funny. Or at least a little corny. You sound like a character in a romance novel."

"I thought women loved romance novels."

"Maybe some women. Not me." She shrugged her shoulders. "All I have time to read are textbooks, anyway."

Richard picked Rebecca's briefcase up off the floor and handed it to her. "Does that mean you're not looking for a guy to sweep you off your feet or rescue you from the dragon?"

Rebecca shook her head and started to walk toward the door. "If any dragons need to be slayed, I want a piece of the action. Why let the guy have all the fun?"

SIX

Rebecca had a smile on her face and an extra pep in her step as she left Aldrich Hall and walked toward her dorm. A breeze picked up off the river and Rebecca pulled her suit jacket tighter around her shoulders. The temperature that day was beautiful for Boston and warm for Richard, but even four years in New York hadn't changed Rebecca's Southern views on the weather. Partly cloudy and low 70s was chilly to her.

I'll warm up once I get moving, she thought. With no classes for several hours, Rebecca was headed to her dorm room so she could change and go for a run along the Charles River. Running was a habit she picked up during college in New York. She loved weaving through the city traffic and parks, feeling the wind whip against her face off the Hudson River. Running was how Rebecca best explored a new city, and she couldn't wait to get to know Boston.

Rebecca was breathing heavier than usual when she took off down the narrow foot path on the banks of the Charles. *This is what I get for not exercising for three months*, she thought, pushing past the burning in her lungs to travel farther into downtown Boston. *It's also what I get for listening to Mother when she said 'people don't run here, honey. It's strange, and no one wants to marry the strange girl'.*

After her college graduation, Rebecca had spent the summer at home in Georgia – three months full of afternoon teas, bridge games, and dates with every eligible bachelor in a fifty-mile radius. The problem was, the few guys she might actually be interested in were off the market: snatched up by their high school or college sweetheart. And Rebecca already had a 'weird' label attached to her, having gone up north to a 'yankee college'. Her mother thought Rebecca was doomed to be an old maid, and her father thought she needed an older, wiser man who could understand her intellectual side.

Rebecca rolled her eyes at the memory of her dad's college roommate, recently divorced, standing on her parents' doorstep to pick her up for dinner.

Having reached Boston Common, a large park that was four miles from campus, Rebecca stopped running and found an open grassy spot to rest for a minute. *They honestly thought I was going to marry someone twice my age with kids older than I am.* The date with her dad's friend was the final straw, and the last few weeks at home had been free of gentlemen suitors. *Much to Mother's chagrin,* she thought.

"I refuse to believe that all the men you went out with were terrible. Surely one or two of them had some redeeming qualities." Rebecca's mother preached at her daughter the entire time she was packing her suitcases for Harvard. "You know that all men are projects, honey. I've been training and refining your daddy for twenty-five years. It's about finding one worth the effort."

Rebecca had sighed, rolled her eyes, and continued packing.

"I saw that, young lady. Don't think you're better than your mother just because you have some fancy college education."

The older woman reached into her dress pocket, pulled out a silver case, and lit a cigarette. Her lipstick turned the end bright pink, and smoke billowed around her coiffed hair that was dyed black to cover the gray. Times were changing in the South, but Beverly Lewis hadn't gotten the memo. Born and bred in Sandersville, Beverly married her high school sweetheart, worked as a secretary while he was in medical school, and threw herself a 'retirement' party on the day Jefferson Lewis became the town's new doctor. Beverly's life looked almost identical to the one her own mother had lived, all the way down to the weekly schedule: church on Sundays, bridge on Tuesdays, hair on Fridays. She belonged to the garden club and the ladies' auxiliary, and all housework was handled by 'the girl' – an African American woman who was older than Mrs. Lewis and married with a

16

family of her own. Now that her children were grown, Beverly's sole ambition was to find a husband for her daughter. She couldn't for the life of her understand Rebecca's interest in school and business.

"I told your daddy this would happen if he let you go up north for college. You'd start thinking like they do. Forget where you come from." Beverly took a long drag from her cigarette and blew the smoke high in the air. "People who aren't from the South like to pretend they're somehow superior, but it's really all the same. At a certain level of society, it's all the same. The only thing that changes is the race of the help. In the South, they're black. In the West, they're brown. And up north, they're white. From all those Soviet countries. The Yankees are the real racists, you know."

Rebecca continued to pack and let her mother ramble, having learned long ago that interrupting would only prolong the conversation. Beverly Lewis would brook no argument with her views on race, class, and regional culture. And even though times were changing and attitudes in Sandersville weren't what they used to be, it was hardly worth her daughter's time to try to change the older woman's mind.

Some views stick around until the people who hold them die, Rebecca thought. Looking out at Boston Common and the beautiful skyscrapers framing the clouds, she smiled. Rebecca stood up, wiped the grass off her legs, and turned back toward Harvard's campus. *Thank God I escaped all of that.*

For her third and final class of the day, Rebecca was once again seated near Richard. This time, though, it didn't bother her. In fact, after the memories of her parents during her run, Rebecca was excited to be friends with her charming British classmate. *Mother might have a stroke*, she thought as she sat down one row in front of Richard. *Her only daughter is in Boston hanging out with foreigners. Oh, the horror!*

17

SEVEN

Richard noticed Rebecca's change in attitude toward him as soon as they sat down. She smiled so big that her blue eyes sparkled, and she said 'hey' with a slow drawl that made the word have two syllables instead of one. Rebecca was as focused as ever on her schoolwork, but Richard could tell he wasn't the enemy anymore. Maybe it was her first day nerves, or maybe she hadn't had enough coffee yet that morning. *Or maybe I simply am that charming*, he thought with a grin. *American girls love an English accent.*

Whatever the reason, Richard didn't waste the renewed opportunity to get to know his classmate – one of six women in their entire school. Rebecca was the prettiest of the group by far, but there was something else about her that intrigued and perplexed him. His other male classmates took turns making passes at the pretty Southerner for the first couple weeks, until word got around that she always said no. But Richard didn't buy the gossip that Rebecca was 'frigid' or a 'man-hater'. *She's jolly good fun as long as she doesn't think you're hitting on her*, he thought.

And that became Richard's approach. If Rebecca refused a date but would eat dinner with a friend, he became her friend – one always up to try a new seafood place on the wharf or Italian spot in the North End. A trip to the movies was a no, but study sessions – even late night, one-on-one – were a yes. When Rebecca mentioned that she would love to find a running partner for her excursions around Boston, Richard jumped at the chance. By the time Midterms arrived, the two were inseparable.

Richard never understood what people meant when they said they 'fell in love'. *What, did you trip?* he thought. Love was an emotion, and emotions could be controlled. He was British, after all. Stiff upper lip, cold greetings, keep calm and carry on.

No, Richard had never understood what people meant when they said they fell in love. Until he met Rebecca. And fell himself.

Although he dated his fair share of girls during university, this was the first time that Richard could remember a woman invading his thoughts like Rebecca did. She was with him when he woke up, with him as he fell asleep, and definitely with him in the classroom.

In Marketing class on the day of midterm presentations, Richard found himself desperately trying to pay attention to his classmates' speeches – to no avail. Rebecca was sitting one row in front of him, diagonal to the right. Try as he might to focus and take notes, Richard couldn't keep his eyes off her.

He watched as she bit her lip in concentration and wondered what those lips would taste like when kissed. Rebecca ran a gentle hand through her hair, pushing it back out of her eyes, and Richard wanted to know, when he touched her hair, if it would feel as silky smooth as it looked. Every time a classmate made a snide remark in a speech about women in the workplace, Rebecca fidgeted back and forth in her chair – and Richard wondered what it would be like to watch her channel all that pent-up passion into something – or someone – she loved.

Stop it, Richard. He shook his head and scolded himself for letting his thoughts wander during class. *Except they don't wander*, he admitted. *They stay on her all the time.*

"Mr. Arrington? Hello?"

Richard snapped out of his daydream to find Professor Craswell standing in front of him. Richard's cheeks turned beet red.

"Ah, there you are. We didn't know if you were going to join us."

"I'm sorry, I – "

"Nevermind that. It's your turn." The professor gestured to the empty lectern in the front of the room.

"Right," Richard replied. "Five minutes practicing the art of persuasion. Convince the class that one's assigned ice cream flavor is the best."

****

Rebecca smiled as she watched her best friend take the podium. Best friend. The thought caught her off guard. *That's what he is, though*, she realized. For the past six weeks, she and Richard had done everything together. Runs on the river. Red Sox games. Study sessions in the library or a dorm room. And seldom a day went by when the pair didn't eat at least one meal together. Rebecca spent time with other friends, especially a fun girl from San Francisco named Emily, but Richard was her person. *The first true best friend I've ever had.*

It hadn't been easy growing up as the nerdy girl with big dreams in a town that wanted her to be a wife and mother by age twenty. Teachers, classmates, and even her own family told her to 'be realistic' and 'let the boys think they're smarter than you'. College wasn't much easier, with her Barnard classmates still mostly comprised of future teachers and MRS degrees. To be an attractive, smart, straight woman wanting to work in finance was off-putting to many around Rebecca . . . and even more off-putting was the defensive personality she developed to protect her dreams.

Richard is different, though, she thought while listening to him expound on the virtues of mint chocolate chip ice cream. *He's never treated me like his inferior. Never laughed when I talk about my plans for the future.*

Richard had even absorbed her stories about family drama without ever making her feel like she was at fault. After a particularly bad phone call with her father, when the older man wouldn't stop complaining about the African American family that moved in next door, Rebecca had begged Richard to go on a long run with her through the streets of Cambridge. Her blue eyes were full of tears while they ran – her talking, him listening.

"That's what's so stupid about Daddy's racism," she had told him. "Half those rednecks are actually redskins. Creek or Cherokee or Seminole. How do you think I got my black hair and high cheekbones? My mom is one-quarter Creek." Rebecca brushed tears off her face and jogged in place at a red light. "Daddy is a hateful man. He always has been and always will be. Mother is better, but she still isn't great. Daddy will come right out and tell you to your face that you're a dumbass no good you-know-what. Mother will smile and be friendly but curse you behind your back."

Richard had taken the whole story in stride, nodding his head and supporting her without ever saying a word.

As he continued to talk about how his ice cream was the best because it didn't need any added toppings, Rebecca smiled again. Richard's eyes were glowing with excitement and he gestured his hands all over the place, looking much more like his fiery Spanish grandmother than his reserved English parents. *He really is handsome*, Rebecca thought. *And kind. And smart. He's . . .*

She stopped herself from thinking the next words. To think it was to admit it. To admit it was to want it. *You're already thinking it, though*, she told herself. *He's the kind of man I could spend forever with.*

EIGHT

That Saturday evening, after their half-term projects had ended, Richard and Rebecca made plans to join some of their other friends for dinner and drinks at the student union. It got dark early in New England, and Richard stopped by Rebecca's dorm so they could walk together to Spangler Hall. She had on high-waisted jeans, a pink sweater, and pink sneakers. Richard smiled and looked up and down her trim body. At 5'7" and a size 2, Rebecca didn't have many curves. *But damn those jeans make her ass look good*, he thought.

"Stop it," Rebecca said.

"Stop what?"

"Looking at me like that."

Richard shrugged his shoulders. "I can't help it. You look amazing. I'm so used to seeing you in a suit or running gear . . . you should dress like this more often."

She smiled and twirled in a circle. "I do look pretty good tonight, don't I?"

You always look good, he thought. "You sure do."

Rebecca laughed and linked her arm through Richard's, making his stomach do somersaults underneath his blue button-down and Barbour jacket. They looked good together, and he knew it.

Does she? he asked himself. Some days he knew he was only a friend, and some days he wasn't quite sure. But moments like this? With her arm wrapped around his and their bodies brushing against each other as they walked . . . moments like this made Richard feel like it was possible to dream of more.

When they arrived at the student union, they walked to a lounge area that had couches and TVs spread out around the room. A few other groups of people were there watching college football games, and Rebecca's friend Emily waved them over to her couch. She was sitting with another friend, Joe, and there were pizza boxes and pitchers of beer on the table in front of them. Emily also had a pile of wedding magazines in her lap.

"My sister is getting married next summer," she explained. "She has no idea what she wants, so I told her I'd cut out a bunch of ideas and mail them to her."

Emily was short and overweight with mousy brown hair, and Richard couldn't help but compare her to the stunning Rebecca seated next to her on the couch. *No wonder all the men are hitting on Becks*, he thought.

"What about something simple for the wedding?" Rebecca suggested. "Family and friends in your church back home?"

Emily shook her head. "We're not really 'church' people. Besides," she added, opening a magazine to a dog-eared page, "I'm thinking she should do a royal wedding." Emily's eyes sparkled as she turned the magazine around to show pictures of Prince Charles and Lady Diana's wedding, along with a story about their new baby, Prince Harry. "I mean, look at her outfit. Ah-mazing."

As the two girls went back and forth on flowers and dresses, Richard tuned them out and tried to watch sports on TV. He had never understood the concept behind American football – *it's so choppy with all the stopping and starting*, he thought as he watched some team in blue smash into a team in white. *Real football is so much prettier . . . so fluid and easy to understand.*

"Richard? Hello?"

Rebecca's voice cut into his thoughts.

"Huh?"

"Emily asked what you think about Prince Charles and Lady Di."

"What about them?"

"Aren't they so cute together?" Emily swooned.

"Really? You think so?" asked Rebecca. "I mean, Diana is gorgeous. But Charles is just so . . . blah."

"He's the next King of England," Emily argued. "He's automatically not blah."

Richard laughed and shook his head. "Being the next King of England makes him more likely to be 'blah' than less likely."

Emily looked at Richard with stars in her eyes. "Do you know them?"

"Charles and Diana?"

"Mmm hmm," she nodded.

"I know Charles as an acquaintance – he's a good bit older than I am. My parents know Earl Spencer, though. Diana's father. They went to the royal wedding."

"Psshh man, my mom watched that whole thing," Joe chimed in. "Woke up at like three in the morning to see it all."

"I think it might work between the two of them," Rebecca said. "Everybody talks about how they don't have any passion, but passion isn't always good. I think a love like theirs is better: something steady and durable. Especially if you're royalty."

Emily shook her head. "No way. I want all the passion," she said, wiggling her eyebrows. "But can we please talk about how your parents were at the wedding of the century? How in the world did they score those tickets?"

Richard laughed. "It wasn't a carnival. It was a wedding. And, like I said, my parents know her parents. My father is House of Lords, so he would've been invited regardless."

Rebecca turned to look at her friend. In all their time spent together over the past several weeks, all the lunches and dinners and studying and runs by the river, Richard had never mentioned anything about having an important family.

"Your dad is in Parliament?"

The pain in Rebecca's voice was impossible to miss. She had told Richard things that she didn't tell anyone – about her struggles to fit in at home and at school, about her father's racist beliefs, about her hopes and dreams for her future. *But he wouldn't even tell me that his dad is in politics?*

Richard tried to convey an apology with his eyes. "House of Lords. He's the Marquess of Dublinshire."

24

"Oh my God," Emily shrieked, "you're royalty!"

"Not royalty. Nobility. It's different."

"So how many people have to die before you become King?" said Joe.

"That's an awful thing to ask," Rebecca replied.

Richard shook his head. "People run the numbers all the time. It's some sort of sick game to them. And I'm not sure. Way too far down the list for it to ever matter."

"But one day you'll be a Lord?" Emily pressed.

"I'm already a Lord." Richard was trying to be nice and answer her questions, but this wasn't how he had envisioned spending his Saturday night. He wanted to grab some food, get himself and Rebecca a bit tipsy, and maybe try for their first kiss. *But now she's mad at me and Emily won't shut up.*

Emily continued to be oblivious to the emotions flying back and forth between her two friends. "How are you a Lord?"

Richard sighed. "I have a courtesy title since I'm my father's heir. I'm Viscount Arrington, or Lord Arrington when using it in conversation. My sister, as the daughter of a marquess, is Lady Sarah Arrington. My parents are The Most Honourable The Marquess and Marchioness of Dublinshire, or Lord and Lady Dublinshire." He shrugged his shoulders. "It's really not that important, absent my father's seat in the House of Lords. The rest of it is just for show."

"It all seems weird to me," Rebecca said, still simmering over his lack of candor.

"Weird because Americans don't have titles?" Richard asked.

"We have titles," she countered. "We just think people should have to earn them." Rebecca stood up and put on her jacket. "I'm tired. Midterms took it out of me. I'm going to turn in."

"Can I walk you back?" Richard asked. "It's dark outside."

"I'm fine by myself."

Richard watched as Rebecca walked out of the lounge and toward the exit doors. "Great job, wanker," he told himself under his breath. "She hates you now."

"She doesn't hate you."

Richard jumped in surprise, having forgotten that Joe was still beside him.

"It's going to take a lot more than a few study sessions and runs on the river to get her to fall for you, though."

"I . . . I don't know what you're talking about."

"Yes, you do. Everyone can see it. You're the only one stubborn enough to not admit you're crazy about her."

"Is it really that obvious?"

Joe nodded. "To everyone but her."

NINE

Sunday came and went without Richard seeing Rebecca at all. His stomach was in a knot by the time their first class started on Monday morning, and she refused to acknowledge him, even though they were sitting right next to each other. *She's even more upset with me than I thought.*

Rebecca was still ignoring him that afternoon in Professor Craswell's marketing class, and Richard could tell that she was angry. *Like she's itching for a fight,* he thought. *All because I was too chicken shit to open up and tell her about my family.* Richard's heart sank and he began drawing slow, lazy circles in his notebook.

Half the class had gone by when the person next to him started pounding on his desk. Richard looked up to discover a fierce debate raging in the classroom. Not surprisingly, Rebecca was in the center of it.

"Why don't you go ahead and drop out?" asked a young man named Andrew. With curly red hair and freckles, the students called him Sniffles behind his back – a product of his cocaine habit.

"Everyone knows that as soon as your boyfriend back home proposes or you trap one of the guys here into getting you pregnant, you'll leave." Andrew leaned back in his chair and crossed his arms over his chest. "You'll get your MRS and be gone. That's the only degree you care about."

Several men pounded on their desks in support, while others jumped out of their seats to challenge Andrew's comments. Richard, for his part, stayed silent and kept his eyes on Rebecca. She didn't move. Didn't flinch. He didn't even think he saw her blink.

When Professor Craswell finally restored order to the classroom, he turned toward Rebecca. The look on her face silenced the instructor, too.

"Are you finished?" Rebecca asked the other student.

He smiled. "Yeah, I'm finished."

27

"What was your name again?" Rebecca asked, even though she knew full well what it was.

"Andrew. Andrew Philip Walters III. Why?"

"I want to make sure I get the name right on the tickets."

"What tickets?"

"Your ugly ass is going to have a front row seat for my swearing in as Chairwoman of the Federal Reserve."

Richard pounded his desk in approval and was soon joined by a chorus of other fists, all proclaiming their support for their female classmate. He had never really understood the point of the Harvard tradition – pound desks for approval, hiss for disapproval – but in that moment he loved it. And he could tell that Rebecca loved it too. Despite her best efforts to maintain her cold and icy glare, Richard saw a small smile creep onto her face.

"Alright, alright," the professor said, "I think we've had enough politics for one day. Let's get back to business, shall we?"

TEN

Later that afternoon, when classes were over for the day, Richard went looking for Rebecca. He had to mend fences; he couldn't stand seeing her mad at him or picking fights with other people because of him.

"It's not like I didn't tell her about my dad on purpose," he muttered to himself as he scoured the dorms and Spangler student union to find Rebecca. "It just didn't come up. I don't talk to him. I don't talk about him." Richard swung open the doors to the library. "She's got to be in here somewhere."

Five minutes later, he spotted Rebecca in a small, quiet corner in the basement of Baker Library. An all-brick edifice with white Georgian Revival columns and a white bell tower, Baker was the centerpiece of campus and loomed over the grassy quad. It was also one of Rebecca's favorite study spots.

Richard took a deep breath before approaching her. He hadn't been this nervous to talk to Rebecca since the first day of classes.

"Hello."

She looked up and nodded her head in acknowledgment. "Hey."

"What are you doing?" he asked, stepping closer and smiling as a peace offering.

"What does it look like? I'm studying."

Despite the hurt she still felt from Richard not telling her about his family, she found it impossible to stay mad at him. *Especially when he smiles at me like that.*

"I can see that you're studying. I meant, why are you studying here?" Richard asked, looking around the dimly lit room with rows upon rows of library stacks.

Rebecca shrugged. "I like it. It's quiet."

"It's spooky."

"Only at night, scaredy-cat," Rebecca grinned.

"Well, regardless, you're coming with me." Richard closed her textbook and started gathering up Rebecca's things.

"What are you doing? I have to study."

"No, you don't."

"Yes, I do," Rebecca said, grabbing her textbooks from his arms. "Craswell hates me. I have to be 100% prepared for every single class."

Richard shook his head and took her books and pens and put them in her briefcase. Then he grabbed her hand. "I know a better way."

At the other end of Baker, in the section that housed professors' offices, Richard loosened his grasp on Rebecca's hand and knocked on a large, wooden door.

"Enter."

"Hello, Professor Craswell?" Richard said, cracking the door open and leaning his head around. "It's Richard Arrington. I spoke with you this morning about Caymus?"

"Ah, yes. Come in, come in."

Richard stepped inside the professor's office, followed by Rebecca. Craswell looked up at them and lowered his glasses. "I know you. The girl in my marketing class."

"Yes sir. Rebecca Lewis."

"Right. Well, Caymus is here," he said, motioning beneath his desk. "Everything you need is on that shelf by the door."

****

Before Rebecca knew it, she and Richard were walking a beautiful, giant Golden Retriever along the banks of the Charles. He was tall, thin, and had a red hue to his coloring – more like an Irish Setter than most Golden Retrievers.

"There's more than one way to curry favor and get ahead," Richard said in explanation. "Craswell will never think your answers are good enough . . . especially as a woman. But," he added, "this dog is his pride and joy. Brings

30

him to campus every day. I saw them together this morning and offered to help with walking him." Richard flashed his trademark grin. "I get all the goodwill without any of the extra studying. And now, you do too."

They walked together in silence for a few minutes before Rebecca stopped and turned to face Richard.

"Why didn't you tell me about your family? I know it shouldn't matter and I know I should let it go, but why?"

Richard also stopped walking, and he let out a deep sigh.

"It wasn't intentional, Becks. I swear. I never meant to hurt you. The last thing I ever want to do is hurt you. I just . . . I don't bring it up. Back in England, everyone treats you differently if you have a title. Besides, I don't talk to my family. We don't have a good relationship. It's hard to when I was sent away to boarding school at eight years old."

"Eight?"

Richard nodded. "It's a different way of doing things. A different world, really. After the first day of class when you told me 'this is America, speak English', I didn't want you to think less of me because of my family."

"How could I think less of you – especially after all the things I've told you about my parents?"

"I don't know. I'm sorry. I should've said something." He stepped forward and put his hands on Rebecca's shoulders, looking down into her eyes. "I've told you everything about me that matters, I promise. You know me better than anyone else in the world."

Rebecca looked up and returned his gaze. A long moment passed and he breathed in slowly, not wanting to blink and break their connection. As Richard started to lean down toward her, a flock of geese flew by and Caymus took off running after them. Richard's arm nearly popped out of its socket as he chased the dog down the river embankment.

"Caymus! Stop it! Get up here!" Richard pulled hard on the leash and got the Golden Retriever back up on the jogging path. "Good grief," Richard huffed. "I thought he was going to pull me into the water."

Rebecca shook her head in disbelief. "No kidding! I'm glad you were holding him. He probably would've drug me in with him."

"Let's go back," Richard suggested. "I think we've had enough walking for today. I know I have."

ELEVEN

The rest of fall semester passed by in a blur and, before the students knew it, finals week had arrived. There were no exams in business school, but they had group presentations to do in each class. For Craswell's Marketing, the final day held a debate on the merits of cold calling as a sales strategy. Richard and Rebecca were assigned to different teams, but fortunately they didn't have to compete against each other. *I'm crazy about her*, Richard thought, *but I'm on track for an A in this class. Plus, she'd hate me if I let her win.* He sat back in his chair and watched as Rebecca's team argued in the negative – that cold calling was not an effective strategy. She was participating, and making some good points, but Richard could tell that Rebecca was holding back. They had prepped each other for the debate, and he knew she could do better.

After class, Richard walked over to her desk.

"What was that?" he asked. "You were way better than that when we practiced."

Rebecca shrugged her shoulders. "I guess I was nervous."

"Bollocks. You could've slaughtered the other team. What gives?"

She sighed. "There's such a thing as being too smart, okay?"

"Also bollocks."

"Maybe for you," Rebecca replied. She leaned down to pick up her briefcase from the floor.

"What's that supposed to mean?"

"Forget it," she said, standing up and walking toward the classroom door.

Richard reached out and grabbed Rebecca's arm. "Talk to me, Becks."

"You can be the smart one and people will still like you."

"People like you."

"Will you shut up for once and listen? You told me to talk, so let me talk."

Richard nodded his head. "Okay. I'm sorry. I'm listening."

"There's such a thing as being too smart . . . for a girl. If you have all the answers, it's because you're smart and a go-getter. If I have all the answers, it's because I'm a bookworm or weird or 'probably hates men'. Or 'wishes she were a man'." Rebecca sighed, and Richard could see that she was on the verge of tears. "If the professor likes you," she continued, "it's because he 'recognizes talent when he sees it'. If the professor likes me, everybody assumes I'm sleeping with him."

"Who said that?" Richard clenched his fists to punch whomever it was.

"It doesn't matter. What matters is what you told me: succeeding in business is about relationships as much as it is intelligence or hard work. It's about becoming one of the guys. And nobody wants to hang out with the smartest girl in school. They flirt with her and ask her to do their homework, but then they ditch her for their friends and the sexy cheerleader.

"I'm trying to find a happy medium, okay?" she added. "Too dumb and I'm an embarrassment. Too smart and I'm intimidating. Did I know the answers? Yeah. But the smarter play was to keep my cards close and my mouth shut. I'm not interested in winning a single hand. I want to win the whole fucking game."

Richard nodded and smiled. "You will win it all. I have no doubt."

He shoved his hands in his pockets to keep from reaching out toward her. Every fiber of his being wanted to take Rebecca Lewis in his arms and kiss her. He loved her passion, her intelligence, and her dreams for the future. He wanted to kiss her to show that he agreed with her and supported her, but he knew that Rebecca wouldn't take it that way.

"What are you smiling about?" she asked.

"You," Richard said, unable to lie this time. "You're amazing."

Rebecca looked at him with mock skepticism. "You aren't flirting with me to get me to do your homework, are you?"

Richard laughed and held up his hands in defense. "You caught me. C'mon, I'll make it up to you by buying you lunch."

"No time for lunch," Rebecca replied as they walked out of Aldrich Hall and into the quad. The area that was green grass when they first arrived in September was now blanketed in December snow. Rebecca pulled a beanie on to keep her head warm. "I have to go back to the dorms and start cooking. Emily's party is tonight, remember?"

"Shit, no, I forgot. What am I supposed to bring?"

"I don't know. Pick up some paper plates and napkins on your way. We always run out of those."

TWELVE

At seven o'clock that evening, Richard and Rebecca got out of a cab at 520 Beacon Street in Back Bay. The six-story, pre-war apartment building was two miles from campus and a major upgrade from the dorm rooms that most students lived in. Rebecca had been there a few times before to hang out with Emily.

"Pretty swanky for a grad student, don't you think?" Richard said as they stepped inside out of the cold winter air. He unwrapped his scarf from around his neck and shrugged out of his overcoat. "At least the heater works."

"Emily said her dad is paying for it. He's does something with import-export in San Francisco."

"You know what that means," Richard said as he knocked on Emily's door. "He's in the mafia."

The door swung open and Emily welcomed them with a smile. Her apartment was decked out in Christmas gear, with everything from blinking lights to a full-size tree in the corner. Richard bumped his head on mistletoe as they walked in.

"Oops, sorry about that," said Emily. "I didn't realize how tall you were!" She batted her eyelashes at Richard, and Rebecca stepped between them.

"Here, I brought dessert." Rebecca held out her trademark chocolate pecan pie.

Emily took the dessert, and another guest handed them both a glass of punch. "Be careful," he said. "It's spiked!"

****

Richard heeded the warning about the alcoholic punch, but Rebecca didn't. By the end of the night, she was laughing and giggling on the couch while more than one male classmate vied for her attention.

And affection, Richard growled. He watched as one guy in particular, David, leaned in and whispered in Rebecca's ear. *Oh, for fuck's sake*, Richard thought.

An hour later, Rebecca weaved and stumbled her way to the door to leave. David was holding her arm, escorting her. Right when Richard was going to step in, someone exclaimed: "hey, you two are under the mistletoe!"

Rebecca and David looked up to see the green plant with white berries tied together by a red ribbon.

"Kiss her!"

David smiled and leaned forward, lips puckered. Rebecca played along and gave him a small peck. It was as far from romantic as a kiss could get, *but it's still more action than I've had*, Richard thought.

****

Although David was the lucky bastard who stole a kiss under the mistletoe, Richard still won the prize of escorting Rebecca home from the party. The punch had done a number, and Rebecca was drunk enough to scoot closer to Richard in the cab and lean her head against his shoulder.

"You wanna know something?" she mumbled, half-asleep. "I didn't like you at first. I thought you were rude and arrogant and only wanted to sleep with me."

"Gee, thanks," he replied.

"No, no, no," she slurred, patting his arm. "That was then. I was wrong. My favorite thing about Harvard is you."

Richard smiled. He leaned over and kissed the top of Rebecca's head. "You're my favorite thing too, darling."

"Merry Christmas," she whispered.

"Happy Christmas."

THIRTEEN

The memory of their shared cab ride carried Richard through the entirety of his two weeks home in England. Through his mother's constant drinking, his father's cold and distant disapproval, and even through the barrage of questions from his best friend, Geoffrey, about his love life in America. Geoffrey refused to believe that Richard wasn't racking up notches on his bedpost at Harvard like he did at Cambridge.

"Things are different there," Richard said one night when he met Geoff for drinks. Richard had driven into London earlier that afternoon and was spending the final few days of his trip in the capital.

"Of course they're different," Geoff replied. "Now you're rich, handsome, *and* have a posh accent."

Richard drank a sip of his beer. He and Geoff had grown up together and were roommates at both Eton and Cambridge. Although his family weren't titled, they were very wealthy and belonged to England's most privileged social circles.

"I'm trying to focus on school," Richard lied.

"Bollocks. There's only one reason why Richard Lord of the Ladies wouldn't be racking them up in America."

Richard rolled his eyes at his old college nickname. "And what's that, mate?"

Geoff raised his glass in salute. "You're in love."

"In love?" Richard scoffed. "No." He shook his head and looked down at the table, spinning his pint of beer in his hands.

"I knew it! You are! Who is she? More importantly, how is she?" Geoff asked, wiggling his eyebrows at the final question.

"I wouldn't know. We haven't gone to bed together."

"Why the hell not?"

Richard let out a frustrated sigh. "It's different, okay? She's different. I don't want one night with her. I want a lifetime."

"What do their lord and ladyship have to say about that?"

"My parents don't know about her. And you bloody well better not tell them."

****

Forty-eight hours after his conversation with Geoffrey, Richard was back in the United States. He wasn't even finished unpacking when he heard a knock on his dorm room door.

"Who is it?"

"Rebecca."

He smiled and walked across the room to open the door. "Hi stranger."

"Hi!" Rebecca smiled in return and threw her arms around his neck.

Richard's stomach did three and a half somersaults before he got it back under control. Every time Rebecca hugged him, or squeezed his hand, or hooked her arm through his while they walked, his heart leapt to his throat and he thought that maybe, just maybe, this time would be *the* time that it meant something. Seeing her again after the two-week Christmas break only intensified that response.

With his arms still around her in a hug, Richard leaned down and drew in a deep breath. *God, she smells good*, he thought. He knew part of it was her perfume – Rebecca wore Chanel No. 5 with its notes of rose, jasmine, and wintry musk. But Richard's favorite part wasn't the Chanel. It was her hair. In contrast to the icy freshness of the perfume, Rebecca's hair was like a warm summer breeze that wrapped its arms around him and wouldn't let go. A floral, fruity smell that he could almost taste – the perfect blend of subtle and bold. *Like Rebecca.*

39

Right when their hug was starting to linger too long and turn into perhaps something more, Rebecca pulled away. The smile on her face and sparkle in her eyes remained, though. *She still has no idea what she does to me.*

"Welcome back!" Rebecca said. "How was your break?"

"Good. Standard English fair: lots of food, parties, and a few days up in London with friends. I must admit," Richard added, "I thoroughly enjoyed Boxing Day this year. I've missed being able to watch football on television."

"Boxing Day?"

Richard nodded. "December 26th. It used to be the day when all the servants celebrated the holiday because they had to work on Christmas. But now it's also become a big day for football matches."

"Why is it called Boxing Day?"

Richard shrugged his shoulders. "Bugger if I know."

Rebecca rolled her eyes. "Your country is weird. But," she added, "speaking of football – *real* football, I mean – a bunch of us are going to Spangler to watch the Holiday Bowl. Michigan versus BYU. If BYU wins, they'll be national champs. Wanna come?"

Richard crossed his arms over his chest and pretended to be offended. "You do know that English football is the real football, right? America is the only country in the world that calls it soccer."

"Yeah, well, you're in America now."

"So speak English, right?"

Both of them laughed at the memory from their first day of class.

"Exactly," Rebecca replied. "So . . . Spangler? I'll even help explain what's going on."

Richard nodded. "Sure, I'm in. Just let me grab my coat."

FOURTEEN

"So, when you said 'a bunch of us are going' what you meant was the entire school?" Richard looked around the packed student union in amazement. "I've never seen it this crowded in here."

Rebecca smiled. "I told you football was a big deal. C'mon," she said, grabbing Richard's hand. "Emily saved us some seats."

"This is pretty exciting," Richard said as they sat down. "Championships are always fun. Some of my very earliest memories are of watching Bobby Charlton play for England in the World Cup. I don't think I've ever seen my dad as happy as he was the day we won."

Rebecca looked over at Emily to see if she had any clue what Richard was talking about. The other girl shook her head no, and they both laughed.

"What?" asked Richard.

"Nothing, nothing," Rebecca replied. "What do you know about football?"

"Real football or American football?"

A classmate sitting nearby snorted in disgust. "American football is real football, man."

Richard shook his head. "Whatever. And not much, to answer your question, Becks."

"Okay, well, you're in luck," she said, scooting closer to him on the couch. So close her thigh was pressed against his.

Richard's heart skipped a beat. *To hell with the game*, he thought. *Just let me sit here and feel you next to me.*

Unaware of her friend's thoughts, Rebecca continued: "I know basically everything there is to know about football. It's a cultural necessity where I come from." She leaned closer to Richard and pointed toward the television. "See the team in white? That's BYU – Brigham Young. And the other team, the one in blue, is Michigan."

41

Richard breathed in deeply, trying to calm his nerves, but caught the fresh scent of Rebecca's perfume instead. *Dear God help me. I'm not going to make it through this.*

Emily stood up to go talk to some other friends, and Richard seized the opportunity to shift over and leave a bit of space between himself and Rebecca.

Unfazed, she continued her football lesson. "Each team will have eleven players on the field at a time. The team with the ball, the offense, has four tries – or 'downs' – to go ten yards. If they don't make it, the other team gets the ball."

"How do you score?" he asked.

"If you run or pass the ball into the end zone – that part on either end that's painted differently – you get six points. A touchdown. If you kick the ball through the U-shaped goal post after, it's an extra one point. And if you kick it through the goal post without a touchdown, that's a field goal worth three points."

"So, this is rugby with a forward pass," Richard concluded.

"Umm . . . sure. If you say so."

"And for whom are we rooting?"

"Well, if you ask my dad," Rebecca said in a whisper, "he's rooting for BYU because their team is all white players."

"Ergo, we want Michigan to win. Go blue?"

"Go Blue!"

FIFTEEN

It didn't take long for Richard to realize that sports were a great way to spend even more time with Rebecca. They started watching the NFL playoffs on Sundays, and even picked up a Celtics game or two on TV. Emily and another friend, Joe, often joined them.

One day, during a halftime news update, the announcer said something about the House of Lords in England. Grainy video footage showed an assembly of men in black suits sitting in an ornate chamber.

"Today's session was televised," Richard explained. "First time ever for the House of Lords."

"Could you see your dad?" Rebecca asked.

"No, they all looked alike from that angle."

Two students seated at a table nearby had been listening to the conversation and walked toward them. "Hey, you're Arrington, right?" one of the visitors asked. "The royal guy?"

Richard shook his head. "I'm Arrington, but I'm not royalty."

"He's close enough," Emily chimed in. "He's a Viscount. And one day he'll be a Marquess."

A pang of jealousy hit Rebecca hard in the stomach, and she cut her eyes over at her friend in surprise. *I didn't know Emily was paying that much attention to him*, she thought.

"How can I help you gentlemen?" Richard asked, turning the group's attention back to their two guests.

"I'm glad you asked. We're putting together a calendar of eligible bachelors, and we think you'd make a great fit."

"Oooh yes, do it!" Emily exclaimed, placing her hand on Richard's arm.

He shook her off and turned his attention back to the television screen. "No thank you. That's not really my style."

Rebecca held back a grin and her jealousy faded away. *He'd never fall for a girl like her*, she thought. *He wants somebody who doesn't care about his family. Someone who only cares about him. Someone like . . .* Rebecca stopped herself from completing the sentence. *He's your friend,* she reminded herself. *Your best friend. Don't screw that up because of some silly crush.*

SIXTEEN

Whether it was a silly crush or not, all Rebecca knew was that she couldn't imagine being at HBS without Richard. Between classes, runs on the river, walking Caymus, trying new restaurants, and now watching sports, there was seldom a moment when they were apart. It became a joke of sorts in their section, with other students referring to them as husband and wife. Rebecca did her best to ignore the gossip, but Richard embraced it. He even referred to her as 'the wifey' in front of their friends.

"Why do you keep doing that?" asked Rebecca one afternoon. They were running on the Cambridge side of the river and could see their campus across the water. "You're encouraging them."

"I disagree," Richard replied. "If they know it bothers us, they'll keep doing it. On the other hand, if I lean in and join the joke, it loses all its power."

Rebecca thought about his argument. "You may have a point there, Lord Arrington."

"Don't. Please."

"Oh, so you can call me your wife when we're not even dating, but I can't use your actual, legitimate title?"

"Glad we're in agreement."

Rebecca laughed. "We're not. But I won't call you Lord anymore."

"Thank you. Oh, by the way," Richard said, jogging in place at a red light, "how did the interview go with Goldman Sachs?"

"Good, I think. They said I should hear back next week."

"Are they your top choice for this summer?"

Rebecca nodded. "Mother is pitching a fit because she wants me to work in Atlanta, but New York is where the action is. What about you? Any chance you'd join me in Manhattan?"

Richard shook his head. "No. Dad expects me to be in London."

"So? My mom expects me to be in Georgia, but I'm not going to be. You're a man. A rich, white, educated man. You have no color barrier. No glass ceiling. No hole or gutter to climb out of. Who cares what's expected of you?"

Richard responded to her in a calm, steady voice – something that irritated Rebecca to no end. Even during an argument, he never raised his voice. Never displayed any, well, any *passion*.

"I may not have a barrier or a ceiling or a gutter," he replied, "but I do have a title. And that title comes with duties and responsibilities that don't go away simply because I don't feel like it. I am my father's heir. I will be the next Marquess of Dublinshire. I have a family and an estate that must be supported, both of which require funds. So, to answer your question, Miss Lewis, I care what's expected of me."

****

After they returned to campus from their run, Rebecca went to the dorms and Richard headed to the student union. "I need a drink," he muttered to himself. He was still stewing over his conversation with Rebecca. *She doesn't get it*, he thought. *She could break from her family's wishes and nothing would happen apart from making her mum cry. If I renounced my claim, Cousin Louis would become the next heir.* Richard shuddered at the thought. *That smarmy kiss ass would run everything into the ground faster than you can say cocaine addict.*

"I'll have a pint, please," he told the bartender. "Budweiser."

Richard found a chair in the corner and sat down with his beer. By the time half the pint was gone, he had started to relax. It was hard to stay mad at Rebecca. And he liked that she stood up to him every once in a while, even though it was never fun in the moment. Rebecca's combination of grit and beauty often reminded Richard of the genteel women in his family. Not his mother, of course, who was a cold-hearted creature. But his grandmother and his father's sisters. Women raised over the years and bred through the centuries to be both lovely and strong, and who knew that true grace required a backbone tough enough to carry themselves and their families without ever missing a step.

He took a long sip of beer and motioned to the bartender to bring him another round.

Mother certainly wouldn't approve of this. 'Drinking in public is for commoners,' Richard thought, remembering what her ladyship liked to say. Victoria Arrington had always been cold and distant - a product of her environment, perhaps. She believed in duty, propriety, and tradition above all else. *Thank God for Abuela*, Richard thought. *Abuela believed in love.*

Isabel María Teresa Castile de Arrington was born in Spain in 1918 to a prominent aristocratic family. Her father fled the country in 1931 with his wife and children when his close friend, King Alfonso XIII, was deposed from the throne. Six years later, the teenaged Isabel met and fell in love with a dashing young Lord Dublinshire, Richard's grandfather. Isabel was the life of the party everywhere she went – a newspaper article once described her as "drinking like an Irishman, eating like an Italian, loving like a Frenchman, and dancing like the Spaniard she was." When Richard's grandfather proposed, he gave Isabel the family ring: a gorgeous, brilliant cut ruby encircled by a falling halo of small diamonds.

Richard smiled at the memory of his beloved Abuela. She adored all of her grandkids, but Richard was special. She loved to show him her engagement ring and tell him about how the English Marquess fell madly in love with the daughter of the Spanish Baron. At the end of the story, Abuela would fix her caramel-colored eyes on Richard, hold out the ring, and say: "Algún día, este anillo será tuyo para regalar a tu amor."

And then I would ask her how to know who the right girl is to give it to, Richard remembered.

"Two souls matched in Heaven are like magnets in a field of sand," his grandmother would reply. "Though the desert will separate them, blow them apart, and trick them with oases along the way, still they will find each other. *Indivisible. Invencible. Destino.*"

SEVENTEEN

Richard found himself thinking about his grandmother more and more as the end of the semester drew near. *Abuela would know what to do about Rebecca*, he thought one afternoon. Classes had let out a little over an hour ago, and the switch to Daylight Savings Time meant it finally wasn't dark at 4:00pm every afternoon. He walked past the dorms and other buildings on the edge of campus and took a right on Kresage Way. In the distance, he could see a tall, thin woman with jet black hair standing at the edge of the pedestrian bridge. Rebecca bent her knee and grabbed hold of her foot with her hand, stretching her thigh muscles. *What should I do, Abuela?* Richard asked, closing in on his friend and running partner. *Risk it all and tell her how I feel?*

When Rebecca saw Richard approaching, she stopped stretching and waved. A smile lit her face and warmed his heart. *I can't lose her*, he decided. *She's the best thing in my life. Even if all I get to be is her friend.*

Rebecca was still smiling when they took off over Weeks Bridge and turned right. They were making a big loop that day, running through Cambridge's neighborhoods until they reached the MIT Bridge, then turning north back along the footpath that ran parallel to Storrow Drive. It was a good medium-distance route and had become one of their favorites over the course of the school year.

"Isn't this weather fabulous?" Rebecca asked. "I love that it's staying light out later."

The warmth of the late April sun filled the two runners with hope and happiness. Everyone in Boston seemed to be in good spirits and celebrating the end of the long New England winter. A few wildflowers had even popped up along the banks of the Charles. Rebecca pointed them out as she and Richard ran.

"Look at that," she said. "Those flowers weren't here on Tuesday."

"Spring has finally arrived," Richard replied. "Thank God. I thought the sky was going to stay gray forever." He tilted his head up and squinted from the glare of the sun. "This is much better."

When they passed another patch of flowers, Richard stopped running, bent over, and picked a handful. He sprinted to catch up to Rebecca and gave her the makeshift bouquet.

Rebecca laughed but took the flowers all the same. "Thank you."

"What's so funny?"

"These are dandelion puffs. They're weeds."

"What? Here, give them back. Or toss them aside." Richard wanted to kick himself. *Well done, Arrington*, he thought. *You're out with the girl of your dreams and the first flowers you give her are bloody weeds.*

Rebecca laughed again and shook her head, turning around to run backward so she could see Richard while she spoke.

"No way. I'm keeping them! After all, it's not every day that a girl can say a British Lord gave her a stack of weeds."

Rebecca turned around and took off down the path, her laughter echoing off the water. Richard hurried to catch up.

"What flowers would you want, if you could choose?" he asked.

"It depends on the occasion, I guess."

"Roses?"

Rebecca shrugged her shoulders. "Roses are pretty, sure. But they're not my favorite."

"What is your favorite?"

"Tulips. Roses are serious flowers. They always have some important meaning attached. And daisies are pretty, but they're almost too happy, you know? Tulips are right in the middle: classy and beautiful but sunny and fun too." Rebecca paused. "Friendly piece of advice, your lordship? You can never go wrong sending a girl flowers."

****

50

After her first class the next day, Rebecca returned to her dorm to find three glass vases full of white tulips sitting beside her door. After working in a flower shop while she was in high school, Rebecca knew that those particular tulips symbolized forgiveness.

She bent down and picked up the card attached to the middle vase.

I'll never again give you weeds when you deserve tulips. xx, R

When she saw Richard later that afternoon, Rebecca cornered him. "You shouldn't have sent me flowers. And you certainly don't need my forgiveness. I loved the dandelions."

"Somebody knows her horticulture," Richard replied. "I thought you said a guy could never go wrong sending a girl flowers?"

"I mean, in theory, yes. But you sent, like, a whole floral shop."

Richard smiled. "I'm their new favorite customer."

Rebecca rolled her eyes. "What's with the xx by the way? In the note?"

"You don't do that here? It's like XO, but only x. Just a friendly sign off." *In a perfect world, I would've signed it Love, Richard*, he thought.

Their professor chose that moment to make his entrance to the classroom.

"Thank you for the flowers," Rebecca said as she took her seat. "But no more, please. People already joke about us being a couple. I don't want any more gossip."

"As you wish," Richard replied. "No flowers. Only friends."

EIGHTEEN

Summer break came and went without Rebecca seeing or hearing from Richard. He gave her his phone number and address in London before they left school, but she hadn't ever worked up the courage to call him. She meant to, and even wanted to, but every time Rebecca picked up the phone, she lost her nerve. *What would I say?* she thought, hanging up the receiver. *It's not like he's my boyfriend or anything.*

That truth hit Rebecca hard. She was getting punched in the gut a lot this summer by thoughts of Richard. And her. And . . . . *Stop it, Becky. He's your best friend. You'll ruin it if he knows you like him.*

She paused in the middle of her apartment hallway.

"I like him."

The words hung in the air and her emotions swirled inside of her.

"Oh my God. I really, really like him."

A minute later, Rebecca shook her head.

"Snap out of it. Stop being such a girl. You'll lose all credibility at school if you start chasing a boy. Not to mention losing the only true friend you've ever had."

****

When she returned to campus in September, Rebecca stayed true to her word and followed her own instructions. Despite her growing attraction and attachment to Richard, she made sure to pull back whenever she felt in danger of exposing her feelings.

After a few weeks of getting the cold shoulder, Richard decided to confront Rebecca. They had taken a cab to Boston's North End and were standing in line outside of Giacomo's, their favorite Italian restaurant.

"When are you going to tell me what's going on?" he asked.

Rebecca furrowed her eyebrows in confusion. "What are you talking about?"

"You've been different ever since we got back. More . . . more distant."

She laughed. "We've hung out almost every day."

"I know. But something's still different. Did you – "

"Did I what?"

"Did you meet someone over the summer? You know, a guy?"

They both stepped forward as space opened in the line.

"No, I didn't meet anyone. Not like that." Rebecca paused, and she got a knot in her stomach. "Did you?"

Richard shook his head. "No." *As if there could ever be anyone but you.* "My family kept trying to set me up with a girl," he added, which was true. "She just graduated from finishing school in Switzerland. Our families are old friends."

The knot in Rebecca's stomach grew larger. "I didn't know finishing school was still a thing," she said, trying to play it cool. "Do you . . . do you like her?"

"No way."

Rebecca breathed a sigh of relief.

"She's young and immature and has no goals or ambition of her own. Plus, she's short and chubby. Mother kept saying she was a handsome woman, but I don't think that's a compliment. Men are handsome. Women are beautiful."

A smile returned to Rebecca's face. Based on Richard's description, she was confident the other woman didn't pose a threat. "You don't think she's beautiful?" she teased.

"No, handsome is an accurate description."

Rebecca laughed.

"She's pretty enough, I suppose. But she's not beautiful. And she's not for me." *You are.*

The door to Giacomo's opened and the hostess motioned for them to come inside.

"Madame?" he said, holding out his arm as an escort.

"Why thank you, sir," Rebecca said in her best imitation British accent.

Richard rolled his eyes and laughed. "Seriously, stop. It's not getting any better. In fact, it might be worse."

Rebecca slapped him on the shoulder with her free hand. "I have a great British accent."

"Hmm. Alright."

"I'm serious!"

"I know," he said with a grin. "But it's still terrible."

NINETEEN

After their conversation in line at Giacomo's, Rebecca decided to let her guard down. She had been worried about Richard finding out she liked him and losing his friendship, but in her effort to hide her feelings she was starting to push him away. *You're going to lose him by trying so hard to not lose him*, she thought. *Besides, if he liked you too, he would've already asked you out.*

Rebecca's return to a close-but-platonic friendship worked well for most of the fall semester. She and Richard were still inseparable, and they would often hug or walk with her arm linked through his, but no lines were ever crossed. Despite all the shared dinners, study sessions, and runs along the river, Richard never tried to kiss her or even imply that they were anything other than the best of friends.

Toward the end of the semester, though, things changed. Richard's hugs lingered longer. He scooted closer to her on the couch when they watched football games. He complimented her constantly, with 'beautiful' and 'gorgeous' and 'amazing' becoming a regular part of his vocabulary. *And the way he looks at me now?* Rebecca shivered. She was sitting in class and could see Richard watching her from across the room.

Rebecca was used to men looking at her. She had always been a pretty little girl and had grown into a beautiful young woman, so it was only natural that men would stare. It bothered her at first, but when she complained to her mom, Mrs. Lewis laughed it off and told her fifteen-year-old daughter to "get used to it, darlin'". And she did.

The way Rebecca got used to it was to ignore it, but with Richard things were different. When she noticed his eyes on her, the creepy-crawly feeling Rebecca normally got was replaced by a tingling warmth that coursed through her. She didn't ignore Richard's staring . . . she embraced it. Wrapped herself in it like a warm blanket to keep out the cold Boston winter.

****

Richard knew he should look away. Knew he should stop running his eyes over Rebecca's body. Knew he should pay attention to the professor instead of imagining what that body would look like naked beneath his.

He knew he should stop, if for no other reason than to save himself the embarrassment of his very obvious attraction at that moment. But he couldn't. *She's too damn beautiful*, he thought. *Too damn wonderful.*

When class adjourned, his friend Joe walked over and sat down next to Richard. "Gonna take you a minute before you stand up?"

"Mmm hmm."

"Probably for the best," Joe replied. "You know, eventually you're going to have to tell her."

"I know. But not yet."

"Make a move, man. C'mon. What do you have to lose?"

"Everything," Richard replied without hesitation. "If I tell her and she says no, I'll lose her completely. I can't handle that. I don't know what it is to exist without her anymore."

TWENTY

By the time Christmas break arrived, Richard was convinced that Rebecca was the love of his life and the woman he wanted to marry. *Our families and backgrounds aren't important,* he told himself as he flew home to England for the holidays. *As long as we're together, that's all that matters.*

A member of the staff at his family's estate met Richard at Heathrow Airport. After loading his bags in the back of the Land Rover, Richard climbed in and they set off in the direction of Rosewood. Located approximately fifty miles southeast of London, the Arrington estate was near the town of Battle in East Sussex. Rosewood had been in Richard's family for over four centuries, and the locals affectionately called it 'the big house'. It was set on nearly 8,000 acres, and cattle and sheep were among the industries that helped support the estate and the local town. The house itself was an enormous, Tudor-style building with a grand ballroom, a picture gallery, and antiques throughout. Many visitors said it favored Althorp, the childhood home of Princess Diana.

It's more like a museum than a house, he thought as he stepped out of the car onto the gravel driveway. He was greeted by one of the footmen, Carl.

"Welcome home, sir," said Carl. "Their lordships are expecting you. They're in the library."

Richard nodded. "Tell them I'm going to change out of my travel clothes first. I'll be down in time for cocktails."

An hour later, Richard walked down the grand staircase and turned right to enter the library. He had changed out his jeans and sweater into a suit and tie.

"I'm glad to see you're still dressing for dinner," his mother commented as she stood up and pressed an air kiss to his cheek. "You look very thin, though. Are you on drugs?"

"It's good to see you too, Mum. And no, I'm not on drugs. I run a lot in Boston. There are some great trails along the river."

Lord Dublinshire shook his son's hand and passed him a glass of whisky. "Here. Catch up. You're behind."

Richard glanced over at the empty martini glass beside his mother's chair. *Oh boy*, he thought. *It's going to be a long night.*

****

Richard's sister arrived the next day in time for lunch. Sporting brown corduroy pants and a red Fair Isle sweater, Lady Sarah looked every bit the part of country aristocracy.

"Thank God," Richard said as he kissed her on the cheek. "I was worried you would show up wearing neon spandex with hair that looked like you stuck your finger in an electrical socket."

Sarah giggled. "I know, right? Fashion now is so horrid."

The siblings took their seats on opposite sides of the dining room table and were soon joined by their parents. Carl and another footman carried in trays of sandwiches and hot soups.

"Richard," his mother said, "I don't want you making any plans for tomorrow night. You're having dinner with Ivy Sinclair-Jones."

"No, I'm not."

"Yes, you are. Her mother and I arranged it. She's a wonderful match for you. Ivy understands what is required for this life."

"So does our estate manager," Richard argued, "but you wouldn't make me marry him."

"Don't be ridiculous," his father said. "You will go to the dinner. You have no appropriate reason to not give Ivy a fair chance."

"What if I were in love with someone else?" Richard asked. "Would that be an appropriate enough reason?" He

58

hadn't planned to tell his parents about Rebecca this early in his trip, but their pressure and attitudes forced him into it.

"Are you in love with someone else?"

"I am," Richard nodded. "Her name is Rebecca. She's beautiful and smart and kind. She's exactly the kind of woman I need by my side."

"Who are her parents?" asked Lord Dublinshire.

"You don't know them. She's an American."

His mother sighed. "Oh, Richard."

"Come on, now," said Sarah, jumping to her brother's defense. "Maybe she'll move to England to be with him."

"Or maybe I'll move to America."

"That is out of the question." His dad looked Richard in the eye. "One day you will be the Marquess of Dublinshire. With all the privileges, duties, and responsibilities that entails. You must marry someone appropriate, son. Not some American from God knows where with God knows whom as relatives."

"Darling," his mom said, "I'm sure she's a lovely girl, but if she's a classmate of yours she cannot be the type of woman who would make a good wife and mother. These 'career women' don't want anything to do with family."

"You don't know her, Mum. She's different."

"She's beneath you," his father stated. "She's disapproved."

"You haven't even met her!"

"Do not raise your voice to me in this house. The conversation is over."

TWENTY-ONE

Richard was still steaming as he walked away from the dining room.

She's beneath you. She's disapproved.

He snorted in anger while his father's words replayed in his mind. "No, she bloody well is not!"

Richard continued his angry march through the picture gallery, down the East Wing corridor, and into the solarium. There he found his wellies, kicked off his loafers, and slipped on the more practical walking boots. It had rained that morning, and no Englishman went walking in the woods without proper footwear – no matter how mad he was.

He heard a clicking sound on the sunroom's tile floor and turned to see his parents' two Bernese Mountain Dogs, AJ and Josie, trotting toward him.

"You coming?" he asked, and the dogs responded by running to the far end of the room where the door led to the gardens.

"I don't blame you," Richard said. "I'm trying to get away from them too."

The dogs' high spirits and squirrel-chasing antics were a welcome distraction from the storm raging inside the future Marquess of Dublinshire. His boots crunched on the gravel path toward the gardens, and every few steps Richard bent down to pick up one of the rocks and hurl it as far as he could.

"If only I could pick up Dad and toss him into the woods," he muttered.

You must marry someone appropriate. Lord Dublinshire's words echoed in his son's mind. *Not some American from God knows where with God knows whom as relatives.*

"Check that," Richard told himself. "I'll throw Dad into a rose bush. That way he's stuck with thorns and Mum can't enter the district flower show."

Richard smiled at the thought. *They deserve a little unhappiness after all they've rained down on the rest of us.*

He realized the dogs had gone quiet.

"AJ! Josie! Come!"

The four-legged pair tore out from under a set of shrubs in the corner of the garden and nearly wiped out as they skidded to a stop in front of him on the gravel.

"Good dogs," Richard said, petting each one on the head. He opened the gate that led from the manicured garden to the larger wooded grounds, and the furry giants raced through.

"Don't go too far," he commanded, knowing that they wouldn't. Even if they did, everything as far as the eye could see – and beyond – belonged to the Arrington family.

Richard passed through the iron gate, shut it behind him, and set off over the damp grass on his way to his secret spot: an old stone house that had all crumbled except for parts of the outer walls. He and his sister played there as young children and hid there as teenagers whenever they needed an escape from being 'Lady Sarah' and 'Lord Arrington'.

He circled around the spot a few times before finding it, overgrown with brush from years of neglect. "I haven't been here in forever. I guess Sarah hasn't either." Richard cleared the weeds and vines off one wall. The three-foot high stacked stone was all that remained of what was once the game warden's cottage.

Sitting down, Richard reached into his jacket pocket and pulled out a 3x3 inch photo of Rebecca. He had taken it while on a team building scavenger hunt, using the school-issued Polaroid camera.

He ran his thumb over the picture and smiled. The scavenger hunt was at Faneuil Hall in downtown Boston. Richard could see the red brick of the historic building in the background, the same spot where early Americans plotted and schemed to break free from his own country. But Richard's eyes focused on the photo's subject, with her black hair glistening in the sun of one of Boston's infamous Indian Summers. Rebecca was smiling at the camera. Not a posed smile, but a relaxed, candid one. Richard smiled himself when remembering how he held the camera up with his finger on the button and called her name to get Rebecca to look his way.

"What's that?"

The question broke through Richard's thoughts, and he jumped up off the wall.

"What the – "

His sister pushed her way through the brush into the opening, followed closely by AJ and Josie. "Sorry, I didn't mean to frighten you." Sarah looked at the picture in Richard's hand. "Is that her?"

He nodded and passed her the photo. "Be careful – it's the only one I've got."

"She's pretty," Sarah said. "Very pretty. I can see why you like her." She handed the picture back to him and sat down on the wall. "Tell me about her."

TWENTY-TWO

"She's . . . " Richard paused and smiled. "Sarah, she's incredible. She's as American as apple pie and shotguns. On the first day of classes, she told me 'this is America, speak English' and that I needed to drink coffee instead of tea."

"And you love her for that?"

He laughed. "I do. I mean, obviously, her attitude toward me has changed since then. We do everything together. Classes, studying, dinners, runs by the river. I don't remember what life was like without her.

"It's more than that, though," he continued. "I don't work without her anymore. She's become the air I breathe. The water I drink. I need her – I need her in order to survive."

Sarah snorted in laughter but stopped when she saw her brother wasn't joking. "You're serious."

Richard nodded. "She's everything to me, Sarah. Without her . . . " His voice trailed off and he looked down at the dirt beneath his feet.

"You'll find someone else."

Richard shook his head. "Not like her. There will never be anyone like her."

"Does she know how you feel?"

"No."

"Why not?"

"It's better that way, isn't it? After what Mum and Dad said?"

Lady Sarah shifted on the wall so she was facing her brother. "Do you truly love her? I mean really, truly?"

Richard sighed. "I do."

"Then fight for her!"

"It's not that simple."

His sister grunted and rolled her eyes. "If you loved her, you'd fight for her. If you won't fight for her, you don't deserve her."

****

Richard sulked his way through a few more days at home before leaving early to return to Boston. He didn't even stop in to see his friend Geoffrey in London. *I don't want to hear how happy he is with his new girlfriend when I'm not allowed to have the same thing.*

Before leaving, on an impulse, Richard went into the back of his closet and pulled out an old shoe box. Underneath some photos was a small, black velvet box. Flipping it open, Richard saw his grandmother's ring. He shoved the family heirloom down in his duffel bag and left his childhood home without so much as a goodbye.

TWENTY-THREE

At the end of January, Harvard's campus and all of Boston was swept up in Super Bowl fever. The Patriots were playing in their first ever NFL championship game, and the city could not have been more excited. Having finished a Cinderella season and surviving a wild card spot in the playoffs, New England now had to face Mike Ditka's Chicago Bears. The Patriots were an underdog, but all of Boston believed.

Rebecca and Richard joined the rest of their classmates in Spangler's student union to watch the game. Four hours later, they walked back outside into the freezing winter night.

"That was a massacre," Richard said. "A literal slaughter."

Rebecca nodded. "I know. Brutal. What was it? Seven sacks allowed and only seven rushing yards gained? Woof. The city is going to be in mourning for a month."

****

The next afternoon, during her usual route through downtown Boston, Rebecca's prediction was confirmed. People hung their heads, stores closed for the day, and there was a general feeling of gloom in the air.

"Good grief," she said after returning to campus. "I know this is a sports town, but nobody died."

Rebecca climbed the stairs in her dorm to reach her room on the third floor. When she exited the stairwell, she saw a middle-aged woman standing at her door. The visitor was wearing a black polka-dotted dress with a red belt and matching red hat, and Rebecca knew enough about fashion to know that the outfit cost more than her entire semester's tuition. The woman heard the door to the stairs close, and she turned to look in Rebecca's direction. A beautiful double

65

strand of pearls draped around her neck and complemented the pearl studs in her ears.

"Excuse me, miss?" the woman said in an English accent. "I'm looking for Rebecca Lewis. I was told this is her room?"

Oh shit, Rebecca thought. *Is that Richard's mom?* She glanced down at her own clothes in horror. Sneakers, green tights, pink leg warmers, blue jersey shorts, and an oversized pink sweatshirt. *With no makeup and my sweaty hair pushed back by a headband.* Rebecca considered lying and pretending to be someone else, but she knew the truth would come out eventually.

"I'm Rebecca," she said, walking forward to shake hands with the other woman. "How can I help you?"

Lady Dublinshire ran her eyes up and down Rebecca's body and huffed in disgust. "He told his sister that you two run together . . . I suppose that would explain your current state of dress." She paused, then said: "I'm Victoria Arrington. Richard's mother. I need to speak with you."

TWENTY-FOUR

Thirty minutes later, Rebecca met Richard's mom at a small coffee shop near campus. She had asked the older woman if it was possible to shower and change before they talked, and Lady Dublinshire happily agreed. As soon as Victoria left the dorm, Rebecca ran down to the phone at the end of the hall and called Emily. Luckily, her friend was home.

"Help! Richard's mom is here!"

"What? From England?"

"Yes!" Rebecca screeched. "She said she needs to talk to me. Oh my God, Em, it was horrible. I walked inside from an hour-long run, all sweaty and nasty, and she's standing at my door looking like a freaking Vogue model."

"What can I do?"

"Come over here and help me pick out an outfit. Also bring some jewelry. Nice stuff."

Standing in the doorway of the coffee shop, Rebecca looked down and nodded. Emily had dressed her in a crimson, knee-length pleated skirt with a cream sweater on top. Black pumps and a strand of pearls completed the outfit, and Rebecca had styled her short black hair to look as sophisticated as possible.

She took a deep breath and walked over to Lady Dublinshire's table.

Richard's mom looked up at her and raised her eyebrows. "Hmm. Much better. Sit, my dear."

Rebecca did as she was told.

"How can I help you, Mrs. Arrington?"

"It's Lady Dublinshire."

"Oh, right. Yes ma'am."

"Yes, your ladyship," Victoria corrected.

"I'm sorry, your ladyship. Aside from Richard, you're the only person with a title I've ever met."

"I don't believe I asked," the marchioness replied coolly.

67

Holy shit, Rebecca thought. *I can't do anything right.*

The two women sat in awkward silence, then Victoria started to speak.

"You can help me by staying away from my son."

"Excuse me?"

"Richard told us about you while he was home for Christmas. He told us that he loves you. That he wants to marry you. Obviously," she said, waving her hand dismissively, "his father and I will never let that happen. Richard is the heir to a very large estate and a very strong business portfolio. He needs someone who understands our world."

Rebecca sat still in her chair. She was stunned. *He loves me?* Ever since she turned him down on the first day of class, Richard had never so much as hinted at their going on a date or being anything other than friends. *I thought I was the one hiding my feelings from him!* Her confidence grew and Rebecca started to smile.

"I could learn to understand your world," she offered.

"My dear, it's not something that can be learnt. You must be born to it."

"Maybe Richard doesn't want that life anymore," Rebecca countered. "Maybe he wants to start over in the U.S."

Lady Dublinshire laughed and shook her head. "That will never happen. If Richard abandoned his claim to the title and the estate, he would be blackballed everywhere. Our family is very powerful . . . on both sides of the Atlantic. And Richard isn't cut out to start over. Has he told you about where he grew up? The world he is accustomed to?"

Rebecca sat up straight in her chair. Her English visitor had offended her in every way possible, disapproving of her outfit, her background, and her life choices. "I don't think you know Richard as well as you think you do," she argued.

Victoria smirked. "No, my dear. It is you who does not know him as well as you think you do."

TWENTY-FIVE

The final months of business school passed by without Rebecca telling Richard about his mother's visit. She didn't see the point. Rebecca knew it would hurt him, and it wouldn't do anything to change the fact that his family disapproved of her. She did take comfort, though, in the news that Richard loved her. Looking back, she wasn't sure how she hadn't seen it before. He never dated anyone else. Never flirted with anyone else. And he was happy to do nearly any activity as long as it was with her.

He even got me these concert tickets, she thought in early April as they drove down to Hartford, Connecticut to see Grateful Dead. The trip was her birthday present, and Rebecca was super excited. The concert didn't start until 8:00pm, so they were also having an early dinner in Hartford before the show. It was the first time they had traveled together outside of Boston, and Rebecca embraced the time alone with Richard. *We'll graduate soon, and he'll leave for London. Just like his family wants.*

Richard looked over at her from the driver's seat. "Are you ready for your birthday extravaganza?"

She laughed. "I'm ready if you are!"

****

When they arrived at the restaurant, Richard told everyone who would listen that it was Rebecca's birthday. The hostess, the waiter, and even people at other tables.

"Will you cut it out?" she asked.

"Why? Don't you like hearing 'happy birthday'?"

"Of course I do, but – "

"No buts. Enjoy it."

At the end of the dinner, their waiter returned and offered Rebecca a choice of free desserts to celebrate. "Take your pick, and I can bring it out with a candle and everything."

"Will you do something else for me instead?"

"Umm, sure."

"You see that couple over there in the corner booth?"

The waiter turned to look. "Yes ma'am."

"Tell them they won a prize as the 500th customer this year, and say their entire meal is on the house. Add their bill to mine."

"But – "

Rebecca waived off the server's objection. "Please just do it, okay?"

He nodded. "Yes ma'am, if you say so."

After the waiter walked away, Rebecca turned to look at Richard. He was staring at her with wide eyes.

"What the hell was that?"

"What was what?"

"The waiter offers you free dessert for your birthday and you say, 'no thanks, what I really want is for you to help me secretly pay for dinner for two total strangers'?" Richard twisted in his chair to look over his shoulder. "They are total strangers, right? That's not your aunt and uncle or something, is it?"

Rebecca smiled. "Yes, they're strangers. Can't a girl do something nice without getting the third degree?"

"Not when that girl is you. You never do anything without a reason behind it. Come on: spill."

Rebecca sighed and leaned back in her chair. "What did you see when you looked at those people?"

"A middle-aged couple having dinner. Why – what did you see?"

"They both have on heavy sweaters rather than layers, they're both drinking water, they didn't order an appetizer, and she borrowed his glasses to read the menu."

"So?"

"So . . . people from the North think that early April weather is warm, even though there's still snow on the

70

ground. Heavy sweaters tell me they're either not from here or don't own a mid-weight jacket for this time of year.

"They're drinking water," Rebecca continued, "because it's free. And they didn't order an appetizer because they can eat the complimentary bread instead."

"What about the glasses?" Richard asked.

"Men forget their glasses all the time," she concluded. "My father was always losing his. Or they don't want to admit that they need glasses, so they borrow their wives'. Women, on the other hand, rarely lose or forget their glasses. Which tells me that his work insurance only covered his vision, not hers. Or he doesn't have insurance but he needs glasses for his job, so they bought some for him but couldn't also afford some for her." Rebecca paused and a wistful look entered her eyes. "Maybe tonight is their anniversary or a birthday or something, or maybe they've been saving up for months to be able to afford a night out at that fancy restaurant they hear people talking about. Except it's not truly a night out because they're still on a super tight budget. But now, with their meal paid for, they can enjoy it like they always hoped, and they'll talk for years to come about that one night at the steakhouse in Hartford."

Richard grinned and shook his head. "Or, they're on holiday from Florida and are wearing the only warm clothes they own, they're drinking water because they're teetotalers, they didn't find the appetizer menu all that appetizing, and she left her glasses at home at their Palm Beach mansion."

Rebecca shrugged her shoulders. "Maybe." She sighed. "I know you don't have much experience with poverty, but I grew up in rural Georgia. I know poor and out of place when I see it. Given how fidgety and uncomfortable they look, I highly doubt they're on vacation from their Florida mansion. But maybe you're right. If so, perhaps this free dinner will prompt them to buy a meal for some other couple in the future."

Richard's grin morphed into a smile, and admiration shone through his eyes. "You, my darling, are a romantic at heart."

Rebecca put her finger to her lips. "Shh. Don't tell anyone. They'll lose all respect for me as a ball-busting businesswoman."

Richard laughed so hard that people at other tables turned to stare. "The hopeless romantic ball-busting businesswoman," he said in a lower volume. "A true woman of the '80s."

Rebecca grinned and raised her glass. "To the women of the '80s."

"To you," Richard replied.

TWENTY-SIX

The concert was as spectacular – and as loud – as Rebecca hoped, and her ears were still ringing as she and Richard exited the arena and walked toward the parking lot. Richard had borrowed their friend Brian's car for the trip, a 1982 Chevrolet Cavalier. The car used to be gold, but snowy New England winters had faded the two-door coup into a color that best resembled urine. Brian called it 'the pee car', but Richard and Rebecca were just happy to not have to take a train to the concert.

When they reached the pee car, they heard a familiar voice from a few vehicles down.

"Arrington! What's up, man?"

Looking over, they saw Joe and his girlfriend.

"Hey, mate," Richard replied, walking over to shake hands. "I didn't know you were coming to the concert."

"I know. We could've ridden together."

"Hi, I'm Sherry," the girlfriend said, reaching out her hand toward Rebecca.

"Hi, so nice to meet you. Joe talks about you all the time. I'm Rebecca."

"How long have you two been together?" Sherry asked.

"What? Oh, no. We're not dating. We're just friends."

Richard knew it was true, but hearing Rebecca say the words still made his heart drop. He should have been used to the statement by now – Rebecca had been responding that same way for almost two years. *Whenever anyone tries to label us a couple*, he thought, *she always denies it.* Richard should've been used to the rejection, but it hurt just as much – if not more – every time it happened.

Sherry shrugged her shoulders, unaware of the loaded nature of her question. "I don't know about you guys, but I thought the concert was amazing. We better get back, though, honey," she told Joe. "I have an early class tomorrow."

"Right. She's a senior at Radcliffe," Joe said in explanation. "I have morning classes too. I guess I'll see you guys then?"

"Yep," Richard nodded. "Safe travels."

As they watched the other couple walk back to their car, Rebecca pulled her coat closer around her shoulders. Even though it was early April and spring in many parts of the country, there was still snow on the ground in Connecticut.

She breathed in the cold New England air and exhaled slowly, sending a cloud of heat into the night sky. Richard smiled, and he knew it was because he felt a kinship with the breath of air that she released. He was also powerless in her grasp, drawn in and warmed through by the deepest parts of her heart and soul. His smile soon disappeared, though, knowing that this magical moment would end and Rebecca would release him too, just as she had the air. Back into the cold world and forever changed by her presence.

TWENTY-SEVEN

The final few weeks of business school flew by for Richard. He was glad to be so busy, though, because it kept him from thinking about the possibility of leaving Rebecca. Between class projects, packing, and making arrangements in London, Richard barely had time to hang out with Rebecca, let alone brood over their potential separation. *We don't have to be separated, though*, he thought. *Not if she says yes*.

Richard's mom and sister made the trip from England for his graduation. Lord Dublinshire stayed home. He blamed it on work, but Richard knew better. *He's never attended any of my school events. Why start now?*

Despite his father's absence, Richard was determined to make the most of graduation week. On the day before the ceremony, he took his mom and sister on the Freedom Trail walk, complete with a stop at Union Oyster House – one of the oldest restaurants in the entire United States. Richard's mother thought the place was 'garish and positively common', but Sarah loved it.

"It's fascinating to think that two hundred years ago people were in these same spots and planning to go to war with our country."

"If by fascinating you mean treasonous," their mother said. "I can't see how you lived here for two years, Richard. At least you'll be back in England in a matter of days." She paused. "I'm tired. I'm going back to the hotel."

After Lady Dublinshire left, Richard and Sarah walked toward the waterfront until they found an open bar.

"Do Americans not believe in day drinking?" Sarah quipped as they sat down in a booth.

"They do." Richard looked at his watch. "Maybe not at 2:00pm on a Wednesday."

Sarah laughed, then looked at Richard in concern. "What is going on with you?"

"What do you mean?"

"You're fidgeting. It looks like you've gnawed off all your fingernails. And you barely touched your lunch at the Oyster House."

Richard let out a deep breath.

"Are you on something?" his sister pressed.

"No. Although part of me wishes I were . . . if only to calm my nerves." He reached into his pocket and pulled out a small, black velvet box.

"That's not what I think it is, is it?"

Richard flipped it open and placed it on the table.

"You're going to propose?!"

"Shhhhh!" Richard grabbed the ring and put it back in his pocket.

"Oh my God, Richard. I mean, oh my God!"

"I know. I'm so fucking nervous."

"Have you two talked about it? Do you have any idea what she's going to say?"

"Yes, hopefully."

Sarah shook her head. "That's not what I meant."

"I know what you meant. We've been close a couple times. She usually brushes it off as not serious, or I'll see the fear in her eyes and I'll change the subject. But I have to ask her, Sarah. I have to know. If I don't, I'll regret it for the rest of my life."

TWENTY-EIGHT

At precisely 8:00am the next day, a man in a gray morning suit and black top hat took the stage in Tercentenary Theatre on Harvard University's main campus. Carrying a long black staff and sporting a gold badge on his left chest, he put his hands on his hips and surveyed the large crowd assembled for graduation. After a few seconds, the man pounded the dais with his staff and, in a booming Boston accent, said:

"As the highhhh sheriff of Middlesex County, I declahh that the meeting will be in orrrrrdaahhhhhhh!"

Rebecca giggled at the graduation tradition, and Richard couldn't help but smile as well.

The dramatic opening of ceremonies was just the beginning. After the sheriff, Harvard's president gave a speech, followed by several invited guest speakers. Once the university-wide part was over, each school returned to its own campus for the actual conferral of degrees.

By the time Rebecca held her diploma in her hand at three o'clock that afternoon, she was exhausted. While standing in place underneath a tree on the campus quad, Rebecca smiled as her parents and brothers took turns taking pictures with her. When they were all finished, Rebecca's cheeks ached from smiling for so long. Her parents asked her if she wanted to grab a late lunch, but she declined.

"I'm sorry. I'm exhausted. I'm going to go back to my room and take a nap before my dinner tonight."

"Who are you meeting again?" her mother asked.

"Emily," Rebecca lied. "I told you about her." She knew her mother would never understand her relationship with Richard, and Emily had already gotten on a plane to Paris for her graduation trip. *There's no way Mother will figure it out.*

****

77

Five hours and a bottle of champagne later, Richard and Rebecca stumbled their way back to campus after having dinner in Central Square. As they walked down the sidewalk, the pit in Richard's stomach grew larger and larger by the minute. He had never been this nervous before in his entire life. *Likely because the rest of my life depends on her answer,* he thought.

When they reached Memorial Drive, the pair turned north toward Weeks Bridge. Halfway through Riverbend Park, Richard stopped walking and drew in a deep breath.

"Marry me."

Rebecca's eyes danced with happiness as she skipped down the dirt path that wove along the river. "What?" she asked, unable to hear over the sound of the wind whipping off the water and the alcohol buzzing in her ears.

"Marry me," Richard repeated, smiling as he said it. He smiled because he was happy, because he graduated from Harvard Business School that day, because he was slightly drunk, and because he hoped that the woman he loved was seconds away from agreeing to become his wife.

Rebecca stopped skipping and turned to face Richard, three yards ahead of him on the path.

"Marry you?" she asked in her Southern drawl.

Richard's heart skipped a beat and he smiled even wider. *Say yes. Say yes. Come on beautiful, say yes.*

Instead of yes, Rebecca laughed.

"Marry you? Are you crazy? No, you're not crazy," she said, shaking her finger and swaying as she walked toward him. "You're drunk. Like me. Mother always said to not make any big life decisions while you're drunk."

"I made this decision two years ago. On the day I met you."

"Yeah right."

"I did." Richard's face turned serious and he started walking toward Rebecca, the gap between them closing as fast as their hearts were racing. "I knew I loved you the first moment I saw you."

78

Richard reached out and pulled Rebecca close, their bodies flush against each other. The movement caught Rebecca off guard and she gasped, but she didn't pull away.

It's now or never, Richard thought. He ran his fingers through her hair, leaned down, and kissed her.

Their lips brushed softly at first – both tentative and unsure. Then Richard pulled Rebecca even tighter and kissed her harder, two years of love and lust exploding in one moment along the riverside. Much to Richard's surprise – and delight – Rebecca's passion matched his. She wrapped her arms around his neck and slid her fingers up through his hair, pulling him down toward her.

Seconds turned to minutes. Minutes that seemed like hours. The world around them disappeared as Richard finally learned the taste of Rebecca's lips and the feel of her curves against his body. A body that grew hotter and more passionate with every passing breath.

"I love you," he whispered between kisses. "Marry me."

Richard regretted speaking as soon as he said the words. The magic of the moment was broken, and Rebecca stepped away from him. She pulled her sweater tight around her shoulders as she walked further back and shook her head from side to side.

"We can't."

"Why not? I lov – "

"Don't say it. Stop saying it. You can't love me."

"Yes, I can," he argued. "I do!"

"We're from two different worlds, Richard. It wouldn't work."

"It would if we wanted it to."

Rebecca's eyes welled with tears. She was torn between the feelings in her heart and the truth in her head. "Be real. You honestly see us living happily ever after?"

"When I look at you, I see my future. I see a lazy Saturday morning, waking up with you in my arms. The two of us making love. Slowly. Passionately. Right before we drift off to sleep again, I see the door pop open and our kids run in, jumping on the bed and asking when they can go outside and play."

"Don't forget the dog," Rebecca said, daring to dream along with him.

"Right. The dog jumped on the bed too and plopped down in the middle of all of us."

Rebecca smiled, bit her lower lip, and reached out to take hold of Richard's hand.

Shit, he thought, as a hundred-pound anvil landed hard on his chest. *She's going to say no.*

A single tear spilled over the edge of Rebecca's eye and rolled down her cheek.

"I'm sorry. I can't marry you." She turned around and took off down the dirt path, stumbling at first before pausing to take off her heels. Once barefoot, Rebecca ran away as fast as she could. When she reached the center of Weeks Bridge, she stopped and turned to see Richard still standing where she left him. Her face and blouse were now soaked wet with tears.

"I love you too," she whispered, watching as he stood in painful disbelief. "I love you too much to let you ruin your life for me."

The conversation with Richard's mom flashed in Rebecca's mind.

"You're not good enough for him, my dear. My son is meant for more. You would only hold him back."

TWENTY-NINE

Richard wandered around Harvard Square for several hours after Rebecca left – finally taking the time to read the plaques and admire the statues dedicated to men who fought to break away from his country. He was standing on the side of Massachusetts Avenue, near Harvard Law School, looking down at gold-plated horseshoes in the cobblestone sidewalk. A sign nearby said this was the path taken by Paul Revere's partner, William Dawes, on the infamous night ride to warn that the British were coming to Boston.

"And if you hadn't ridden," Richard asked aloud, "would I be here today? The first son and heir to an English peer?" He paused. "Would she be here?"

Richard kicked himself for believing that Rebecca would say yes. He had fallen so hard for her, and his feelings were so strong, that he was convinced she felt the same way too. For the past two years, his life had been consumed by Rebecca. He dreamed about her, talked about her, and thought about her. But, scariest of all, Richard had allowed himself to plan.

For the first time in his life, when he thought about his future, there was someone else in it. The nameless, faceless mannequin who was a stand-in for 'future wife' was suddenly a black-haired beauty with eyes the color of the oceans. When he thought about his children, they all had sparkling smiles and high cheekbones like their mother. Rebecca.

She was the first woman to ever break through the fortress around Richard's heart, and instead of marshalling his defenses to repel the intruder, he welcomed her with open arms. Richard allowed himself to wish and hope and dream and plan in a very specific way, and those wishes and hopes and dreams and plans shattered his heart into a thousand little pieces.

It was well past midnight when Richard returned to his dorm room on the Allston side of campus. After strolling around the law school, Richard cut back through Harvard Yard and gladly accepted beer from undergraduates partying outside their dorms. He walked across Weeks Bridge – stopping at the same point where Rebecca did hours earlier. Richard reached into his pocket and pulled out the small velvet box that had been burning a hole in his trousers all night long.

He flipped open the box with his thumb.

The full moon that night made his grandmother's ring shine brilliantly over the Charles River below.

"I can't marry you."

Rebecca's words echoed in Richard's mind and he snapped the ring box shut, nearly tossing it in the river before shoving it in his pocket in an angry huff and finishing his march back to his dorm room.

THIRTY

Love in general is a wonderfully miserable phenomenon. The object of one's desire occupies all of one's thoughts, even when one doesn't want him or her to. Love drives people to do and say ridiculous things, and – rather than being embarrassed – be proud of their lunacy. Love fills a person with incredible joy and infuriating irritation; a warmth unlike any other and a pain worse than the human heart was designed to endure.

And all of that is when the other person loves you too.

Unrequited love violates the law's ban on cruel and unusual punishment.

It's the kind of torture the Geneva Conventions were drawn up to prevent.

Unrequited love . . . well, one had to search no further than the look on Richard Arrington's face to see what it meant.

After returning from his late-night wanderings through Harvard Square, Richard finished off every bottle of alcohol he had in his room and, unable to sleep, organized the remainder of his belongings for his trip home to England. And now he was sitting on the ledge of his dorm room window, watching below as Rebecca and her parents packed up a rented moving truck. Becks was going straight to New York and starting at Goldman Sachs the next week. *Full steam ahead, as always*, he thought. *No breaks. No distractions*.

Richard was both light-headed and heavy-chested at the same time, as if he were floating above himself while also having a pallet of bricks stacked on top of him. Some of that was the hangover, he knew, but most of it originated from the Southern siren in the courtyard below.

After a few more minutes, Richard forced himself to get up from the window and go take a shower. His heart wanted to keep watching Rebecca – to catch every last glimpse of her that he could before she disappeared forever. But his head knew he needed to stop. Needed to focus on something else to keep his tears at bay. Excited and full of love a day before, Richard now faced a future of sunken emptiness, with a hole in his heart that refused to go away.

THIRTY-ONE

Four months later

Richard settled into his life in London and buried himself in his work. He had lined up a job as a junior analyst at an investment firm, and he logged between 80 and 100 hours per week. Richard didn't mind the work, though. It kept his thoughts busy and off of her.

Richard still couldn't say her name. The pain of Rebecca's rejection was too raw. *That's not the worst part, though*, he thought one day on his lunch break. *I can live without being her husband. I can't live with not even being her friend.* Over the last two years at Harvard, Rebecca had become Richard's closest confidant. His person. Now, when he had a bad day at work or saw something funny on the street, who could he tell? *No one gets me like she did.*

He returned from lunch and gave a friendly nod to his secretary, a woman named Tricia. In her mid-thirties and married to a police officer, Tricia was average height with red hair and wore large-framed glasses when she worked. Having gone to secretarial college after her state secondary school, Tricia was qualified and experienced enough to assist far more senior members of the investment firm. But, given Richard's good looks and high profile, Tricia was assigned to him. "The boss knows that I won't fall for Lord Arrington like all of the younger girls in the office," Tricia explained when her husband asked why she was working for 'a kid'.

Richard paused at his doorway and turned to face Tricia. "I'll be here late again tonight. Go home when your work is done. Please. There's no need for you to stay until I leave."

"Sir, office policy says – "

"I know what office policy is," Richard interrupted. "It also says I can change that rule if I want to. And I do. If I catch you here past six, I won't be happy."

****

At midnight that night, Richard turned off the light in his office and went home. *The biggest benefit of staying late*, he thought as he rode in the back of a taxi, *is that there's no traffic at this hour.*

The cab pulled to a stop in front of a beautiful row house on Lower Belgrave Street between Eaton and Chester Squares. Richard paid the tab and stepped out into the brisk night air. It was early October, and the weather was starting to turn cold.

Richard stood on the sidewalk for a moment and admired his home. Three low, wide steps led from the street up to the ground floor entrance. To the left of the black door was a wrought iron fence with a gate and stairs leading down to the lower ground floor. There were two bedrooms and two baths in the basement flat, with another three bedrooms and three baths upstairs. Some of his neighbors rented out their lower ground floor as a separate apartment, and some used it as the servants' quarters. Richard didn't need rental income and didn't want nosy servants. In another life, he and Rebecca would've lived upstairs with their children while a housekeeper and nanny lived downstairs. But that was in another life. The one that was now only a dream.

Richard went inside and walked upstairs to the drawing room. He poured himself a glass of whisky and collapsed on the couch, exhausted from another long day at the office. The London Stock Exchange was set to deregulate at the end of the month, and the world of finance was in an uproar trying to prepare.

As he was starting to drift off to sleep, Richard heard a knock on the door. He ignored it, but the person kept knocking.

"Who the bloody hell is calling at this hour?" he grumbled as he marched down the stairs.

Richard looked through a side window and saw his buddy, Geoffrey, leaning against the door. "What the fuck, mate?"

"Richard!" Geoff said with a smile. "You're finally home! I came by earlier and you weren't here."

"I was working."

"Working shmorking," replied Geoff. He stumbled forward and pushed past Richard to go inside. "All work and no play make Richard a very dull boy."

"Well then, I guess that's me."

Geoff shook his head. Newly single after breaking up with this girlfriend, he had been on a tour of London's hottest nightclubs for three weeks straight.

"C'mon mate. You need to get out."

"No," Richard replied, "I need to sleep. I have to be back at the office first thing tomorrow."

Geoffrey made his way into the kitchen and poured himself a glass of wine. "You're acting like a bloody poof, Arrington. So the girl said no? Who gives a shit? Move on. You're a multi-millionaire. Your father is a fucking peer. This city is full of women who will do whatever you want them to. Don't let one American twat ruin your life."

Richard crossed the room and had Geoff pinned against the wall before his friend knew what was happening.

"Don't you *ever* talk about her like that again. Do you hear me?"

Geoff tried to wriggle free but couldn't escape the hold Richard had on his shirt and jacket. "Chill out. I only meant . . ."

"Say it," Richard growled. "Say 'I'll never talk about her like that again.'"

"Ok, ok. I'll never talk about her like that again."

Richard gave his friend one final shove before releasing him and stepping back from the wall. He ran his hand through his hair and sighed. "Get out of here. Go have fun. Double the fun on my behalf."

"You sure I can't convince you to join me?"

87

"Not tonight, mate. Not tonight."

THIRTY-TWO

Across the Atlantic in New York, Rebecca was having
dinner at one of Manhattan's most spectacular spots –
Windows on the World. Located in the North Tower of the
World Trade Center, the restaurant had floor-to-ceiling
windows with sweeping views of the city below. Rebecca's
table was right next to the glass, and she felt like she was on
top of the world. She looked across the table at her date and
smiled. "This place is amazing. Thank you so much for
bringing me here."

John Bailey smiled back at her. "Of course, honey. Only
the best for you!" He raised his glass and clinked it against
Rebecca's. "Cheers. To us."

"To us."

Rebecca took a sip of her martini and tried not to think
about the last time she said cheers with a man at a restaurant.
It was Richard, of course, during their trip to Hartford. *Stop
it, Becky. That's over. You're here with John.*

Dr. John Bailey was also from Georgia, and he could not
have been any more different from Richard. At five foot nine
with blonde hair and green eyes, John was good looking but
not strikingly so. He attended the University of Georgia for
college and Emory Medical School after that, and he was
now doing his residency at New York-Presbyterian Hospital.
The only child of an unremarkable family in the Atlanta
suburbs, John met Rebecca through mutual friends and
pursued her relentlessly until she agreed to go out with him.
Rebecca liked that about John. *He knows what he wants, and
he goes after it. He wouldn't sit around for two years without
making a move.*

Again, Rebecca shook her head to clear the thoughts of
Richard.

"Are you okay, honey?"

"Hmm? Oh, yes, I'm fine. Just dealing with a lot at work
right now."

"You know," John said, leaning closer to her, "you won't have to work if we get married."

Rebecca almost choked on the olive in her drink. "Married? John, we've known each other for two months."

"And?"

"And . . . I like you, very much, but I think talking about marriage is a little premature."

John shook his head. "I disagree. In fact, I wanted to ask you tonight what your plans are for Thanksgiving. I figured we could start out with my family in Marietta and then drive down to Sandersville to see your folks."

"Umm . . . I . . . "

"Come on, baby. Why waste time when we're such a good match? We're both Southern. We're both good looking. We get along. What else do we need?"

Rebecca sighed. *Passion? Friendship? Love?* she thought. "You're right," she lied. "We don't need anything else."

He's hard working, he's nice, he's handsome, and he wants me. That's as much as I have any right to ask for. Richard was a fairy tale. John is real.

THIRTY-THREE

Richard stayed in London for Christmas. He had a lot of work to do, but he also didn't want to be around his mother's drinking or his father's judgments. His sister, Sarah, joined him on Boxing Day to watch the football matches.

"I come bearing gifts," she said as she walked inside. "Beer, fish, and chips."

Richard took the food and drink into the kitchen while his sister shrugged off her coat and scarf.

"How was Rosewood?" he called out.

"Same as always. The Sinclair-Joneses came by last night, though. We all got drunk and played sardines."

"The drinking part doesn't surprise me," Richard replied. "Are Mum and Dad still trying to push Ivy on me?"

Sarah walked into the kitchen. "Who knows. I'm just hoping that I find somebody to marry before they start arranging a match for me. Speaking of weddings," Sarah added, "who is this for?"

She held up an envelope with Richard's address written in fine calligraphy.

"No one. Put that down."

Sarah ignored his instructions, opened the envelope, and pulled out an engraved invitation.

"Ooh, fancy. 'Dr. and Mrs. Jefferson Lewis," Sarah read, "request the honor of your presence at the marriage of their daughter, Rebecca Leigh Lewis – "

Sarah paused and looked at her brother. "What? She's getting married?"

"Apparently so."

"You're going to go and stop her, right?"

He shook his head. "No."

"Richard!"

He picked up his plate and started walking toward the living room. "She made her choice. I may not like it, but it's done. She's happy. It's not my place to interfere."

"Of course it's your place. Forget the fact that you're in love with her. You're also her best friend!"

Richard let out a deep breath. "I asked her, okay? On graduation night, I asked and she said no."

"Richard – you need to try again."

"It won't work."

"You don't know that."

"Leave it alone, Sarah. I already sent my regrets."

THIRTY-FOUR

In April of 1987, the day after Rebecca's birthday, she joined five of her best friends and bridesmaids for a pub crawl through Manhattan.

"Because somebody's getting marrrriieeeeeddddd!"

Rebecca laughed at her friend Julia's excitement. They had been roommates together at Barnard and now shared an apartment as working women in New York. Julia was a teacher at a prestigious prep school on the Upper West Side and was dating one of John's co-workers at the hospital.

On their third stop of the night, the girls grabbed a table in the corner of a bar in Soho and ordered two rounds of tequila shots.

Emily, Rebecca's friend from Harvard, slammed her empty glass down on the table and motioned to the waiter to bring more. "Now, future Mrs. Dr. Bailey, here's what I want to know."

Rebecca giggled. "What?"

"Whatever happened to Richard?"

The other bridesmaids perked up at the mention of a different man. "Who's Richard?"

"No one," Rebecca said. She glared at Emily.

Undeterred, Emily replied: "he's most certainly not no one."

"Shut up, Em. Nothing happened."

"Nothing happened to him? He disappeared?"

The other girls laughed at Emily's drunken line of questioning, but Rebecca wasn't amused. "He didn't disappear. He's in England. Doing quite well for himself trading stocks and bonds, last I heard."

"Who is this?" asked Marsha, a friend from back home.

"Her ex-boyfriend," Emily volunteered. "Tall. British. Gorgeous. I tried to land him for myself, but he only ever had eyes for the bride here."

"No," Rebecca said, shaking her head. "He was just a friend. We went to business school together."

"Just a friend my ass. You two were inseparable."

"Number one," Rebecca replied, raising her finger, "'were' is the key word. Past tense. And B," she added, eliciting giggles from her friends, "he was never my boyfriend."

"Is he coming to the wedding?" Marsha asked.

"No. He said he's really busy at work and couldn't get the time off. Besides, that's a long way to travel for a weekend."

"To attend your best friend's wedding?" said Emily. "Nowhere is too far for that." She alone saw how close Rebecca and Richard had gotten, although no one knew about graduation night. And Rebecca intended to keep it that way.

The bride-to-be sighed. "Can we please stop talking about Richard? I'm engaged to John. I'm marrying John. Now where's the waiter? We need more shots."

THIRTY-FIVE

Two months later, a day arrived that Richard was dreading. He had almost forgotten about it, but as soon as Tricia handed him his mail that morning, the pit in his stomach returned.

"Hold my calls, please," he said, before walking into his office and shutting the door. He threw the mail down on his desk, sorted through it, and picked up a magazine. It had thick paper stock, a crimson border, and the words HARVARD printed across the top in gold font.

Richard flipped through the pages until he found the one he was looking for: Class News. In bold type, under the heading 'Class of '86', was the note that took Richard's nearly-healed heart and smashed it to bits once again.

Marriages
Rebecca Lewis (B'86) married Dr. John Bailey in Sandersville, Georgia on Saturday, June 6, 1987. Dr. and Mrs. Bailey, both from Georgia, now reside in New York City. He is a Gynecologist and Obstetrician at New York – Presbyterian, and she is an associate at Goldman Sachs.

Reading the words – seeing it in print – made Richard's stomach twist in knots.

A doctor from Georgia, he thought. *Of course that's who she would marry. A Viscount from Britain – a future Marquess – wasn't good enough. But a doctor from Georgia?* Richard shook his head and closed his eyes. *Pull yourself together, man.*

He knew she was getting married. Rebecca even dared to send him an invitation, which he politely declined. *All very civilized*, he thought. But a part of Richard had hoped, somehow, that the wedding would get called off. That someone would stand up and object or Rebecca would ditch John at the altar and show up on Richard's doorstep.

"You alright, sir?" asked Tricia, poking her head into his office.

Richard snapped the magazine shut to hide its contents. "Yes, perfectly fine. Thank you."

"Okay. Don't forget you're due in the conference room in five minutes."

"Shit. On my way."

****

By the time Richard arrived in the conference room for his client meeting, the only seat remaining was next to Penelope Stuckey.

As if today couldn't get any worse, Richard thought.

Penelope looked over at him and smiled. "Good morning. I wasn't sure if you were going to join us."

"Just some last-minute preparation," Richard lied. He started reading the papers in front of him in an effort to ignore his colleague.

Penelope made no secret of the fact that she had a crush on Richard. Distantly related to the newly minted Duchess of York, Sarah Ferguson, Penelope thought her royal connections made her a great match for Richard, Viscount Arrington. She often found excuses to stop by Richard's office, and when he told Tricia to make her leave, Penelope started visiting while his assistant was out at lunch.

"I like your tie today," the young woman offered. "It reminds me of your eyes."

Richard looked down at his red tie. *Right, because red and blue have so much in common.* Their boss picked that moment to enter the room, saving Richard the trouble of responding to Penelope. As soon as the meeting ended, though, she resumed her pursuit.

"Since we're working together on this client, I was wondering if you'd like to grab lunch with me tomorrow. We can talk about the portfolio . . . or not." Penelope stepped closer to Richard and batted her eyelashes.

96

"Sorry, I can't. I have lunch with my sister tomorrow."

"Aww, that's so sweet. What about one day next week?"

Richard sighed. *She's going to make me say it, isn't she?* "I'm trying to focus on my career right now," Richard said. "I'm flattered, but I'm not interested. I'm sorry."

He turned and walked toward his office, not wanting to deal with whatever counterargument Penelope would throw at him. Sitting down at his desk, Richard threw the alumni magazine in his rubbish bin. *Work*, he told himself. *Work is the antidote.*

The next morning dawned bright and beautiful – a gorgeous summer day in England's capital. Birds were chirping, children were playing, and it was 1:00pm in the afternoon before Rebecca crossed Richard's mind. An improvement, he supposed, since thoughts of her usually began before breakfast. The time span was starting to expand, though. Working such long hours didn't leave as much time or space in his head for Rebecca. She was always there . . . just not in the forefront. Richard's friends noticed the change more than he did. He was happier, less explosive, and more likely to live in the present and think of the future.

It didn't take much for Rebecca to return, though. Today's culprit? Tulips. Rows upon rows of tulips in Kensington Gardens where he was meeting his sister for lunch.

"Tulips are my favorite," Rebecca said. "Tulips are right in the middle: classy and beautiful but sunny and fun too."

Richard smiled at the memory. "You are a tulip, Becks," he whispered to himself as he walked through the garden. "Classy and beautiful; sunny and fun. Not too serious. Not too happy."

"Who are you talking to?" asked Sarah. She snuck up on Richard while he was lost in his daydream.

"Hmm? Oh, nobody. Myself. Happens when you get older," he added with a wink and a smile.

"Yeah, you're super old. Everything is downhill after twenty-four."

Richard laughed, slung his arm around Sarah's shoulders, and walked them toward the restaurant. It had become somewhat of a Friday tradition to meet his sister for lunch near Kensington Palace when the weather was nice.

"Sarah is the one person in the world who can understand what it was like with my parents," he had told Geoff a few weeks earlier. "Plus, it's nice to spend time with a girl around my age who isn't trying to get something from me."

As for Sarah, she loved the impact that his time in America had on her brother. *He's much more respectful toward me now,* she thought as the pair sat down at a table on the outdoor veranda. *Not quite feminist, but he treats me like I'm a person and an adult.*

She smiled and leaned forward in her chair. "So . . . before we get to me, what's the story with you?"

"How do you mean?"

"I went by your office a few days ago to pick up the keys to the house, remember?"

Richard nodded, half listening while gazing at the nearby flowers.

"You were in a meeting and your assistant was at lunch, but this other girl came over to help me find them. Tall, blonde, very pretty, very into you."

Richard responded with a growl. "Her name is Penelope Stuckey. And there is no story."

"I don't believe you, big brother."

"You should, little sister. Penelope may want there to be a story, but there isn't. And won't be."

"Why not?" Sarah asked. "She's pretty. Friendly. Obviously keen on you."

"She's keen on anyone with a title."

Sarah rolled her eyes. "Would you stop with your conspiracy theories? If you insist on believing that all women who fancy you only do so because of your rank or money, you'll never be married."

"Not all women," Richard muttered under his breath.

"Right," Sarah said sarcastically. "I forgot about Saint Rebecca . . ."

"Don't!" Richard shot back, slamming his fist on the table. "Don't ever talk about her like that."

99

"Okay, okay," his sister replied, holding her hands up in the air in surrender. She looked around at the other people eating in the restaurant. "Don't make a scene."

Richard snorted and glared at his sister.

Beyond the anger, Sarah saw pain in his eyes. She softened her tone. "I'm sorry, Richard. Truly. At some point, though, you will have to accept that she's moved on. And that it's time for you to move on too."

Richard swirled his water glass in his hand, watching as the liquid rose and fell around the edges.

"Perhaps you're right. Perhaps it is time. But that doesn't mean I'm ready yet."

THIRTY-SEVEN

Later that night, Richard met Geoff for drinks at Wedgies nightclub in Chelsea. It wasn't Richard's usual scene, but Geoff convinced him to step out of his comfort zone. Although neither man needed to work for an income, Geoff had embraced the trust fund life and gave a friendly greeting to the bouncer at the door of the club.

"Welcome back, Mr. Kirkland," said the security officer.

Inside, neon lights flashed through a haze of cigarette smoke and a DJ spun a remix of Queen and Madonna. A pretty brunette escorted them past the dance floor and up a flight of stairs to Geoff's usual spot. Richard looked over at the table next to them and saw a man and woman taking turns snorting cocaine.

"How often do you come here?" Richard asked.

"I don't know. Once a week, maybe. But enough about me," he said. "Tonight is about you. You're going to get drunk, get laid, and wake up with the wonderful realization that this city is chock full of beautiful women who would love to love a future Marquess."

Richard shook his head. "I don't think one night of drunken debauchery can cure a broken heart."

Geoff's face turned serious. "As your oldest friend, I promise to stand by you through as many nights of debauchery as you need. No matter how many pints we have to drink or women we have to screw, I'm here for you."

Richard couldn't help but laugh. "I'm sure you are. And thank you, but no thank you. I'll have one drink and then I'm headed home. It's been a really long week."

****

One drink turned into five, and by the time Richard made his way home he could barely stumble up the stairs to his bedroom.

"Mrs. Schonberg is going to pitch a fit," he mumbled as he undressed and fell into bed. His housekeeper, an older German woman, hated it when he left clothes lying around on the floor.

"You vill never find a vife if you live like a slob," Richard mimicked her accent and favorite saying.

He rolled over onto his back and put his hands behind his head. "Why do I need a wife?" he asked aloud. "Maybe Sarah and Geoff are right. Maybe it is time to move on. Becks is clearly enjoying her life – why shouldn't I?"

The next night, Richard returned to Wedgies. The night after that, it was Annabel's. The famous, exclusive nightclub in Berkeley Square was more to Richard's taste, and he recognized a number of faces from Eton and Cambridge among the crowd. *So this is where all of my friends have been hiding,* he thought as he sat down and ordered a double whisky, neat. It wasn't long before a cute blonde in a tight miniskirt asked Richard if she could join him. Mary seemed like a sweet girl at the club, but she turned into a naughty vixen when they left and went to her apartment. Richard woke up the next morning with the young woman's arms wrapped around his waist, and he knew his lonely nights were over. *This is so much better than moping around my house by myself.*

****

For the next several weeks, Richard accompanied Geoff to whatever bar or nightclub was most popular, ordered a few drinks, and went home with the prettiest girl he could convince to sleep with him. But the disco lights, overpriced drinks, and rampant drug use weren't Richard's scene. He was a social smoker in college but quit his final year, and he never tried the hard stuff. *I hate needles and I hate things going up my nose,* he thought one night as he watched a tray of powder being passed around the table next to him. *There has to be a better method than this.*

102

In September, Richard pulled strings as a Viscount and arranged a long-term reservation for a room at The Savoy Hotel. He had gotten tired of sleeping in strangers' homes, and there was no way he was going to bring his conquests back to his house in Belgravia. *They'll get one look at the address and never leave*, he thought. The room at The Savoy was the best of all worlds: he had a clean, safe location where he could bring his dates. The girls never saw his real home. And he could keep clothes and toiletries there to get ready for work the next morning. *It's perfect.*

By the time the new year of 1988 came along, Richard had also selected a handful of upscale yet lowkey places where he would go on the hunt. The thrill of the chase was the most exciting part, and the bars in Mayfair, Soho, and Covent Garden were full of young co-eds and gorgeous tourists looking to have a night or two of fun.

Two nights was Richard's preference, and as the months went by his nighttime activities started to resemble actual dates with dinner and sometimes dancing. The caliber of women he pursued changed as well, moving from the easiest of yeses to a more sophisticated crowd. Richard liked the challenge. Sometimes they ended up at The Savoy on the first night, and sometimes the woman made him wait. They were always there by night two, though. *They don't call me the Lord of the Ladies for nothing.*

THIRTY-EIGHT

In the summer of '89, Richard met a tall blonde named Jenny. She worked as a nursery teacher, and they frequented the same sandwich shop near his office and her school. After several weeks of flirting, Richard asked the young woman if she'd like to have dinner with him.

"Absolutely," Jenny replied with a smile.

Their first date was at San Lorenzo, an Italian restaurant made famous by the Princess of Wales. She and Prince Charles were dining there the same night, which impressed Jenny to no end. "I love Lady Di," she cooed in delight. But even the proximity to royals couldn't persuade Jenny to go to bed with Richard that night.

"I think it backfired," he told Geoff the next day. The two friends had met up for a lunchtime game of tennis. "She was more focused on Charles and Diana than she was on me. I looked like chopped liver compared to them."

"Maybe next to Diana," Geoff replied, "but definitely not Charles. I say this as a confident heterosexual man – you're much better looking than he is."

Richard laughed out loud. "Thank you. I appreciate that."

"Where's date number two?"

"I think Kensington Place," Richard replied between backhands. "It's new and trendy but less pretentious."

"Where you can shine in comparison," Geoff concluded. "I like it. Can't wait for the report after. From what you've said, this Jenny girl is a knockout."

****

Dinner at Kensington Place was everything Richard hoped it would be. Modern British cooking, a bustling crowd, and no royals in sight. When they finished their meal,

Richard and Jenny walked hand in hand through Kensington Gardens and Hyde Park before catching a cab to The Savoy.

Richard nodded a greeting to the front desk staff. He knew they all thought he was a rake, but he didn't care. *They would do the same thing if they were me.*

He led Jenny back to the hotel bar and ordered them a bottle of wine. The conversation was easy and relaxed, and Richard realized that he enjoyed Jenny's company. *Maybe more than any woman since – "*

A shadow crossed his face.

"Are you okay?" Jenny asked. "You look pale."

"Hmm? Oh, yes, I'm fine."

Richard smiled and picked up the wine to pour his date another glass. He was about to ask if she wanted to order a second bottle when the tall blonde smirked and said: "I guess this is it for us, huh?"

Richard stared back at the girl, confused. "I don't understand."

"This is our second date."

"Yes . . . and I thought it was going rather well."

"Me too," Jenny replied. "Absolutely. But this is our second date, and you don't ever go out with a girl more than twice."

"That's not – " Richard started to argue then paused, thinking back over the past two years and his torrid run through London's ladies.

Jenny smiled. "It's fine. I knew that before our first date. You've done the same thing with three of my best friends."

"Why did you still go out with me?"

She shrugged. "All of your girls say they have a great time. And you are fun to be around. Plus, I guess, well, I guess we all kind of hope that we'll be the one who breaks the pattern and wins you over."

Richard sat back in his chair and gulped down the rest of his wine. A large pit appeared in his stomach, and he got the same nervous, nauseated feeling that he used to have before being punished in boarding school.

After a long silence, Richard sat up straight and let out a deep breath.

"Jenny, you're a lovely girl and I would be honored if you would have dinner with me again this Saturday."

"Because you genuinely like me or because you're trying to prove a point and not feel bad?"

"Does it matter?" Richard asked.

Jenny smiled, shook her head, and reached across the table to hold Richard's hand. "Thank you, but no thank you. I don't want a pity date."

THIRTY-NINE

Richard escorted Jenny to the taxi stand in front of the hotel, kissed her on the cheek, and sent her home. As her car drove away, he sighed. *Definitely not what I was hoping for this evening.*

"One for you as well, Lord Arrington?" asked the doorman. He worked most evenings at The Savoy and recognized Richard as one of its frequent guests.

Richard looked back toward the hotel bar and then up into the night sky. "Not tonight, Simon. I think I'll walk."

Richard left the hotel and walked down to the Victoria Embankment at the riverside. He shuffled his feet along the concrete path and was in no hurry as he made his way home.

I didn't realize I had a reputation, he thought. Richard's mind replayed all of his activities for the past two years. "How could you not have a reputation, you wanker? Those girls see you coming from a mile away." *And yet they still go out with me. And sleep with me.* He shook his head. *Women.*

By the time he reached Westminster Abbey, Richard had started trying to justify his two-date rule. *One date gets boring,* he thought. *You say the same things on every first date, and at three dates people start to get ideas about futures and feelings. Two dates are perfect. A little variety, a little fun.* Richard grinned. *A little more fun upstairs if she's willing – and they usually are.*

He glanced over at the church and winced. "Sorry, God. I guess you got your payback, didn't you? Making me the talk of London."

Richard stopped walking and leaned against the Abbey's rail. The Palace of Westminster was to his left, with Westminster Bridge beyond that. Behind him was St. James's Park and the stark contrast of his present and his future: the glitz and glamour of Mayfair's clubs next to the stodgy government buildings of Whitehall. Richard knew that one day he would have to take his father's place in the House of

Lords and deal with the Whitehall bureaucracy. "But not tonight," he said. "Not tonight."

Richard continued walking until he reached Belgravia and his house that betrayed no signs of being home to London's most notorious womanizer. The five-story, freehold house had been in the Arrington family for generations, but Richard didn't let any of the neighbors know that. As far as they were concerned, he was a bachelor tenant who worked long hours and had few visitors. He liked it that way. *I'm not Lord Dublinshire yet*, Richard thought. *Not bloody yet.*

FORTY

Richard changed his habits after his encounter with Jenny. He got rid of his standing reservation at The Savoy, and he only dated on occasion. His run as London's most elusive bachelor was fun, to be sure, but the last thing Richard wanted was to bring shame to his family. He had two years of memorable conquests to help keep his mind off Rebecca, and Richard knew he was lucky to escape the time period without any unwanted diseases or children.

"It's time to be a grown up," he told himself as he looked in the mirror while getting ready for work. He was twenty-six now and, as the Dean of Harvard Business School once told his class, the time for youthful indiscretions was over.

For the next several years, Richard poured himself into his work. Without nighttime escapades clouding his mind, Richard rose through the ranks at his firm and was made a full partner days before he turned thirty-one. He also developed a taste for politics and was watching the rise of the Labour Party with keen interest. His family, like most of the aristocracy, were Conservatives. But Richard's time in America taught him the importance of seeing both sides, and Labour's offer to lower taxes made the business-minded Richard even more interested in the party. He didn't tell his father that, though, when he asked to start sitting in on parliament staff meetings. Richard merely claimed he wanted to start the learning process since the House of Lords seat would be his one day.

"I'm glad you're finally coming around, my boy," his father said after one of the meetings. "It's important for people like us to take our positions seriously. We have a legacy to uphold. Speaking of," he added, "I think it's time you find a wife and produce an heir."

Richard groaned. "Do you really have to phrase it like that, Dad? Can't there be any mention of love or romance?"

"No. Not in our world, son."

"Fine," Richard replied. "I'll start the search."

FORTY-ONE

Three weeks later, Richard was an hour late to work. Tricia, his assistant, was beginning to worry. Then he started walking down the hall.

Tricia smelled Richard before she saw him. Even at the height of his dating life, he usually did a better job hiding his escapades from the night before.

Today is a definite exception, she thought.

Richard's hair was tousled, his clothes disheveled, and a scruffy shadow emerged from his normally clean-shaven face. Richard walked past Tricia's desk, and she was hit by a wave of cheap beer and cigarettes . . . a combination that she knew meant last night was particularly bad. Most evenings, Richard left his office in The City and either went home or made his way to Soho or Mayfair for a quiet dinner with friends.

But cheap beer and cigarettes? Tricia shook her head. Those things meant that Richard, Viscount Arrington spent the night before in a grungy dive bar that would have kicked him out if they knew he was the son of a peer.

Richard stopped in his doorway and mumbled a gruff "coffee" to Tricia before going into his office and shutting the door.

His assistant delivered Richard's coffee a few minutes later. She placed the drink on the desk and stepped as far away as she could. *He smells awful*, Tricia thought, resisting the urge to cover her nose. "Dare I ask?" she ventured.

Richard raised his head up from the desk to sip the coffee. Still wearing yesterday's suit, he grabbed a newspaper article and tossed it toward his assistant.

Tricia looked down at the paper in her hand, which she saw was the latest edition of the Harvard Business School alumni newsletter. Underneath a picture of a mother and baby was a caption:

Mrs. Rebecca Lewis-Bailey, Class of 1986, and her husband are pleased to announce the birth of their son, Jonathan Hubbard Bailey. Born October 2, 1994, in New York City. Jonathan joins older sister Sarah, age two.

"She gave him a son," Richard said. "A fucking heir."

Tricia knew better than to respond. Instead, she counted to five in her mind, placed the article back on Richard's desk, and left the room.

So that's who she is, Tricia thought as she sat down at her desk. She knew her boss had been in love once before – a deep, painful love from which he never fully recovered. She gathered that much over the years from bits and pieces of conversations. But never a name. Or when or how Richard knew the woman.

A business school classmate. An American, no less, Tricia thought. *Or at least she lives in America now.* The assistant shook her head. *Poor Richard. The love of his life just gave birth to a son and heir . . . only it wasn't his son or his heir.*

112

FORTY-TWO

Upstate New York
2001

Rebecca spent her fourteenth wedding anniversary alone at her cabin in the Hudson River Valley. Both of her kids were at summer camp in Maine, and she and John were supposed to have a romantic weekend by themselves. But Dr. Bailey, now an attending physician at New York-Presbyterian Hospital, changed his plans at the last minute and claimed he couldn't get away from work. Rebecca didn't know if it was true or not, but by that point in her marriage she wasn't surprised.

What would have surprised me, she thought as she stepped outside onto the cabin's porch, *is if we actually had a romantic weekend. Here or anywhere.* Rebecca bent her leg backwards and stretched out her quad, then switched and did the other leg. After warming up, she stepped off the porch and ran to the left, down a dirt path that was two feet wide.

The cabin was Rebecca's happy place – where she went to escape the rigors of her job as a partner at Goldman Sachs. The ten-acre property in Wappingers Falls, New York reminded Rebecca of her small hometown in Georgia, only with less humidity, fewer mosquitos, and no gossip from nosy neighbors.

Rebecca's other stress release was running. She was as thin, if not more so, than she had been in business school and stayed that way by running at least three times a week. When they bought the cabin, Rebecca hired contractors to cut a trail through the property. There was a five-mile loop that started at the house and wound through the trees, past the pond, and along the riverbank before making its way back to the cabin.

She did some of her best thinking while running, but today's thoughts swirled in dark clouds about her troubled marriage. Everything looked perfect on paper, and things were good in the beginning. But when Rebecca refused to stop working and began making more money than John, the relationship turned sour. He started working longer hours and traveling to more and more medical conferences. Rebecca knew he was probably seeing other women, but she didn't have any proof. And she didn't want to find any. Not with two young kids at home.

"I haven't succeeded because of John," she said aloud as she ran. "I've succeeded in spite of him. We were never a good match to begin with."

There was a part of Rebecca's personality that ran deeper than anything cotillion and sweet tea could wash away. A spirit in her blood that spoke of moccasins rather than heels, beads rather than pearls, and red skin rather than white. Rebecca's mother called herself 'Black Irish', but the truth was she was part Creek. And Rebecca was part Creek. The part of her that struggled and fought and yearned to be free.

John Bailey, on the other hand, was as English as English could be – with one set of grandparents immigrating after the First World War and the other after the Second. A piece of bitter irony, Rebecca knew, since the man she rejected and the man she married had so much in common. *Ethnically, anyway*, she thought.

John had wanted a pretty trophy wife who would bear him even prettier trophy children, and he gambled that he could convert Miss Lewis from a Harvard-educated career woman into a proper Southern housewife. "A smart wife means smart kids," he told his friends at his bachelor party. "Besides, she's from Georgia. All good Southern girls eventually turn into their mothers."

FORTY-THREE

By the end of the summer, John and Rebecca were still on speaking terms but lived more like roommates than spouses. The detached approach to their marriage lifted some of the tension in their home, and everyone – including their kids – seemed happier.

If Rebecca had her way, her family would live in Rye or White Plains or some other sleepy suburb of the city. Not for her sake, of course. Rebecca hated to commute. But for her children's sake. She wanted them to have the kind of upbringing she did: slow, calm, and as protected as possible. *The exact opposite of what they have here*, she thought while she sipped her morning coffee from the balcony of their Manhattan condo. She and John bought the three-bedroom apartment on the Upper East Side when their daughter Sarah was born. It was nice, to be sure, and provided the family with everything they needed. *But it's still the city*, Rebecca thought as a police siren screamed by on the street below. *Central Park is nice, but a private yard is better. The Subway is great, but learning to ride a bike in a quiet, tree-lined neighborhood is a slice of Heaven.* The investment banker sighed. Living in Manhattan was another trade-off she made in life – this one in order to please her husband. Others, like working full time or traveling for business, were decisions she made for herself. But the fact that they were her choice didn't lessen the anguish or guilt she felt on days like today, when the nanny had whisked her kids off to school while Rebecca was still in the shower. She felt the pain especially hard today since she was headed down to DC for meetings for the rest of the week.

Mommy guilt, Rebecca thought. *My kids' nanny and teachers know them better than I do. And certainly spend more time with them.* Rebecca blinked her eyes to hold back tears. She didn't have time to redo her makeup before she left for the airport. *You chose this, Becky. Anyone can change a*

115

diaper or drive carpool – very few people can do what you do at work. You didn't put yourself through everything at HBS just to sit home and knit.

The last thought hit Rebecca hard, and she knew she would be fixing her mascara in the taxi en route to LaGuardia. Not because she hadn't enjoyed her classes or her time at the world-famous business school. But because of another trade-off she made; another 'what if' that haunted her on days like this. *Richard.* Her first love. *My only true love, if we're being honest*, she thought. *I loved him too much to let him throw it all away for me*, Rebecca reminded herself. *Besides, that's long done now.*

FORTY-FOUR

A mid-September morning dawned bright and beautiful, and Richard admired the weather outside his office window. As the day continued, his thoughts turned to leaving the office early and getting in a game of tennis with Geoff. Richard opened a new email draft to propose the idea to his friend, and a news alert popped up on his screen: PLANE CRASHES INTO NYC WORLD TRADE CENTER.

Holy shit, Richard thought, quickly turning on the small TV in his office. BBC One was beginning coverage of the crash, and Richard turned up the volume. Tricia walked into the room to join him.

"What happened?" she asked.

"I don't know. They're saying it was an accident, but I don't see how you accidentally fly into a skyscraper."

Twenty minutes later, Richard and his assistant watched live as a second plane flew into the other World Trade Center tower.

"Oh my God," Tricia whispered, covering her mouth with her hand.

Richard's thoughts jumped straight to Rebecca. "She has to get out of there."

He looked up the office number for Goldman Sachs and called it, but no one answered. After several tries, Richard opened his desk drawer and started pulling out pieces of paper, throwing them over his shoulder when they weren't what he was looking for.

"Where the bloody hell is my business school thing?"

"What thing?"

"You know, the alumni one with all of the names and contact information."

Tricia left the room for a minute and returned with a small white booklet.

"Here you go, sir. It was in the file cabinet."

Richard snatched the item from Tricia's hands and flipped through the pages until he found the directory.

"Here she is," he said, picking up his phone. "Rebecca Lewis-Bailey."

Richard dialed her cell phone number. No answer. He tried again. Still no answer. In the frantic minutes and hours that followed, even as his own office was evacuated in an abundance of caution, Richard continued to try to reach Rebecca. He didn't care what it looked like, didn't care that they hadn't spoken in years, and didn't even care what Rebecca or her husband would think. He had to reach her. Had to know that she was okay. That she was alive.

****

In New York City, Rebecca was walking north on Broadway – part of a sea of dust-covered zombies exiting the war zone that was Manhattan's financial district. She saw that people were trying to call her from all over the country and the world, but Rebecca wasn't interested in answering. She was focused on making one call: to her children's school.

Rebecca's feet were beginning to hurt, and it was only then that she realized she left the Goldman Sachs building wearing her four-inch Manolo Blahnik heels. She kept a pair of ballet flats at her office and wore those when walking to lunch or other errands, but everything had happened so fast that she barely remembered to grab her cell phone and house keys before running for her life.

The first two Duane Reade stores that she passed were abandoned by frightened workers. It wasn't until the corner of Broadway and Grand, over a mile north from her office, that Rebecca gave up and ducked into a drugstore. She grabbed the first pair of cheap, plastic flip-flops that she saw. The bright purple, polka-dotted shoes were hideous, but they felt amazing on her blistered feet. Placing a $50 bill on the abandoned checkout counter, Rebecca and her $4.99 shoes continued their march north toward her children.

118

It was 3:00am in London before Richard finally reached Rebecca. He had stopped trying to call, and instead stayed awake watching news coverage and keeping an eye on the black screen of his phone – praying for it to ring.

He picked up as soon as the small, silver Nokia flashed her name.

"Rebecca??"

"I thought it might've been you," she replied in a tired voice. "Twenty-eight missed calls from the same number in London."

"I had to know you were okay."

"I'm alive," Rebecca said. "'Okay' is going to take some more time."

Worry replaced the relief that Richard had been feeling. "Are you injured?" he asked.

"No, no, I'm fine. Well, I have nasty blisters on my feet from walking so far. But all things considered . . . "

Her voice trailed off and Richard could hear muffled sobs on the other end of the line.

"I'll let you go," he said. "Thank you for calling me back. I really just needed to know you made it out."

"Is it . . . is it alright if we stay on the phone a little longer? The kids are asleep and John is at the hospital. He probably won't come home for days. I'd just . . . I mean, it's nice to have someone to talk to. To fill the quiet."

"Of course," Richard replied. "Of course, darling."

Rebecca heard the term of endearment but didn't object. She was alive when thousands of others weren't. If the day had taught her anything, it was to stop pushing people away.

"How are your kids?" Richard asked, trying to find a good subject to discuss.

"They're shaken up. Sarah is nine and Jonathan is only seven, so it's hard to explain to them what's going on.

They've never been alive during wartime . . . they don't understand what it is to have an enemy like this."

"What happened, Becks?"

She let out a long, trembling breath. Richard wasn't the first person to ask her to recount her harrowing experience – her parents, brothers, and friends all had as well. But there was a comfort in Richard's voice. Comfort in his concern for her, and a trust built many years earlier that let her know she would be safe with him.

"My office is at 85 Broad. A five-minute walk from the Towers. We're downwind, though, so all of the smoke and debris was floating by in the sky outside my window.

"We didn't know what it was, at first. Maybe a bomb. Maybe an accidental plane crash. Nobody knew anything." She paused. "Then the second plane hit."

Richard wanted to respond, wanted to reach through the phone and wrap his arms around her in a hug. But instead, he stayed silent and listened.

"We all evacuated at that point. The trains had stopped running, so I walked. I left my office in such a hurry that I forgot to grab the flats I always keep underneath my desk. I walked in my heels, and after that I walked barefoot until I found a Duane Reed that was open where I could buy a pair of plastic flip-flops. Then I walked some more. No cabs anywhere to be found.

"I finally got ahold of the school about thirty minutes into the walk. The kids were fine . . . they were all being held in their classrooms until a parent or nanny came to get them." She scoffed in disbelief remembering the day. "It took me two and a half hours to walk from my office to Trinity School. It would normally take about thirty minutes by car. Two and a half hours in a dusty, sweaty business suit and $5 flip-flops from the drug store. Plus another fifteen minutes home after that."

"Oh my God, Becks."

"I'm not complaining. I'm not. I'm alive. I'm safe. My kids are safe. John is safe."

"Just because you survived doesn't mean you're not a victim, too. It's okay to not be okay."

The phone went silent, and again Richard heard muffled sobs on the other end of the line.

"I'm trying so hard to hold it all together," Rebecca said through her tears. "John has been at the hospital ever since it happened, and the kids are scared and don't understand. I told our housekeeper not to come in . . . there's no point with us all home. I just . . . I just . . . "

"You need to not have to be strong. Even if only for a few minutes."

"Is that horrible of me?"

"No," Richard replied. "It's human of you. And I'll be your rock. Whenever you need me. I'm here."

FORTY-SIX

London, England
2006

Richard's cell phone buzzed in his pocket, and he pulled it out to see the name 'Becks' flashing on the screen.

It was unusual for Rebecca to call him. After their late-night conversation on 9/11, Richard and Rebecca resumed a cordial but distant friendship. Happy birthday and Merry Christmas text messages were exchanged, along with the occasional email about a current event in global finance. But they very rarely talked on the phone.

Richard justified the communications in his mind as being business savvy – after all, he and Rebecca were key players at their respective firms and even had some clients in common. *As long as we keep it surface-level, I'm fine*, he told himself. It had now been twenty years since he'd seen Rebecca in person, and he was finally able to think about her and speak to her without spiraling into a puddle of heartbreak.

"Hi, Rebecca," he said as he answered her call. "To what do I owe the surprise?"

"Well, it's you that surprised me. I had an email alert a few minutes ago from the HBS alumni association. It seems Richard Arrington, Class of '86, is running for Parliament?"

Richard chuckled. "Indeed, he is."

"I thought you were already in Parliament?"

"Eh, sort of. I inherited my dad's seat in the House of Lords when he passed away last year. But I resigned from that so I could run for a spot in the House of Commons."

"You were already in the upper house and gave it away to maybe join the lower house?"

Richard laughed. "It sounds a bit crazy when you phrase it like that. But yes."

"Why?"

"After the 7/7 bombings last year, I wanted to do more. We've got terrorist attacks and wars going on, and I didn't feel right sitting by not doing anything. Britain needs its best people leading the charge right now. Maybe it's arrogant of me to say, but I believe I'm one of those people."

"Of course you are," Rebecca replied. "Good for you. That's great. I only wish I could fly over and vote for you myself."

Richard smiled, and Rebecca could hear the happiness – and nerves – in his voice. "Thank you, Becks. Hopefully there are a lot of other people out there who want to vote for me too!"

FORTY-SEVEN

Richard struggled early in the polls, finding it difficult to overcome his aristocratic background. Halfway through the campaign, he hired a brash young man from Liverpool to be his manager. Tripp Taylor had a public school education but never attended university, choosing instead to work on political campaigns. At a mere twenty-one years old, he already had three years' experience under his belt and an impressive 14-2 winning record.

Tripp made Richard change out of a suit and wear jeans and a button-down with the sleeves rolled up. Richard's dog, Buddy, became a regular fixture at campaign events. People loved the goofy yellow lab, and they started to love Richard as well. His poll numbers began to climb. For the final two weeks of the campaign, Richard and Tripp spent ten hours a day canvassing his district, knocking on doors and asking for votes.

By the time election day arrived in mid-December, Richard won in a landslide.

After all the votes were counted and all the hands shaken, Richard and Tripp went back to Rosewood. The grand hall was decorated for Christmas, with garland wrapped around the staircase and a giant tree in the middle of the room. Richard breathed in the smell of fresh pine and smiled. *I love Christmas trees.*

The staff of Rosewood all gathered in the hall and greeted the new Lord Dublinshire, MP with cheers of congratulations. Carl Guinn, the former footman who was now the butler, escorted Richard and Tripp into the library where Richard's mother and sister were waiting for them.

"Well done, my boy," said the Dowager Marchioness. Victoria Arrington had aged a lot in the last year, with the death of her husband taking a hard toll, but she was still a commanding presence. Not a hair was out of place on her head, and Richard knew that her outfit cost more than he paid Tripp for the whole campaign.

"Congrats, bro!" Sarah chimed in. She was Lady Sarah Miller now, having married a university professor fifteen years earlier. Sarah had two boys, Carter and William, who were both away at boarding school. Carter, as Richard's closest living male relative, was heir to the Dublinshire title and Rosewood estate.

"I knew you could do it!" Sarah exclaimed. "Here, have a drink. Celebrate!"

Sarah handed him her glass and went to the bar cart to make herself another one.

The party of four – Richard, Tripp, Victoria, and Sarah – lasted for about an hour before the two ladies called it a night.

After they left the room, Richard poured two fresh glasses of whisky and walked over to the couch, handing one to Tripp.

"Cheers," Richard said. "To you. I never would've won this thing without you."

Tripp smiled and clinked glasses with his boss. He took a deep breath and said: "About that. I've been thinking. I really enjoyed this election, and I'm tired of bouncing around from town to town running different campaigns. Would you have any interest in keeping me on as a member of your staff?"

Richard leaned back in his seat. "I'll do you one better, kid. How does chief of staff sound?"

"I . . . umm . . . I'm honored," Tripp managed to say. "I was not expecting that at all. I would love to – but I don't know what I'm doing. I've never worked on Parliament staff before."

"And I've never been a MP. We can learn together," Richard said. "It's much more important to me that I have staff I can trust. We'll figure out the rest as we go."

A huge smile crossed Tripp's face. "Yes sir." He took a long sip from his whisky glass and shook his head when the liquid burned going down.

"Not used to the hard stuff?"

"I'm a broke, twenty-one-year-old campaign manager. Expensive whisky doesn't sit high on my shopping priorities."

"Well, stick with me and that'll change." Richard laughed. "Or just stick with me and drink mine."

"Cheers to that," Tripp replied. He paused. "Can I ask you something? Now that I'm your chief of staff and all?"

"Sure."

"Why have you never been married? We got that question all the time during the campaign. Even had to fight off the rumors you were gay. What's a smart, rich, good-looking guy like you doing still single?"

Richard sighed and placed his glass down on the table in front of him. "Truth? I've been in love with the same woman for the past, shit, for the past twenty-two years."

"What? But – "

"Don't believe everything you see."

Tripp stared at his boss, dumbstruck. "Never married. No kids. A different woman on your arm for every big function. But in love with the same lady for over twenty years?"

Richard nodded his head. "She's beautiful. Smart. Funny. An incredible combination of compassion and warmth wrapped around a spine of steel." He smiled and picked up his drink to take another sip. "She could probably beat me in a footrace, bakes the best chocolate pie I've ever tasted, and a long time ago, if I was lucky – if I was *really* lucky – she would look my way and smile." Lord Dublinshire paused and twirled his glass in his hand. "My world stopped spinning, my cold English heart warmed over, and for that brief moment in time I felt like the luckiest man in the world. All because she looked my way and smiled."

"If you feel that way about her . . . "

126

"Why am I sitting here alone?"

"Well, yeah."

Richard sighed and took another long, slow drink of whisky. "She's taken. At first, I was afraid of her. I see that now. She was too spirited. Too challenging. Then, she was afraid of me. Afraid that what we had together might make her lose sight of who she was and who she wanted to be."

"And then?"

"Then some bloke came along who wasn't afraid of her. And didn't scare her. And marked off every damn little box on her future husband checklist.

"So, she's taken," Richard concluded. "Despite what my political opponents say, I'm not a total bastard. I'm not going to steal another man's wife."

Tripp leaned back in his chair and stared at his boss. A finance wiz turned political master. A man who would've been knighted for his economic efforts if he hadn't already inherited a title. And a man who lived and worked for over twenty years under the weight of a broken heart.

"Dude, that sucks."

Richard downed the rest of his drink. "Want to know the bloody worst of it all? She's taken, but so am I. She has my heart. I'm ruined for anyone else." He paused. "All because she looked my way and smiled."

FORTY-EIGHT

A few minutes later, Tripp said goodnight to his boss and went upstairs to the guest room he had been using during the campaign. Richard ran in his home district near the town of Battle, so it made sense to use Rosewood as the base of operations.

After saying goodbye to Tripp, Richard pulled loose his bowtie and unbuttoned the top of his shirt. Walking over to the drink cart in the corner of the library, he poured himself another glass of whisky. The square crystal container clanged against the metal cart when he put it back down, and for half a second the newly elected MP thought he might've broken it. But the family heirloom held, the liquor stayed put, and Richard breathed a sigh of relief.

"At least one of us isn't broken," he said, lifting his glass in salute to the decanter. He took a large gulp and relished the burn as the alcohol worked its way down his throat. "On what should be the best day of my life, Rebecca is still haunting me. How's that new song go?"

The melody to Rascal Flatts' 'What Hurts the Most' played in his mind. "What hurts the most was being so close," he sang aloud. "Having so much to say. Watching you walk away. And never knowing what could have been."

Richard smiled, but not because of the lyrics or the whisky or the pain in his heart. He smiled because it was a country song, and Rebecca loved country music. After hearing so much of it in her dorm room during school, Richard had grown to like it too.

The smile faded, though, as it always did when his thoughts turned to her. Lord Dublinshire – now officially Richard Arrington, MP – gulped down more of his drink as he walked from the corner of the room to the sofa and sat down. He reached to undo the second button of his evening shirt but stopped when he noticed a stack of Christmas cards lying on the coffee table in front of him.

Hmm. Guinn must have put them there this afternoon, he thought.

Richard leaned forward and picked up the collection of holiday greetings.

Best wishes and Happy New Year.
Sir Arthur Walsh

"Same to you, old man," he replied, lifting his glass to his lips again.

The next card had a picture of Rudolph the Red Nosed Reindeer on the front. Scribbled inside was: "Happy Christmas – remember, you're weird and none of the other kids like you."

Richard threw his head back and laughed. He loved the tradition that he and his sister had of sending insulting cards instead of loving, mushy ones.

He finished off his glass before looking at the third card. A beautiful manger scene was on the front, and when Richard picked up the card, a photo fell out onto the floor. He bent down to get it, but the whisky in his stomach and the image in his hand combined to give Lord Dublinshire a swift punch to the gut.

The card was from her.

Who else? he thought.

"Of course she sends the prettiest card. And of course she includes a picture of her and her kids and her goddamn husband."

Anger and jealousy poured out of Richard, even more so the longer he looked at the family portrait. *Husband, wife, son, and daughter*, he thought. *So fucking perfect.* Richard set his jaw and let out a deep, frustrated growl. *She got everything she ever wanted. And he got everything I ever wanted.*

****

129

Three thousand miles away, Rebecca sat in the back of a Lincoln town car as its driver battled afternoon rush hour. Her head was buried in her cell phone, and her thumbs moved at warp speed to respond to the incoming flood of emails. While December meant holidays and winding down for many people, for Rebecca it was full steam ahead. She was the partner in charge of Goldman Sachs' most complex mergers and acquisitions, which meant that the rush to beat the end-of-year made her work life miserable. Adding on top of that were a dramatic teenage girl and a very active pre-teen boy. *Don't forget the husband with an image to maintain*, she thought. It was John who needed her today for a holiday party at his hospital, which was why Rebecca found herself in a car at 4:30pm instead of behind her desk.

I don't know why I still do this shit for him. He never lifts a finger for me. Rebecca shook her head to clear her thoughts. *Work. Focus on work.*

A few minutes later, though, as the car inched along Manhattan's busy streets, Rebecca's mind returned to her marriage. She knew John was busy. He was an attending physician at New York-Presbyterian. *But I'm busy too*, she thought. *I'm a partner at fucking Goldman Sachs.* She let out a deep breath to calm her nerves. *Don't walk into the party upset. That will hurt you more than it hurts him.*

Rebecca put her phone down in her lap and looked out the window. "That's what my mother would say," she told herself.

"What was that, ma'am?" asked the driver.

"Nothing, nothing. I'm just talking to myself."

Mother would say something like that, though, Rebecca repeated, this time remembering to keep her thoughts silent. *'Go to the bathroom and fix your face. A man who doesn't want to be involved won't care if you're upset. And people won't remember him standing quietly at the party. They'll remember you in tears. And hold it against you.'*

If anyone knew about being in a marriage with a distant husband, it was her mother. Her dad, Dr. Lewis, was a walking contradiction in their small Georgia town: a tough, hard man who preached family values at the dinner table but often left after to go to 'work', which was usually code for his mistress' house. A brilliant doctor guided by ignorant prejudices. A devout Christian who rarely graced the doorway of a church. And a bigoted racist who was the only doctor in the area who would treat African American patients.

Rebecca grew up surrounded by her father's contradictions and her mother's tireless efforts to bridge the gaps and sweep up the messes they left behind. As a result, Rebecca developed an uncanny ability to read people and situations. To see not only what others wanted her to see, but also the truth beneath the surface. Her knack for predicting future events earned her a reputation on Wall Street as something of a psychic, but in reality Mrs. Lewis-Bailey was reading signs and cues that others didn't realize they were giving.

She had seen the writing on the wall with John for several years now, but she didn't have the courage to confront him. *Or the evidence*, she thought. *Besides, I'll be alone with him or alone without him. The only difference is the damage a divorce would do to the kids.*

Her car continued to work its way north on First Ave toward the Lenox Hill neighborhood where John's hospital was, with horns honking and voices yelling their daily traffic melody. On the right, standing tall against the waterfront of the East River, was the United Nations' headquarters. The light gray building with bright blue windows glistened in the December afternoon sun. Rebecca's eyes wandered to the rows of international flags, and one flag in particular. The Union Jack always reminded her of Richard.

I wonder if he won his election?

Rebecca picked up her Blackberry and searched his name in Google.

'Hereditary Lord Elected MP'

'Arrington Wins'
'A Marquess in the Commons'

England's newspapers were having a field day with articles covering Richard's win. *It is quite the story*, Rebecca thought. *He's born into a seat in their Senate and he gives it up to run for a spot in the House?* She smiled. *He did it, though!*

"We're here, ma'am," said the driver. Looking up, Rebecca realized that they had been sitting in front of New York-Presbyterian Hospital for several minutes.

"I'm sorry. Thank you so much. I don't know where my head is today." Rebecca smiled as she exited the car, thanking the driver once again for the smooth ride.

"I do know where my head is, though," she muttered under her breath. "It's in England. With him."

A group of doctors' wives spotted Rebecca and called her name, forcing her to put Richard out of her mind. *You're married to John*, she thought. *And you have no one to blame for that but yourself.*

FORTY-NINE

One month later, after end-of-year close, Christmas morning, and New Years' Eve parties had all passed, Rebecca found herself thinking once again of Richard. This time, though, she had a somewhat reasonable excuse. She had been invited to give a guest lecture at the London School of Economics, and her plane left the next morning for seven days in England. *A full week without my kids and without John. In the same city as Richard for the first time since we left Harvard.*

Rebecca shivered at the thought of their graduation. The crisp night air. The sound of the river flowing by. The feeling of Richard's body and lips pressed against hers.

She shook her head to try to clear the memory, but it came roaring back. Forcing her to think about the smell of Richard's cologne. The soft waves in his hair. The way the world around them melted away as they were lost in each other's arms.

"Rebecca? Hello?"

She turned to see her husband standing in the doorway of their bedroom.

"Are you alright? You look flushed."

"Huh? Oh, yeah, I'm fine. Just a little stressed trying to figure out what to pack."

"It's a business trip. You go on them all the time."

"I know, I know. But I'm giving a lecture. And it's England – they're more particular about their clothes."

John rolled his eyes. "You're a partner at Goldman Sachs. You have two children. A husband. An elderly mother. You have more important things to worry about than your wardrobe."

After he left the room, Rebecca closed her eyes and let out a deep breath. *Bastard.*

****

Goldman Sachs' Gulfstream V landed at London City Airport the next day. The firm had splurged and sent Rebecca on its private plane, since they viewed her speaking engagement as a way to recruit new top talent in England. A black town car was waiting at the private jet center and took her from London's east suburbs into the heart of the city. She was staying at The Savoy – one of London's finest hotels that was also a mere ten-minute walk from the campus where she was speaking.

On her second day in town, Rebecca finished her speech, grabbed her purse from underneath the podium, and headed in the direction of the nearest subway stop. She had decided to take advantage of being in a foreign city by herself, and she rode the Piccadilly line to Green Park Station. Climbing up out of the underground tube into the cold January air, Rebecca smiled. In front of her was the massive Green Park, and on the other side of that sat Buckingham Palace.

Despite the dreary weather, Rebecca spent the entire afternoon being a tourist. She hit all the major spots: Buckingham Palace, Westminster Abbey, Parliament, and the London Eye. It was a fifteen-minute walk from the Eye back to her hotel. Halfway across the Golden Jubilee Bridge, Rebecca felt her cell phone buzz in her coat pocket.

I SAW THAT YOU'RE SPEAKING AT LSE THIS WEEK. WHY DIDN'T YOU TELL ME YOU WERE IN TOWN? LET'S GRAB A DRINK WHILE YOU'RE HERE. FOR OLD TIME'S SAKE. XX, R

FIFTY

At eight o'clock the next night, Richard walked into Rebecca's hotel. His body tensed, recognizing sounds and smells from the many, many evenings he spent there years earlier. Richard didn't want to meet Rebecca at The Savoy – didn't want to associate her in any way with his torrid run through London's dating pool. But she suggested the hotel bar, and he was so happy she agreed to meet with him that he didn't want to do anything to mess it up.

The hotel manager recognized Richard and walked into the bar to say hello.

"How are you, sir? It's been a long time."

"It has," Richard nodded. "I'm meeting a friend here, and she doesn't know anything about my dating past. I'd like to keep it that way."

"Yes sir. Absolutely. Not a word."

As the manager left the room, he walked past Rebecca going the opposite direction. She smiled at him and nodded in greeting, and Richard's stomach spun into knots.

Good Lord. She's more gorgeous than ever.

Rebecca was forty-four, but she easily passed for thirty-four as she walked toward Richard's table. Tall and thin, she was wearing a knee length dress with a slit high enough to see her toned and sculpted thighs – the product of her frequent running. The bright blue color of the dress made Rebecca's eyes pop, and she let her long black hair cascade over her shoulders. The only thing Richard didn't approve of was the diamond ring on her left hand.

****

Rebecca reached his table, smiled, and threw her arms around Richard in a hug. Out of instinct, she breathed him in and was filled with warm, happy memories. Unlike her husband, who often smelled of tequila and cigars, Richard smelled the same as he did in business school: a musky, sandalwood cologne and a hint of peppermint.

Rebecca stepped back from Richard and gave him a once over. "How are you? You look great, by the way."

"Not as good as you," he replied. "You might be in even better shape now than you were at HBS, which is hard to believe."

Rebecca shrugged her shoulders and sat down in her chair. "I still run a lot. Keeps me in shape and helps relieve stress."

"Hmm, maybe I should take it up again." Richard paused as their server arrived with a bottle of red wine and two glasses. "I ordered for us. I hope you don't mind."

"Not at all. You've always known more about wine than me."

Rebecca picked up her glass and held it in the air. "What should we cheers to? Old friendships?"

Richard nodded. "That works. To old but renewed friendships."

They clinked their glasses together and Rebecca took a sip of the wine. "Oh wow, that's delicious. What is it?"

Richard grinned. "Caymus."

"Aww, Caymus. I loved that dog. He was so sweet." She drank more of her wine, and added: "I wish we could get a dog, but John's allergic."

Richard tensed at the mention of her husband, and Rebecca kicked herself for bringing him up. "Do you have any pets?" she asked, trying to find a happy subject.

"I do. A yellow lab named Buddy. If you ask my campaign manager, Buddy is the reason I won. Hard to say no to that goofy smile of his."

"I bet," Rebecca said with a laugh. "Dogs are the best."

A silence fell over the table, and neither one of them knew what to say. *So much for things never being awkward between us*, Rebecca thought. She took another sip of wine and noticed that Richard had already finished his glass. *I guess he's nervous too.*

Richard broke the ice by asking about her speaking engagement, and they talked business for a few minutes before Rebecca mentioned her kids.

"It's Sarah and James, right? How old are they now?"

"Sarah and Jonathan. Sarah is fourteen and full of raging hormones. Jonathan is twelve and plays sports year-round. It's basketball season right now."

"Sounds like they keep you busy," Richard said. He poured himself another glass of wine and offered some to Rebecca, but she shook her head no.

"I have some emails to catch up on tonight. I promised myself I'd only have one glass."

Richard nodded. "Smart. As usual."

"What about you?" Rebecca asked. "What keeps you busy these days, aside from work?"

"That's about it, unfortunately. Work and Buddy and the occasional game of tennis with Geoff. Although he doesn't play much anymore now that he's got a wife and three kids."

Rebecca opened her mouth to speak, but stopped. *Ask him*, she thought. *You know you want to.* "Why didn't you ever settle down?"

"I think you of all people should know the answer to that question."

He can't mean . . . ? Surely not? Rebecca smiled nervously. "You can't be serious."

"I've always been serious about you."

"That was twenty years ago. A lifetime ago."

Richard shrugged his shoulders and drank a large gulp of wine. "They say true love lasts a lifetime, right?"

True love? Rebecca felt a cool, tingling sensation rush through her body. It seemed as if the rest of the room went silent as the pair looked into each other's eyes.

A minute later, Rebecca blinked and the moment was lost.

"This is ridiculous," she said. "I'm married. I have children. I shouldn't even be here."

"Of all the things you shouldn't do, being here with me is one you absolutely should."

Rebecca shook her head and turned around to grab her purse off the back of her chair.

"No. No. I have a husband. I have children."

"Do you love him?" Richard asked.

Ignoring his question, Rebecca stood up from the table and placed her purse strap over her shoulder.

"Goodbye, Richard."

For the second time in his life, Lord Dublinshire watched Mrs. Lewis-Bailey walk away from him. It was a calmer exit this time – walking instead of running; words rather than tears; a public audience instead of a passionate riverside kiss.

But still . . . she's gone.

Richard let out a long, frustrated sigh and motioned for the waiter.

"Double bourbon. Neat."

The waiter nodded. "Will the lady be returning?"

"No. She's gone."

FIFTY-ONE

New York, New York
2016

Cristina Dominguez smiled as she walked the busy streets of New York's West Village. The day was cloudy and gloomy with an approaching rainstorm, but Cristina was all smiles. Twenty-six years old with dark, wavy hair and bold brown eyes, the native of Puerto Rico skipped past skyscrapers and apartment buildings. Her good mood continued as she entered a small preschool at the corner of Greenwich and Barrow Streets.

"Hi Gloria," she said to the receptionist at the front desk. "How'd my boy do today?"

"Wonderful, as always," the older woman replied in a strong New York accent. She pressed a button on the speaker in front of her. "Nito's mom is here."

"What's got you all happy today, honey?" asked Gloria.

Cristina smiled even wider. "I got a job!"

"Oooh girl, congratulations! What are you gonna be doin'?"

"I'm an assistant at a catering company. I don't have to cook or anything – I just help organize who is working when and where and all that. It's only part time, but it's something! I've been trying to convince Nito's dad to let me work for so long. He finally said yes, and I'm so excited to have something to do while Nito is at school."

"That's great, honey. You'll be great at that."

Both women turned as the door to the classrooms opened. "Here's the little man," Gloria said. "We'll see you both tomorrow!"

Cristina bent down to be at eye level with her son. "¿Qué tal la escuela, mijo?"

The little boy gave her a big, toothy grin. "¡Muy bien!" he exclaimed, telling his mom that school was great that day. "Escuchamos mi cancion favorita: Wheels on the Bus."

Cristina smiled and grabbed hold of Nito's hand. "I love Wheels on the Bus, too. Do you want to sing it for me while we walk home?" She looked back over her shoulder, smiled, and winked at Gloria.

"Hasta mañana, Señora Gloria," said Nito as he followed his mom out the door. The three-year-old – three and a half if you asked him – began singing the warbly tune as he and his mom walked south on Greenwich Street and then turned left to head east on Morton.

Cristina smiled at her son and at the passersby who were amused by the little boy's singing. With his mom's olive complexion and curly brown hair, and his dad's bright green eyes, Cristina had been approached several times by talent scouts wanting to turn little Juanito into a model. His father refused. "I will not have my child displayed on billboards and Facebook ads for all the world to see."

It was hard enough convincing him to let me work outside the home, Cristina thought with a sigh. *He'll never agree to modeling, not in a million years.*

Ten minutes later, the pair arrived at their home: a tan-colored brick building with a donut shop on the ground floor and five levels of apartments above it. Cristina, Juanito, and Juanito's dad lived in a two-bedroom unit on the third floor. Forty-five minutes later, after a snack and an episode of Thomas the Train, Nito laid down for his nap. Cristina called her mother in Puerto Rico to celebrate her new job.

Several hours later, Cristina heard keys rattling by their front door and called out to her son, who was playing in his room. "Mijo, Daddy's home."

When the door opened, Dr. John Bailey of New York-Presbyterian walked inside.

****

140

Over two hundred miles away, at a non-descript office building in suburban Washington, DC, a young political intern knocked on his boss' door. Cameron Birdsong was in his second year at George Mason University, and he spent two afternoons each week working at a consulting agency. Mostly running Google searches to find dirt on clients' opponents.

He knocked again.

"Yes, yes, I heard you. Come in."

Cameron peeked his head around the door, still not wanting to show his boss the results of his latest research. He knew this information was huge – life changing, really – but his supervisor was a frightening, middle-aged man who believed interns should be seen and not heard.

"Stop standing there like a dumbass, Birdsong. What do you want?"

"I finished the oppo research on Rebecca Lewis-Bailey."

"And?"

Cameron stepped all the way into the office and handed the other man a manila folder. "She's clean," he said, "but her husband isn't."

"Drugs? Money? Whores?"

Cameron shook his head. "He has a whole second family. A mistress and a kid in the West Village."

His boss sat up straight in his chair and started reading the folder's contents. "Are you sure? This is the third check we've run on Lewis-Bailey . . . nothing has come up before."

The intern nodded. "Yes sir. It was hard to find, but once I knew what I was looking for, all kinds of stuff popped up."

"Such as?"

"I did all the traditional name and address searches but didn't find anything. So I did a reverse image search for Mrs. Lewis-Bailey, her husband, and her kids. The husband showed up on a 'Donuts with Dad' post for a preschool's website. I called the school and talked to a receptionist named Gloria. She broke like ten different privacy laws telling me all about the boy and his parents.

141

"It was easy after that," Cameron continued. "The boy is three. He has his mom's last name, but they call him Juanito, or John Jr. I have a friend who is working for New York City this summer and she got into the public records database. John Bailey is listed as the father on the birth certificate. The apartment was paid for in cash and is in the mom's name. He covered his tracks well. It's all in there," he said, motioning toward the paperwork.

"Thank you, Birdsong. That'll be all."

FIFTY-TWO

The manila folder holding John Bailey's dirty little secret was stamped with 'HIS EYES ONLY' and traveled from one suburban Washington office to another under lock and key. Inside the second office, the leading candidate for President read the report with a look of shock on his face.

"This is impossible. I know John Bailey. He delivered two of my grandchildren. He's the best. There's no way."

"We triple checked the sources, sir. Even spoke to a few neighbors who know the mistress and the boy. Unfortunately, it's true."

The presidential candidate let out a frustrated sigh. "Does the other side have it?"

"Not that we're aware of."

"Good. I want her to hear it from us, not some sleazy reporter." He picked up the folder and handed it back to his aide. "Tell her, then let her decide if she still wants the job when we win."

His assistant nodded and couldn't help but smile. There was no doubt in his boss' mind that he would be the next President of the United States. Which also meant there was no doubt he wanted Rebecca Lewis-Bailey to become his chief financial advisor.

****

In New York City, Sarah Bailey walked from Starbucks to her office at 200 West Street in Battery Park City. The twenty-four-year-old was the spitting image of her mother – blue eyes, black hair, tall, and thin. More than one man on the street turned to stare as she walked by, but Sarah ignored the looks and catcalls like her mom taught her to.

Walking into the tall skyscraper, Sarah nodded hello to her coworkers and scanned her Goldman Sachs employee badge to open the security gate.

"Frappuccinos today?" the guard asked.

Sarah nodded. "Double shot for the Boss. One of those days."

The Boss was her mom. When she first started at Goldman Sachs as one of Rebecca's assistants, Sarah was fresh out of college at Princeton and not well-liked by the other employees. Everyone knew she got the job because she was the Managing Partner's daughter, and they treated her poorly because of it. But after two years of hard work, friendly smiles, and very, very long hours, Sarah had earned the respect of her peers and was a valued member of the team.

When the elevator reached the forty-fourth floor, Sarah stepped out into the executive suite and scanned her badge once again. Only those with special clearance were allowed past the bullet-proof glass and into the leadership offices.

"Here you go, Jamal," Sarah said as she handed her mom's senior assistant a cup of coffee. "Extra caramel sauce."

"You're an angel," he replied. Jamal was five years older than Sarah, a Cal-Berkeley grad, and had taken her under his wing when she started at the investment firm. He was also her best friend in the city and considered a rising star at their company. His attention to detail and strong business acumen led to him leaping over more senior assistants to land the job supporting the top boss.

"Is she in?" Sarah asked, nodding toward Rebecca's door.

"Not right now. She'll be back soon, though. You can leave the coffee here for her if you want."

"Perfect," Sarah replied, placing the cup on Jamal's desk.

He leaned forward and dropped his voice to a whisper. "I got a call for you, by the way. From our friends down in DC?"

Sarah knew that was code for the presidential campaign. They were vetting her mom for a White House job, but the potential role was a secret from the rest of Goldman Sachs' employees.

"What'd they want?"

"They're sending somebody up to talk to you. Said it's urgent but confidential. They'll be here first thing tomorrow."

FIFTY-THREE

At ten-thirty the next morning, Sarah Bailey sat on a bench in Rockefeller Park and watched as ferries and tugboats passed by on the Hudson River. Tourists milled around her, most of them making their way to or from the nearby 9/11 Memorial, but Sarah didn't pay them any attention.

"Your father has another family."

The political aide's words replayed over and over in Sarah's mind.

"The mistress is Cristina. The little boy's name is Juanito. They have an apartment in the West Village where your father spends several nights a week."

Sarah's face turned pale. She ran from the bench to a trash can and hurled the contents of her stomach into the bin. After she vomited a second time, Sarah made her way back to the bench and sat down in a broken heap.

The campaign worker had apologized, given her a folder full of evidence, and left to catch his train back to DC. "You're her most trusted aide," he told her. "We didn't know who else to give it to."

Sarah had nodded silently and stared into space for a few minutes before telling Jamal that she didn't feel well and needed some air. *Understatement of the century*, she thought.

An hour later, Sarah returned to her office. It was small – a 7x7 foot space that barely had enough room for a desk, a chair, and a stack of shelves. But it had a door and a small window, and no one else was assigned to it, so Sarah was happy. It was far better than the cubicles that most of her friends and co-workers were given.

She heard a knock on her door and looked up to see Rebecca standing in front of her.

"Are you okay, honey? Jamal said you weren't feeling well."

Sarah shook her head back and forth. "No, I'm not okay." She picked up the manila folder and handed it to her mom. "They told me to tell you, but I don't know how. I'm so sorry, Mom. I'm so, so sorry."

FIFTY-FOUR

Rebecca left her office not long after she read the report on John. Sarah saw her mom walking toward the elevator, but the look on Rebecca's face told her to stay away. The younger woman picked up her cell phone and sent a text to her brother.

CALL ME. ASAP. 911. EMERGENCY.

Jonathan, a student at Columbia, called his sister as soon as he got out of class. After his tirade of cuss words and promises to kill their father subsided, the two siblings agreed to meet an hour later at their parents' apartment.

"Mom needs us," Sarah said. "We'll deal with Dad later."

When they walked inside their childhood home, they found their mother sitting outside on the balcony. Barefoot but still in her business suit, Rebecca was swaying back and forth on the small rope swing she installed when they were kids. Black tears ran down Rebecca's cheeks.

Her kids joined her on the balcony and the three sat in silence, each attempting to process the news of John's betrayal.

"I'll never understand why we have to make the world so complicated," Rebecca finally said, digging her manicured toes into plastic green astroturf and pushing off backwards again on the swing. "Do me a favor, will you?"

"Anything," Sarah replied.

"Find a copy of the poster that says, 'Everything I need to know I learned in kindergarten'. I want to frame it and put it up at work. New office rules."

Sarah nodded her head. "I'm on it."

Rebecca dragged her heels through the ground to stop herself. "Look at me. Sulking like a child. Are y'all okay?"

Jonathan managed a half-smile. "It's okay to sulk, Mom. To be upset. Yell. Scream. Throw things."

Rebecca nodded. "I called in a favor at the FBI. I'm going to their indoor shooting range tonight."

Her son's smile broadened. "See, there you go. Blow off some steam. Maybe they can make a custom target in the shape of Dad's head."

"I was planning on taping his picture to the paper target."

Jonathan laughed, walked over, and wrapped his arms around his mom's shoulders. "Just leave a few shots for me, okay?"

Sarah looked at her brother and then her mom. "We've been talking," she ventured. "You and Dad haven't been happy for a long time. Not that it excuses what he did, not at all. But – "

"Why did you even marry Dad in the first place?" Jonathan blurted out.

Rebecca sighed. "He was handsome. Stable. Mature, or so I thought. He had nice parents and a similar upbringing as me. The life we would have together wasn't scary . . . it was familiar." She paused. "Besides, your dad was a catch."

Sarah rolled her eyes.

"No, really. That's what everyone would tell me when we were dating and after we got engaged. 'You're so lucky – he's such a catch.' And they were exactly right. Because you know what you catch? Fish. Cold, lifeless, smelly fish."

****

After the shooting range, Rebecca and her kids ordered Chinese takeout for dinner. While Sarah set the table, Jonathan went to the liquor closet and pulled out his father's 1800 Colección bottle of tequila.

"Who wants a shot?" he asked, holding up the $2,000 extra añejo, one of only forty bottles in the world.

"Fuck yes," Sarah replied. "Bring it on."

149

When the tequila was half-empty, Rebecca pulled out three large, black trash bags. "Here," she said, handing one to each person. "Throw all of your dad's shit in these. I'll messenger it over to him and his whore in the West Village."

FIFTY-FIVE

The next morning, Rebecca was back on her swing, drinking coffee and looking out over Manhattan. For the first time in her entire career, Rebecca called out sick from work when she wasn't physically ill. *The kids are always telling me I need to take mental health days*, she thought as she took another sip of coffee. *This time, they're right.*

Her cell phone buzzed in her pocket, and she pulled it out to see that the front desk of her apartment building was calling.

"Hi Mario. What's up?"

"Good morning, Mrs. Lewis-Bailey. Umm, Dr. Bailey is here, and he wants to go upstairs."

Rebecca let out a deep breath. "Fine. Send him up."

She hung up the phone, and then a thought hit her. She dialed the front desk's number.

"Hello, Mrs. Lewis-Bailey. He's already in the elevator, if you changed your mind."

"No, thank you Mario, I didn't change my mind. I'm just wondering why you called at all. John still lives here – technically."

The security guard paused, and Rebecca could feel his discomfort through the phone.

"Umm, well, Sarah and Jonathan talked to me yesterday. At first, I said that I couldn't stop an owner from going up to his apartment, but then they told me what happened. And that you kicked him out. I mean, good for you, ma'am," added Mario, gaining confidence as he spoke. "If it were me, I would've – "

"Thank you, Mario," Rebecca said, cutting him off. "I appreciate it."

After hanging up, she had to resist the urge to throw her phone off the balcony. The only thing that stopped her was the thought of it injuring someone on the street below.

"That's the last thing I need," she muttered to herself as she walked inside toward the front door. "My husband has a second family; my kids are telling everyone about it . . . I don't need to get arrested on top of that."

John used his key to open the door and strode inside like there was nothing wrong.

"Really?" Rebecca asked. "You aren't even going to pretend to be sorry?"

John took off his suit jacket and sat down on the living room couch. "Come on, Rebecca. We've both known our marriage was over for a long time."

"We have? Huh. That's news to me. Because the last time I checked, I'm still your goddamn wife!"

"Go ahead, pitch a fit. I don't care."

"That's the first true thing you've ever said. If you cared, you wouldn't have lied to me for all these years. If you cared, you wouldn't have kept a second fucking family in the same fucking city!"

Rebecca picked up a pen off the kitchen counter and threw it across the room.

"Was having one son named after you not good enough?" she continued. "You had to have a second boy and give him your name too? Bastard."

"Hey, hold on," John objected. "You can't call Juanito that. He didn't do anything wrong."

"What? No, I meant you're the bastard. I feel sorry for the kid."

"He's great, Becky," John said with pride. "You'd love him."

"Go fuck yourself."

This time it was Rebecca's phone that went flying across the room, shattering into pieces when it hit the wall.

John ducked out of the way and looked at her with an evil smile. "Yikes, baby. The Senate won't look too kindly on a White House advisor with a temper."

152

Rebecca set her jaw and glared at him. "You know that's how I found out, right? Background research by the campaign?"

"Maybe it's better this way, Rebecca. I wouldn't have given up my job to follow you to DC anyway." He sighed and ran a hand through his balding hair. "There's no passion anymore. We look great in a photo op and we made two beautiful kids, but there's no substance. No romance."

"And you blame me for that?"

"There's no one to blame."

"Ha! Like hell there isn't! You know what," she said, picking up his suit jacket and walking to the door, "fuck you. Or, actually, fuck her. Because you definitely won't be fucking me anymore." She opened the door and threw his jacket in the hall. "Get out. And stay out."

FIFTY-SIX

In December of that year, Rebecca packed up her belongings and moved south to Alexandria, Virginia. Her candidate had won the election, and Rebecca was in charge of his finance team. She was a political novice but an investment whiz, and it was an open secret that she would one day take over as Treasury Secretary. Rebecca was a shoo-in for the top job: having spent thirty years at Goldman Sachs, she was well-known and well-liked on both sides of the aisle. She was also scandal free, with the press thus far unaware of the nastier details of her separation from her husband. The only reason reporters knew about the split at all was because Rebecca dropped 'Bailey' from her last name.

Rebecca and Sarah settled into a three bedroom, four bath townhouse in Old Town Alexandria, just across the river from DC, and went to work on the president-elect's transition team. It was their job to prepare to take the reins when the new administration began.

After spending a year by the President's side at the White House, Rebecca Lewis was sworn in as Secretary of the Treasury in late January of 2018 – three days after her divorce became final.

The next morning, Rebecca woke up early. Her townhome faced the East, and she loved watching the sun rise over the Potomac River. Her new place wasn't all that big, only 2,800 square feet, but after living in Manhattan for so long it seemed like a mansion to Rebecca and Sarah. Especially because they didn't have neighbors above or below them. The red brick, three story townhouse had a front-entry garage and a small back patio that was large enough for a grill. That last detail thrilled Jonathan to no end, and he always grilled out for them when he came to visit.

Rebecca opened the French doors in her bedroom and saw grass, trees, and water. Best of all, after years of car horns and city yelling, she heard birds chirping. Rebecca breathed in the fresh air and smiled. *God, I love it here.*

After finishing her coffee, Rebecca dressed in leggings, a quarter-zip, gloves, and her favorite sneakers. She walked downstairs, pulled a beanie on top of her head, and stepped out into the cold winter air.

"Good morning, ma'am," said a tall, muscular man standing on her front porch.

"Good morning," Rebecca replied to the Secret Service agent. "I guess you're coming with me?"

"Yes ma'am. I'll be five yards behind you the whole time, with the car another ten behind me."

Rebecca looked to the street and saw a black Chevrolet Tahoe idling at the curb. "Is that really necessary? I mean, I get it when I'm exercising. But do y'all really have to sit outside in a running car all the time no matter what? Even in the middle of the night?"

"Yes ma'am. We could need to leave in an instant."

Rebecca sighed and shrugged her shoulders. "If you say so. Ready to go?"

The Secretary and her security detail started off in Rivergate City Park across from her townhouse. They ran north along the river through a handful of other parks and residential streets before reaching the Mount Vernon Trail: a wide, paved path that went alongside the George Washington Memorial Parkway in Northern Virginia. From Rebecca's house to Reagan National Airport and back was a five-mile loop, which was about all her knees and back would let her do these days.

"Never get old," she huffed to the Secret Service agent when they returned to her house. "It's hell on your body."

The younger man laughed. "So is chasing after a freakishly fast Cabinet member."

Rebecca smiled. "Touché." She held out her fist and bumped knuckles with the agent. "Alright. Shower, then office."

155

Across the pond in London, Richard joined his longtime friend, Geoffrey, for dinner that night. They met at a small Italian bistro in Chelsea called Il Trillo, best known for its handmade pastas and romantic back patio. Geoffrey first discovered the place when he was dating his now-wife, and the two friends ate there several times a year. Geoff liked it because it was close to his house, and Richard liked it because no one cared who he was. The owners had watched him grow up from a brash young analyst into a refined, successful MP. When he was named Chancellor of the Exchequer that past summer, the owners of Il Trillo sent him a plate of prosciutto and an order of pasta to celebrate.

On that particular evening, Richard noticed a young couple seated at a corner table. They were nervous enough to be early in their relationship – *maybe even a first date*, he thought.

"Excuse me, Giovanni?" Richard asked, getting the waiter's attention.

"Yes sir?"

"You see that couple out on the patio? In the corner?"

Gio turned to look. "Yes sir, I see them."

"Put their bill on mine."

The waiter looked back at Richard. "You sure?"

"I am. But don't tell them it was me. Say they're the millionth customer or something like that and they won a prize."

Giovanni shrugged his shoulders. "Okay. If that's what you want."

After the waiter walked away, Richard looked across the table and saw his friend staring at him.

"What the hell was that?"

Richard smiled, remembering when he asked the same question the first time Rebecca bought a meal for strangers.

"Just a nice gesture."

"But why?"

Richard shrugged his shoulders. "Because I can."

"I don't get you, mate. Hard-charging politician by day – secret Santa by night."

"I don't see a conflict between the two."

"Your colleagues in Parliament might. For instance, voting to cut welfare subsidies?"

Richard wagged his finger back and forth. "Completely different. That bill was bollocks. And even if it wasn't, what I choose to do with my own money is my business."

Geoff looked across the table skeptically. "If you say so. But really – how often do you go about buying dinner for strangers?"

The Chancellor smiled, his thoughts again flashing back to the night in Hartford with Rebecca.

"Occasionally," he answered. "A good friend of mine in business school used to do the same thing. Except she always attached some sort of story to it as well. Said the couple was celebrating their anniversary or down on their luck or whatever it may be."

"Okay," his friend replied. "So, what's going on with the people over there?"

"Bugger if I know."

Geoff laughed. "No story?"

"No. I deal with enough people playing make-believe every day at work. I don't need that here, too."

Their dinner arrived soon thereafter, and Richard and Geoffrey focused their attention on the food. The two men usually got half orders of two or three different pastas and shared them. This time was no different, with plates of tortellini, ravioli, and pappardelle crowding the small table.

"Next time, I'm getting my own pappardelle," Richard said between bites. "With the wild boar marinated in chianti? Mmmm," he groaned in appreciation. "Amazing."

Geoffrey grabbed the plate away from Richard. "Next time, go for it. Tonight, you have to share."

"Bastard."

"I am not. I'm just a man who loves to eat."

Richard drank some of his wine and smiled. "You better not let Amanda see you this happy about someone else's cooking."

Geoff shoveled more pasta into his mouth. "She knows. She likes Il Trillo better than her own cooking, too." He paused to swallow the food. "That's what you need. A wife to bring here so you can steal all of her pasta instead of taking mine."

"I think my find-a-wife days are over."

"Oh, mate!" Geoff slapped the table in excitement. "I can't believe I almost forgot. She's single!"

"Who?"

Geoffrey lowered his voice. "The one you've wanted all along. She's Treasury Secretary now . . . you're equals."

"She's married."

"That's not what I heard. Kept it out of the papers, but a nasty split. Husband had a whole second family, apparently."

Richard stared at his friend in disbelief. "No fucking way."

****

Richard finished dinner with Geoff and tried to maintain his composure, but inside his emotions were raging. He hadn't seen or even spoken to Rebecca in over ten years. *Not since our disastrous meeting in London*, he thought. In an attempt to calm his nerves, Richard drank too much that night – *and I ended up blowing it*, he concluded. Rebecca had seemed so distant, so confident in her marriage and her children. *But if she's divorced now . . .*

No. Richard shook his head as he climbed inside his government-issued car. He had a full-time security detail ever since being named Chancellor of the Exchequer. *Don't get your hopes up. She might as well have told you to go fuck yourself the last time you saw her.*

"Straight home, your lordship?" asked his driver.

158

"Yes. Straight home."

As the black car rumbled through London's busy roads on its way to Downing Street, Richard continued to war with himself over the news of Rebecca's divorce. "A whole other family?" he muttered under his breath. "I knew I never liked that arsehole."

Richard's driver glanced in the rearview mirror but didn't say anything. He had been a protection officer for fifteen years, which meant he was used to pretending not to hear the personal moments of the famous and powerful.

"She probably doesn't want to talk to anyone right now," Richard continued. "Not if her whole world just crashed down around her." *Then again*, he thought, looking out the window, *maybe a friendly face is exactly what she needs*.

FIFTY-EIGHT

The next morning, Rebecca was reading an email from her chief deputy when her assistant, Jamal, beeped in on the intercom. The young man had followed her from New York to DC and partnered with Sarah to provide the Secretary the support she needed.

"Excuse me, ma'am?" said Jamal. "You have a call from Lord Dublinshire's office? The British Chancellor of the Exchequer?"

Rebecca raised her eyebrows in surprise. *Wow, Richard. I haven't heard from him in forever.* "Put him through," she said.

A second later, the phone rang. Rebecca picked it up. "Yes, please make this quick. I'm busy and extremely important."

She could hear Richard's laugh from the other side of the Atlantic. "I hate to break it to you, Madam Secretary, but I'm equally busy and important."

It was Rebecca's turn to laugh. She slouched back in her chair and twirled a strand of hair between her fingers.

"What's up, Richard? To what do I owe the surprise?"

"I never would've thought 'what's up' would be part of your vocabulary, Miss Barnard and Harvard."

"I have two Millennials as my children . . . I'm down with all the slang."

"I'm sure you are," Richard replied with a chuckle. "How are they, by the way?"

"Good. Sarah is twenty-six and working for me. Jonathan is twenty-four and in his senior year at Columbia. He took a gap year before college so he's a little older. How's Buddy?" she asked, referring to Richard's beloved dog.

"Buddy passed a few years ago. I have a chocolate lab now. Gus."

"Aww, I bet Gus is a cute little guy."

"He weighs nearly six stone. There's nothing little about that dog."

Rebecca leaned forward and opened a new browser on her computer, typing 'stones to pounds' in the search bar. "Eighty-four pounds. Wow!"

"You just looked that up online, didn't you?"

Rebecca smiled and shook her head. "You know me too well."

"That I do, Becks," he said. "That I do."

A silence fell over the phone as the two old friends reached the end of their pleasantries. Unlike her calls with other people, though, this silence wasn't awkward. Rebecca realized that she liked knowing Richard was on the other end of the line, whether they said anything or not.

"I've missed this," she blurted out before she could stop herself.

"You've missed what?"

"Talking to you."

Rebecca knew she was headed down a rabbit hole, but she didn't care. Newly single for the first time in three decades, she liked being able to talk to friends – male or female – without worrying what John would say.

"I've missed talking to you too," Richard replied. "We should do it more often. Especially because we're both finance ministers now. But only if John wouldn't object," Richard added. He was testing the waters. Geoffrey told him that Rebecca and her husband split, but Richard didn't trust the rumor. He wanted to hear her say it.

"John and I are divorced," Rebecca replied. "So his objections wouldn't matter anyway."

"I'm sorry, Becks. Truly."

"Don't be. I . . . I don't want to get into it right now – not when I have a meeting in a few minutes – but don't be. It's for the best."

"Okay," Richard said, knowing better than to push any further. "And I won't keep you any longer. I have a call at the top of the hour as well. I just wanted to say hello and wish you luck in the new job. I'm sure we'll be talking more soon. I know our predecessors interacted with each other a good bit."

"I look forward to it, your lordship," she said, doing her best impersonation of a British accent.

"Oh, please. You were never any good at that."

They both laughed, and another warm silence settled over the phone.

Finally, Richard said: "I'll talk to you soon, Becks."

"Bye, Richard."

Rebecca smiled as she hung up. Her first real, true smile in longer than she could remember. It was amazing how the love of a good man could make a woman feel beautiful even in the midst of her darkest hour.

FIFTY-NINE

Richard texted her again the next day at the same time to say hello and wish her a Happy Thursday. Rebecca knew what he was doing, but this time she didn't care. *I need a little joy and friendship right now*, she thought.

The next morning, day three, her phone rang again. Rebecca looked at the clock on her computer. *Ten a.m. sharp*. She smiled as she picked up the receiver.

"This is starting to be a habit, don't you think?"

"What are you talking about?"

Rebecca's smile vanished at the sound of the deep American voice.

"What do you want, John?"

"Who did you think I was?" he pressed.

"None of your business. You forfeited your right to know that or anything else about me."

Her ex-husband grunted into the phone. "Fine. If that's how you want us to be, fine." He paused. "I'm calling because I got an email from Sarah with a bunch of documents to sign. You're selling our apartment in New York?"

"I told the kids they could decide what to do with it. I don't want it, and you don't need it since you're living with *them* now."

"We bought that place together," he countered. "Surely I should have some say in the matter."

"I don't give a shit, John. And honestly, I have better things to do than talk to you about this. I'm a big fucking deal. I have Secret Service protection, I can sign official Treasury orders, and I have my own damn flag that flies on my motorcade car. I'm sorry if you can't handle the fact that I'm more important than you now, but that doesn't change the fact that *I'm more important than you now*." Rebecca picked up a folder from her desk and lifted her purse off the back of her chair. "Now, if you'll excuse me, I have a meeting to go to. At the White House."

163

Rebecca hung up on John and sauntered down the hallway of her office with an extra sway in her hips. *Jackass*, she thought. As Rebecca climbed into her car, her cell phone buzzed.

GOOD MORNING, BEAUTIFUL! BUSY DAY FOR ME. I HOPE THINGS ARE GREAT WITH YOU. XX, R

SIXTY

Two weeks later, the calls and texts from Richard stopped. It was a busy Wednesday morning, and the 10 o'clock hour nearly passed before Rebecca even noticed the lack of a message from him. Walking back to her office from a conference room down the hall, Rebecca hung her head in disappointment. *He's probably having a busy day too, Becky*, she told herself. *You can't expect him to keep this up forever.*

When she passed Jamal's desk, Rebecca noticed an odd grin on the man's face. Once inside her office, she realized why: an enormous bouquet of pink, purple, and red tulips was sitting on Rebecca's desk. She opened the card displayed on the top.

I'm roses serious when I say that I hope you have a daisies happy day.

Rebecca's eager assistant had followed his boss into the office and now stood admiring the flowers.

"The card isn't signed," said Jamal, reading over her shoulder.

"It doesn't need to be," Rebecca replied with a smile. "I know who sent them."

"Your kids?"

"No. These are from my best friend."

Jamal used his pen as a pointer and counted the flowers. "There are 34. Shouldn't it be 24 or 36? Multiples of a dozen?"

"I guess the florist messed up," Rebecca said, sitting down at her desk.

"Weird. Well, do you need anything, ma'am?"

"No thank you, I'm fine right now."

After Jamal closed the door behind him, Rebecca stood up and leaned over her desk toward the flowers. She breathed

165

in their fresh scent and read the card over and over. *Thirty-four tulips. One for every year we've known each other.*

Not for the first time, Rebecca thought back to her years at Harvard with Richard and wondered what might have been.

If she said yes.

If he chased after her.

If they were two normal people to begin with and could have been together from the start.

"But you wouldn't be here, Madam Secretary," she told herself. Putting the card back in the flowers, Rebecca sat down in her chair. "You definitely wouldn't be here."

Rebecca picked her cell phone up off the desk and opened a new message chain.

THE FLOWERS ARE BEAUTIFUL. THANK YOU. XX, B

His response came instantly.

I FIGURED ENOUGH TIME HAD PASSED AND MAYBE THE RULES HAD BEEN RESET. STILL TOO MUCH? OR AM I ALLOWED TO SEND FLOWERS NOW?

She smiled and started typing back with her thumbs.

I WAS RIGHT THE FIRST TIME AROUND. YOU CAN NEVER GO WRONG SENDING A WOMAN FLOWERS.

SIXTY-ONE

Apart from his assistant Tricia, who coordinated the flower delivery, no one in Richard's life knew about his renewed pursuit of Rebecca. All they could tell was that the Chancellor of the Exchequer was happier than they had ever seen him. Vacation days were approved. Clever nicknames were assigned. And there was laughter in the halls of Number 11 Downing Street for the first time since Richard took the oath of office.

Perhaps the biggest change, though, was the addition of 'family dinners'. On the first Friday of every month, Richard invited his senior staff and their families to have dinner at Number 11, which served as both his office and his residence. Richard's sister and brother-in-law joined the group for the first dinner, and Geoffrey brought his wife and kids to the next one.

After the second dinner was over and all the staff and guests had returned home, Richard and Geoff walked out to the back patio with cigars and whisky in hand.

"This was nice," Geoff commented as he sat down on the outdoor furniture. "Your staff seemed to enjoy it." He paused as he lit a match and held it to the end of the cigar, drawing in hard on the first few puffs. "It's good to see you like this."

"Like what?"

"Relaxed. Happy. I don't know what her name is, but I'm a big fan."

Richard raised his whisky glass up to his mouth and cut his eyes over at his lifelong friend. "I don't know what you're talking about."

"Mmm hmm, sure. Tell me this, old man, is she young enough to give you a little Richard Junior running around?"

"Hypothetically," Richard said, "*if* there were a woman *potentially* in my life . . . no, she's not young enough."

Geoff blew rings of smoke into the night air. "That probably bodes well for the relationship, since I don't see you putting up with a dimwit twenty-something. Although," he added with a grin, "it is a shame you won't be able to pass along those devilishly handsome good looks."

Richard shook his head and drew in a long breath from his own cigar. "Children weren't in the cards for me. Sarah's eldest will be the next marquess."

Richard was so unassuming and down to earth, and they had known each other for so long, that Geoffrey often forgot about Richard's title. Forgot that, in addition to being Chancellor of the Exchequer, he was also Lord Dublinshire.

"Do we like him?" Geoff asked. "The heir?"

"He's a sniveling little shit. Calls me 'Dick' and is content to waste away his youth on the hopes that I will die young like my father did. He's twenty-six and blowing through his trust fund trying to 'make it' as a professional sailor." Richard huffed his disapproval. "His younger brother, on the other hand, is a great kid. Went through Sandhurst and is stationed on Gibraltar as a First Lieutenant.

"If William were my heir," he continued, "things would be different. I'd be content to die young, content to leave the estate intact, confident in the knowledge that the family – and the family name – would be well represented. But William is the second son, not the first." Richard raised his glass to the sky. "So I must live forever."

Geoff roared with laughter at his friend's dramatic declaration.

"Tell me this, Mr. Live Forever, can immortals play tennis? I won't be fit for much of anything early tomorrow, but I can probably sneak out in the afternoon."

Richard shook his head. "Can't. I'm driving to Rosewood first thing in the morning. I've got my monthly lunch with the Dowager tomorrow."

"You mean your mum?"

"She prefers I call her the Dowager. I think she likes to rub in the fact that there's not a current Marchioness of Dublinshire, only a Dowager Marchioness."

"Chancellor of the Exchequer and heir apparent to be Prime Minister, but still not good enough because you haven't got a wife?"

Richard nodded. "That's my mum for you."

SIXTY-TWO

The next day, promptly at noon, Richard was shown into the dining room of the Dowager House for lunch with his mother. As the widow of the former Marquess, Victoria Arrington lived in a house on the edge of their property that was reserved for surviving spouses. Richard would have been more than happy to let his mother continue living at Rosewood – *I'm rarely there anyway*, he thought. But Lady Dublinshire insisted on following protocol, and she moved to the Dowager House the week after Richard's father died. "It's the appropriate thing," she had told him, using her late husband's favorite word for what members of a family like theirs should or shouldn't do.

Both of her children had command performances once a month with their mother – Richard the first week and Sarah the third. Victoria said it was to keep an eye on them, but Richard suspected it was the eighty-one-year old's way of giving herself something to do. With a family raised and a husband gone, life could get rather lonely in the countryside.

Richard walked into the dining room and found it empty. *No surprise*, he thought. *She loves to make an entrance.*

Five minutes later, his mother walked in.

"Darling! So good to see you," she declared, opening her arms wide for the mandatory hug. *Except it's not really a hug*, Richard thought, since their bodies never touched and their hands barely grazed the shoulders of the other.

"We're having beef stew today," Lady Dublinshire continued. "It's still so cold out. I was hoping for a warmer March than this."

Richard nodded and waited for the butler to pull out his mother's chair before sitting down himself.

"It'll warm up soon," he replied. "April is always when it turns."

A very boring but very *appropriate* conversation continued for several minutes, through the first course salad and on into the beef stew. The weather, the upcoming garden show, his sister's kids . . . the topics never changed. Richard let his mind wander to work meetings and emails he needed to return, nodding and smiling enough to convince his mother that he was paying attention.

As lunch drew to a close, Lady Dublinshire said: "Oh, dear, this might interest you. I couldn't sleep the other night, so I turned on the channel that used to show your father's House of Lords sessions. They were talking about the world economy, and there was an interview with the American finance minister. She made some excellent points – a very impressive woman."

Richard froze mid-bite and turned pale for half a second before lowering his spoon to the table. He set his jaw and let out a fierce breath.

"Darling, what on Earth is wrong? Have you choked on something?"

"You were impressed by the American finance minister?"

"I was. Very smart, obviously competent and prepared. Far more elegant and less brash than most American politicians. And quite pretty, too," Victoria added, dropping a not-so-subtle hint for her bachelor son.

He nodded his head up and down in approval. "She's almost aristocratic in a way, no?"

"I suppose you could say that about her, yes."

Richard stood up from his chair so fast that it slammed to the floor behind him. He closed his eyes and took a deep breath, trying to regain his composure. A moment later, Richard stalked out of the room, down the stairs, and out of his mother's house. He was so angry he couldn't speak.

Back inside, Lady Dublinshire stared bewildered at the door. "What on earth was that?" she asked the family's longtime butler, Mr. Guinn, who had been serving them lunch.

"If I were to wager a guess, your ladyship, I would say it had something to do with the American politician in

171

question. I believe she is the woman his lordship was in love with during business school. I was only a footman at that point, but I do remember talk of it amongst the servants."

"What the devil are you talking about?"

"If I recall correctly, Lord Dublinshire informed your ladyship and his late father of his desire to marry the young woman."

Victoria gasped. "That's right. There was someone. That's her? The finance minister?"

"I believe so, yes ma'am."

Richard's mother sighed and shook her head. "The same girl I ran off when I visited Boston. I can't believe he's still bitter about that. They never would've worked. They're from two different worlds. It would be like me marrying . . . marrying you, Guinn." The elderly woman laughed at the thought. "Preposterous."

"Yes ma'am. A union against nature, no doubt."

The sarcasm in his voice was lost on Lady Dublinshire. "Exactly, Guinn. A union against nature."

SIXTY-THREE

Richard stopped answering his mother's calls, and he skipped the next month's lunch. He couldn't bear to hear her voice, let alone see her face. *After all this time*, he thought. *After all those years of pain and loneliness, she decides Becks is 'appropriate' after all*. He snorted in disgust. *Bitch*.

Rather than fight with his mother, Richard focused all his attention on his two favorite things: work and Rebecca. The Chancellor of the Exchequer was a popular figure in Parliament and Whitehall, and newspapers were starting to speculate that he would be the next Prime Minister. But Richard's pride in his work accomplishments paled in comparison to the joy he got from his renewed pursuit of Rebecca.

He was still texting her every day at the same time; occassionally even calling when he could come up with a decent work-related excuse. He was particularly proud of himself for her birthday gift: tulips sent to her office (anonymously, of course) and dinner delivered to her home in Old Town Alexandria. *But not just any dinner*, Richard recalled with a smile.

He and Tricia worked for weeks to iron out the kinks. A long-distance courier picked up the food from Rebecca's favorite restaurant during business school: Giacomo's in the North End. The courier then hopped on the American Airlines shuttle from Boston Logan to Reagan National. By the time Rebecca arrived home from work, dinner was waiting. Fried calamari to start, followed by homemade fusilli with lobster, shrimp, and a spicy red sauce. The *pièce de resistance* was a box of assorted cannolis from Mike's Pastry, the famous bakery down the street from Giacomo's.

****

When Rebecca and her daughter walked in the door from work that evening, they found Jonathan busy setting a table with delivery containers, plates, and wine glasses. He had flown down from New York for his mom's birthday but quickly discovered that he wasn't the only surprise.

Rebecca threw her arms around her son and hugged him tight. "What are you doing here?!"

"It's your birthday. Of course I'm here."

She pulled back to examine the dining room table. "And you brought dinner?"

Jonathan shook his head. "I brought the wine. The food got here about thirty minutes ago. Delivered by a courier. The guy said he didn't know who hired him, but it was the craziest order he'd ever done."

"Craziest how?" asked Sarah.

At that moment, Rebecca recognized the label on the takeout containers. She smiled and shook her head. *I can't believe he did all of this.* "The food is from Boston," Rebecca said in reply to her daughter's question. "It's Giacomo's . . . my favorite Italian place."

"How did it get here?"

Rebecca shrugged her shoulders. "Must've been my friend Emily. She's a professor at HBS now. Giacomo's was one of our favorite spots during school."

As soon as she could, Rebecca snuck away to the bathroom and pulled out her cell phone.

It's amazing. You're amazing. My kids are here tonight, but I'll call tomorrow. Seriously – unreal.

He texted back almost immediately, having stayed up late to find out what Rebecca thought of the surprise.

Happy birthday, Becks. You're the amazing one.

SIXTY-FOUR

After breakfast with her children, commuting in with Sarah, and a full slate of morning meetings, it was nearly noon Eastern Time before Rebecca had a moment of privacy. She put her computer status as 'do not disturb' and picked up her personal cell phone.

Richard answered on the second ring. "Happy belated birthday, Madam Secretary."

Rebecca smiled and looked at the bouquet of tulips still sitting on her desk from the day before. "Thank you, Chancellor. And thank you a thousand times over for the flowers and the dinner. I can't believe you did all of that!"

"I was gutted that I couldn't be there in person to celebrate, so I wanted to make it up to you. Lobster fusilli was your favorite, right?"

"It was. Plus the cannolis, which you would always buy but never eat."

"I hate ricotta cheese," Richard confessed, "and I knew you secretly wanted to eat two of them. I'd buy one and give it to you – "

"Pretending to be too full from dinner," Rebecca said, finishing his sentence.

"So how was it?" he asked. "As good as I remember?"

"Even better. Although, you could've warned me about it," Rebecca added. "I had to come up with a lie on my feet when my kids asked who sent the food. I couldn't even say it was from my office, because Sarah works here with me and would've known about it."

"Oops, I didn't think about that. What'd you tell them?"

"Remember Emily? She's a professor at Harvard now. I said she must've done it."

"Clever girl," replied Richard with a smile. "Well played."

Jamal knocked on Rebecca's door to remind her of her lunch meeting.

"Uh oh, I have to go. Real quick, though: you'll be at the G7, right? So I can buy you dinner to say thank you?"

Silence hung over the line, then Richard responded.

"Is that a date, Secretary Lewis?"

His voice was deep, sexy, and different than it had been for the rest of the conversation. Rebecca's stomach did a somersault. She knew they had been walking a fine line with the text messages, phone calls, and flowers. But things had stayed friendly and platonic, at least on the surface. The current underneath was raging and carrying them swiftly toward something very serious, but Rebecca had been able to pretend it wasn't happening as long as it stayed unspoken. Richard's question, though, brought things forward in a way Rebecca wasn't quite sure she was ready for.

"Becks?" he asked, breaking the silence.

"It's a date," she responded, pushing herself toward the bravery she didn't have thirty years earlier. "I'll see you in Canada."

SIXTY-FIVE

The 44th G7 Summit was held on June 8th and 9th, 2018, in Charlevoix, a small resort town in Quebec, Canada. A mere hour and a half drive from Quebec City, the Fairmont Le Manoir Richelieu was a large, gray manor with a green roof that was home to over 400 hotel rooms, four restaurants, and a sweeping view of the St. Lawrence River. As the top finance ministers for their respective countries, Richard and Rebecca were in attendance at the summit along with presidents and prime ministers from the top seven advanced economies in the world: Canada, France, Germany, Italy, Japan, the United Kingdom, and the United States.

Richard arrived with the UK delegation on the evening of the 7th of June. As a leading dignitary, his staff checked him in and prepared his suite of rooms before he got there. Stepping out of his motorcade car and into the hotel, Richard barely acknowledged the beautiful lobby with wall-to-wall windows overlooking the river. His focus was on his iPhone and reading the final draft of his speech.

"It's wonderful to be here with you all – ooof!"

Not watching where he was going, Richard slammed straight into a person walking in the opposite direction. He bent down to pick up his phone off the floor and looked to see who his victim was.

"Becks!"

Richard couldn't hide his excitement. He stood up and enveloped Rebecca in a huge hug. He knew people were watching them and gossip would spread about their greeting, but *I don't fucking care*, he thought, breathing in Rebecca's long-lost scent of perfume and breezy shampoo.

"My God, I've missed you," he whispered in her ear.

"You haven't changed one bit," Rebecca said, taking a step back and holding his hands wide to get a better look at Richard. "Not one bit."

And he hadn't. Even his outfit was the same: brown loafers, khaki slacks, and a button-up shirt. Rebecca knew, if the weather were cooler, he would also be wearing a navy blazer – or perhaps tweed with elbow patches. *If the events of the day called for casualwear*, Rebecca thought with a smirk, remembering how he used to describe his clothing choices.

"What?" asked Richard.

"Nothing, nothing. You really do look exactly the same."

He laughed. "Yeah, plus about twenty pounds and a lot of gray hair and wrinkles."

Rebecca shook her head. "You look the same to me."

"And you look fantastic," Richard replied, taking his own appraisal of his longtime friend. Wearing a blue shift dress and white summer blazer, Rebecca looked every bit the world power player that she was. *Rebecca Lewis*, he thought with a smile. *No longer Rebecca Lewis-Bailey, either. Even better.*

"Hello?"

"Huh?"

"I asked what you're doing tonight," Rebecca said.

"Work, unfortunately. I have a lot of emails to get through."

"Yeah, I've got a pile of call sheets to return as well. I'm so glad we bumped into each other, though," she added with a smile.

"Literally," Richard said, and they both laughed.

"Yes, literally. I'll see you at the conference tomorrow, right?"

Richard nodded. "That's why I'm here."

"Excellent. See you then!"

Rebecca rose up on her tip toes, gave Richard a quick kiss on the cheek like she used to in business school, and scurried off in the direction of the American block of rooms.

Richard resisted the urge to run his hand over the spot where her lips branded his skin. Instead, he shook his head and smiled. "Always in a hurry."

SIXTY-SIX

Later that same evening, after finishing her work for the day, Rebecca decided to explore some of the hotel. *I can't sleep, so I might as well make the most of the trip*, she thought as she left her room. *Better than sitting in bed watching Netflix.*

She took the elevator down to the basement to find the exercise room. Peaking her head inside, Rebecca saw a row of treadmills and ellipticals facing the windows. *Perfect. I'll be able to see the river when I run tomorrow morning.* Next to the gym was the spa. Rebecca grumbled. *No time for that this trip. Even though I could desperately use a massage.* She had even gotten her daughter, Sarah, to call the hotel spa and find out if they were having special hours during the G7 summit.

"No such luck," Rebecca muttered to herself as she walked back toward the elevator. "They could make a fortune doing massages late at night."

She rode up to the main floor. Having changed out of work clothes into a more comfortable red blouse, skinny jeans, and espadrille wedges, Rebecca looked more like a tourist than a Cabinet Secretary. There weren't any tourists to be seen, though, since the entire hotel was rented out for the conference. Between dignitaries, staff, and security, there weren't any rooms to spare. The 'ring of protection' approach to the G7 was why Rebecca was able to explore the property without her Secret Service detail. Since no one was allowed to enter without proper credentials and a background check, attendees had more freedom once inside the bubble.

Walking through the lobby, Rebecca noticed that the bar was still serving drinks. *Oh, so they leave that open late but not the spa.* She stepped inside the lounge. Dark leather tables and chairs complimented the cherry wood bar. In the middle of the room, a grand piano sat ready for someone to play its keys. Although the bar was crowded, most of the

179

people were near the windows that overlooked the river. Rebecca spotted an empty table in the back corner.

A waiter soon appeared. "Can I get you something, ma'am?"

"I'd like a Moscow Mule. With a splash of orange juice, please."

The waiter nodded. "Preference on vodka?"

"Tito's is fine."

"And I'll have an Old Fashioned. Bartender's choice on the whisky."

Rebecca looked up to see Richard standing beside her table.

"That is, of course, if the lady will invite me to join her."

Rebecca smiled and nodded her head. "Of course, please." She motioned toward the empty chair opposite hers.

"Anything else?" the waiter asked.

"No, that'll be all," Rebecca said. "Thank you."

Richard sat down and leaned toward her. "Thank God you're here," he said. "I was worried for a second that I would have to spend the night talking about monetary policy with some kiss-ass staffer."

"What makes you think I don't want to talk about monetary policy?" Rebecca held a straight face for a second before a smile broke through.

"Phew," Richard said, sitting back in his chair. "You had me there for a minute." He ran a hand through his shaggy hair.

"I see we're still refusing to get a proper cut," she commented.

Richard patted the top of his gray hair and grinned. "At my age, if you have it, you want to keep it. Besides, it was my father who made me cut it. With him gone, the impetus isn't there."

"Doesn't your image consultant or assistant get on you about it?"

"Image consultant? The day I'm made to have one of those is the day I retire from public life." He paused. "My

180

assistant schedules me a quarterly cut. But the hair is part of my rogue, boyish appeal, right? Helps with the female voters." Richard winked.

"You forget how well I know you, Richard Arrington. That disaffected charm won't work on me."

Their waiter arrived and placed the drinks down on their table. "Still all set?" he asked.

"Yes, thank you."

Richard took a sip of his drink and nodded his head. "That's a good Old Fashioned. And you're right. You always saw through my charm . . . and me. Much to my chagrin."

"You did quite all right with me just by being yourself."

"Not well enough," Richard said.

A look of darkness flashed across Rebecca's face and Richard regretted his words. "I'm sorry, Becks. I didn't mean — "

"No, no. Don't worry about it." Rebecca smiled again, but this time it didn't reach her eyes. "Keep the shaggy hair," she added. "You wouldn't be you without it."

A minute of silence passed as the pair drank their cocktails and watched the other people in the bar.

Don't fuck this up, Richard told himself. *You're finally with her again. Get back on solid footing.*

"I've kept tabs on you, you know," he said. "Goldman Sachs and then fundraising chair in the last election. And now . . . look at you." He raised his glass toward her in salute. "You hold the keys to the biggest, most powerful bank in the world."

Rebecca smiled at him from behind her copper mug. "Your bank isn't too bad either, Mr. Chancellor."

"That's Lord Chancellor to you," he quipped, and Rebecca rolled her eyes. Richard let out a deep breath and looked toward the windows. "Did you ever think we'd get here? All those late nights studying for Craswell's marketing projects or Pritcher's econ quizzes?" He turned back toward Rebecca. "Did you ever think we'd end up here?"

181

"Where? Sitting together in a bar in Canada, preparing to represent our countries at the G7 tomorrow?" She laughed and shook her head. "No. Did you?"

"Well, the together after thirty years part certainly crossed my mind a time or two."

"Richard."

He put up his hands in defense. "You asked. But both of us as Cabinet-level finance ministers? No. I never imagined that." He paused. "You saw yourself here, though. You said so in our class when that wanker told you to get married and leave."

"Technically, I told him I was going to be Chairwoman of the Federal Reserve. But you're right. And I did track him down."

"Seriously? For your swearing in?"

Rebecca grinned. "Andrew Philip Walters III had two front row tickets for the ceremony. He didn't show, of course, but the seats were reserved. I took a picture of the empty chairs and emailed it to him after."

"Nice. Vindictive, but nice!" Richard finished the last of his drink and put his glass down on the table. "I need to turn in soon. Long day tomorrow."

"Yeah, me too."

Richard opened his mouth to say something, but stopped.
"What is it?"

"I was just . . . I was wondering if you're still wanting to have dinner together while we're here."

Rebecca looked around and lowered her voice. "You mean our date?"

He nodded. "If you still want to."

"I do. Tomorrow around 8?"

"Perfect. I'll get us a table at one of the restaurants."

SIXTY-SEVEN

Rebecca couldn't hide her smile as she walked out of the bar, across the lobby, and toward the elevators. *I forgot what it was like to spend time with him.* She pushed the elevator button for her floor and leaned back against the wall. *Even when it was awkward it was still . . . right.* Her cell phone buzzed in her pocket.

YOU LOOK BEAUTIFUL, BY THE WAY. I KNOW WHAT I'M DREAMING ABOUT TONIGHT.

Rebecca shivered in response. She pressed the button for a blowing kiss emoji, then deleted it. She typed 'goodnight,' and deleted that too. Rebecca's stomach was in knots. *I've never had to flirt by text message before. This is hard!* She looked down at her phone again and started typing.

SWEET DREAMS. XX

Rebecca smiled as she slipped her iPhone back into her jeans pocket and turned the corner down the hall to her room.
"Where have you been?!"
Sarah stood up off the floor and walked toward her mom. "I called you. I texted you. I walked around the whole hotel looking for you."
"You didn't look very hard," Rebecca responded. "I was in the bar in the lobby."
"Why didn't you answer your phone?"
"I bumped into an old friend. I put my phone on silent so we could talk in peace. Why? What's going on?"
Sarah let out a frustrated breath. "Nothing is wrong. I came to your room to say goodnight, but I couldn't find you anywhere. Your security detail said you were 'somewhere in the hotel', which is ridiculous."

Rebecca pressed her key against the pad to unlock her door. "We can come and go as we please as long as we don't leave the property. I think it's nice to have some alone time. And, as you can see, I'm fine."

"Was it Richard Arrington?"

"Huh?"

"The friend you saw in the bar," Sarah pressed. "Was it Richard Arrington?"

"You mean Lord Dublinshire, the Chancellor of the Exchequer? Yes, as a matter of fact, it was." Rebecca stepped inside her doorway. "It's nearly midnight, honey. I'm tired. Go to bed."

****

Sarah Bailey stood in the hallway until she heard the 'click' from the deadbolt on her mom's hotel room door. *She's lying. Mom never puts her phone on silent. Ever.* Even when Sarah was in college and would drunk dial her at 2:00am, Rebecca always answered. *She's hiding something.*

Sarah first noticed the change in her mom's behavior after they moved to DC. She smiled more. Said yes more. Took longer runs and held shorter meetings. For the first several months, Sarah thought the change was due to her new job and living in a new city. *Plus getting rid of my dad*, Sarah thought. But then the flowers started to arrive. And the phone calls. And her mom suddenly being very possessive of her cell phone.

By March of that year, everyone on Rebecca's senior staff knew that their boss had a secret admirer. Sarah enlisted the help of Rebecca's other assistant, Jamal, to try to figure out who it was.

"It doesn't help that she does so much on her personal phone," the young man said one day over lunch. "All her calls that come through me are work-related. Cabinet secretaries, her deputies, her counterparts in other countries. Like that British dude."

"What British dude?"

"You know, the British treasury guy. The . . . " Jamal snapped his fingers trying to remember the correct name. "The Chancellor of the Exchequer."

Sarah had leaned forward in her seat. "He calls her?"

"Sure. Every once in a while. But so do the ones from Germany and Canada and all over."

"Maybe so . . . but Mom didn't go to business school with the people from Germany and Canada."

Jamal pulled out his cell phone and googled 'chancellor of the exchequer'. Richard's Wikipedia profile popped up, along with several pictures. "Is this him?"

Sarah looked at the screen. "I guess so. I've never met him."

Jamal turned his phone to look at Richard's pictures again. "Damn, that boy's fine. I mean, if your mom doesn't want him, I'll take him. Shit."

Sarah had laughed and rolled her eyes. "We'll see him at the G7 in June. If Mom is still acting strange, we should be able to find out more then."

SIXTY-EIGHT

The next day dawned bright and beautiful in Quebec. It was summer, but they were so far north that the nights still turned cold and a hazy mist rose off the river in the morning. Since he didn't have any official meetings until ten o'clock, Richard stayed in his hotel suite to get some work done. He was buried neck deep in economic reports when he heard a knock on the door. "Come in."

Expecting to see one of his advisors, Richard was surprised when a younger version of Rebecca stepped through the door.

"Hello, sir. I mean, umm, your lordship?"

He smiled. "Richard will be fine. You must be Sarah."

The young woman smiled in return and walked further into the room. "Yes sir, I am. How did you know?"

"You look exactly like your mother."

"Yeah, true. Umm, do you have a minute? My mom is actually what I wanted to talk to you about."

"Is she okay?" Richard asked.

"Yes sir, she's fine. I just think maybe she could be even better." Sarah paused and fidgeted back and forth, picking at her fingernails.

"Please, have a seat. Tell me how I can help."

Sarah sat down and took a deep breath to settle her nerves. "If I'm overstepping here, please tell me. I'll leave and pretend like this never happened. But I noticed that you've been calling my mom a lot lately. Every time she talks to you, she's in a good mood the rest of the day."

"Really?" Richard smiled. *I knew it was going well, but not that well.*

"She told me you were friends in business school, but I can't help thinking that there was more to it than that. Or there could be more to it now."

Richard rubbed his hand through his hair. "Perhaps."

"So perhaps you could ask her to out to dinner?"

"You're a little behind the game, young lady. We already have plans for tonight."

"You do?!"

Richard nodded. "We do."

Sarah leaned forward in her chair. "What happened? Really? Were you two together? Did you love her? Do you love her?"

Richard let out a deep breath. *Might as well tell her the truth. She's already figured it out anyway.*

"Have you ever heard of the LiveAid concerts?"

Sarah shook her head no.

"They were a series of concerts in the '80s held in London and Philadelphia to benefit charities in Africa. I attended the one in London in 1985, the summer after our first year of business school. But anyway, the concerts were a big deal, and everybody knew they were going to happen. At the end of our first year, a few months before the actual events, our class decided to hold our own LiveAid gala. It was quite a to-do . . . formal attire, dinner, dancing. The works. Exactly what you would expect from a bunch of Harvard students. We held it at a hotel in downtown Boston.

"After the event – bear in mind, we all had a good bit to drink by this point in the night – we decided to explore the campus of a nearby school. Whatever possessed us to do so, I'll never know. But there we were, four of us in our very best evening wear, traipsing around the grounds of a primary school. Trespassing, truth be told."

"Mom did that?"

"Oh yes," Richard replied with a nod and a smile. His thoughts returned to that night in April in Boston. He hadn't wanted to explore the school grounds or run the obstacle course that they came across on the playground. But Rebecca was leading the charge, and at that point he would've jumped off a cliff if she told him to.

When Rebecca kicked off her right shoe and then her left, Richard had known she was serious. Ignoring the prying eyes of her male companions, she lifted up the hem of her

187

gown until her hands reached the top of her thigh-high pantyhose. Those soon joined her stiletto heels in a pile on the muddy ground. Rebecca hiked up her dress once more, again to mid-thigh, but that time she gathered the excess material and tied it in a knot below her right hip. Glancing down, she had nodded in approval.

Joe and Brian, the other two students in their group, laughed at their friend's new fashion statement. "Look out Paris!" Brian had joked. "That style will be all the rage soon."

Richard, for his part, remained silent.

"What – no wise cracks from you?" Rebecca asked.

"No," he said with a shake of his head. "I think you look great."

His memory was a bit hazy, but Richard still swore he felt the air shift between the two of them that night. At the time, he was glad that the other two guys were too drunk to notice.

Rebecca had turned away from him, but not before Richard caught a glimpse of her flushed cheeks in the moonlight.

My God, she's beautiful.

"Are we gonna do this or what?" asked Joe.

"Yes. Let's go," Rebecca replied. Finding a stick on the ground, she drew a line through the mud. "Start here. First one to finish the obstacle course and touch the wall of the building wins. Ready?"

Four of Harvard's best and brightest stumbled into their starting positions in the half-frozen mud.

Richard had stolen a glance at Rebecca, who was lined up right beside him.

Blue eyes fixed on the target ahead. Her jaw was set and focused, which accentuated her high cheekbones even more. And her arms and legs, toned from their regular runs along the river, rippled in ready anticipation.

Richard was mesmerized.

"On your mark," said Rebecca. "Get set. Go!"

188

****

"There's no way."

Richard woke from his memories to see Rebecca's daughter staring at him. "There's no way my mom ran through an obstacle course in an evening gown and heels."

"Well, technically, she was barefoot. But she did it."

"You're making up all of this."

"I am not. I promise." Richard paused. "We were all standing there at the end, and I looked over at Rebecca. She had her hands on her hips, her dress hiked up to her knees, muddy feet, and a smile on her face that – well, let's just say I didn't need a torch or the moon that night. My whole world was lit by her smile."

Richard stared across the room, lost in his own memory. "That's when I knew," he said. "That's when I knew that I would always love your mum. That there could never be anyone else."

SIXTY-NINE

After Sarah left, Richard went downstairs to the conference rooms. He had a full slate of meetings that day, and he couldn't afford to be caught daydreaming. There was too much at stake for his job and his country. *Rebecca will have to wait*, he thought, and locked her away in a compartment in his mind.

Nine hours later, when work for the day was complete, Richard returned to his suite and sat down at his desk. His chief of staff soon followed him into the room.

"Would you like me to order some room service, sir?" Tripp asked. "I noticed that you didn't eat anything at the cocktail hour."

Richard shook his head. "No, thank you. I'm meeting a friend for dinner at eight."

"Nice. Who is it?"

Richard knew there was no point trying to keep the dinner a secret. "Rebecca Lewis. The American Treasury Secretary. We went to business school together," he added. "It will be nice to catch up."

Tripp nodded his head without suspicion. "Sounds good. I'll leave you to it, unless you need anything else from me?"

"Not tonight. Thank you, Tripp."

As soon as the other man left, Richard started getting ready for his date with Rebecca. *I haven't been this nervous in a long fucking time*, he thought as he showered, shaved, and walked to his closet to pick out his clothes. Having worn a suit all day, he wanted to be more casual at dinner. *But still look good enough to impress her*. He picked out khaki pants, a green oxford shirt, and his trusty navy blue blazer. Richard slipped on his Ferragamo loafers for the final touch and looked in the mirror. "Good," he told himself. "Now don't fuck this up."

****

Three floors above him, Rebecca was doing battle with the butterflies in her stomach. She had also showered to wash off the stress of the day, and now she stood staring at her closet while wrapped in the hotel's robe.

"What the hell am I doing?" she asked herself. "I haven't been on a date in thirty years." She pushed her outfit choices along the hanging rack. "No, no, no." Rebecca let out a frustrated sigh. "He's going to look gorgeous because he always looks gorgeous. I'm going to look . . . ughhhh."

The door to her hotel room opened and Sarah walked inside.

"Here, wear this."

Rebecca spun around to see her daughter carrying a dress over her arm. "I brought this for me, but you should wear it tonight."

Sarah held up the clothing for her mom to see. The emerald green midi dress had cap sleeves, a fitted bodice, and a relaxed skirt with a slit that was high but not scandalous. A portion of the back was cut out, giving the dress a modern flare.

"I can't wear that," Rebecca said. "I'm a Cabinet secretary."

"There's no cleavage, it's well below your knees, and your shoulders are covered," Sarah argued. "Besides, Richard will love it."

Rebecca's eyes opened wide. "How did you – "

"I saw him this morning and he told me you were having dinner together." Sarah stepped forward and took her mom's hands in her own. "I think it's great. He's great. You deserve to be happy."

SEVENTY

Thirty minutes later, wearing her daughter's dress and her own white Jimmy Choo pumps, Rebecca arrived at Vices Versa restaurant in the nearby town of La Malbaie. Richard had texted her the address, with both of them agreeing that eating away from the hotel would offer the most privacy and least chance of gossip.

Rebecca got out of her car and smiled. The small bistro was located in a brick building on Rue Saint Étienne, a main thoroughfare in the small French-Canadian town. As she stepped inside the restaurant, Rebecca ran her hand over her hair. She had curled it into soft waves and put on more makeup than usual, which made her blue eyes shine even brighter.

Richard was waiting for her by the hostess stand.

"Wow," he said, running his eyes over her body. "You look incredible."

Rebecca blushed. "Thank you. It's my daughter's dress," she said, rubbing the bodice nervously.

"You should get one for yourself. You're a knockout."

"Puis-je vous aider?" the hostess asked. Seeing their blank faces, she switched languages. "Can I help you?"

"We have a reservation," replied Richard. "Arrington party of two."

"Yes, right this way."

Richard stepped back and held out his arm, motioning for Rebecca to walk ahead of him. He was trying to be chivalrous and polite, but he also wanted to admire her backside as they walked to their table. The years had been kind to Rebecca's body, and she was as fit and toned now as she had been over thirty years earlier.

Richard shook his head to clear his thoughts and calm his body. *Relax. You're having dinner in a public place. It's not like you can press her up against the wall in front of the entire restaurant.*

His body tightened even more at that visual. *Get it together, Richard. Stop acting like a bloody teenager.*

The waitress led them to a small booth in the back corner. Looking over her shoulder, Rebecca saw her security detail grab a seat at the bar while Richard's protection officer loitered by the back exit.

"This place is great," Rebecca said as she sat down at their table.

"It is," Richard agreed. "But anywhere would be great with you."

A waiter came over and poured their water glasses. After he left, Rebecca said: "I must confess, I'm a bit nervous. I can't remember the last time I did this."

Richard leaned forward and lowered his voice. "The last time you went on a date?"

She nodded.

"It's just me, Becks," he replied. "No need to be nervous. I have an idea," he said. "Why don't we both look at the menu for a few minutes and decide what we want while our nerves settle down. Then we can order all at once and have the wait staff leave us alone."

"Perfect."

SEVENTY-ONE

Fifteen minutes later, Rebecca was sipping a glass of
rosé while Richard swirled an Old Fashioned in his hand.
They had ordered the seared scallops and shoulder of lamb,
with 'crazy style tomatoes' to share.

"I don't know what they are," Rebecca said, "but the
description sounds fabulous."

"I'll try anything," Richard replied. "English food
doesn't get very crazy, so a little tomato variety will be
good."

"John hated tomatoes," Rebecca said, then regretted her
words. "I'm sorry. I won't talk about him."

"It's fine. Really. You were married to him for a long
time. You can't erase his memory entirely."

"If only," she replied as she drank more of her rosé.

Richard noticed that she was finishing the glass rather
quickly. He reached over and grabbed hold of her hand.
"You're safe now, Becks. Everything will be okay."

Rebecca nodded and sighed before slipping her hand out
of his. "We probably shouldn't do that. Someone will see
us."

Richard looked around the restaurant. "No one knows us
here. But I'll keep my hands to myself."

"Thank you. For listening to me. And seeing me," she
added. "I don't think John ever truly saw me. Not the real
me. He put me up on a pedestal and left me there dangling
my feet."

"Pedestals aren't all bad."

"No, they're not. But the trouble is, once you're there,
you can't move. You can't do anything except sit still and
look down while your husband makes a mockery of your
marriage."

Rebecca stopped talking when she saw their waiter
approaching with the appetizer.

After he left, Richard grabbed a tomato from the plate. "Why didn't you say something?" he asked between bites. "Confront him? Leave him?"

Rebecca shrugged her shoulders. "I did confront him a few times in the beginning. About his working late and mystery phone calls and what not. But he wasn't going to change. I saw that. I made him promise to at least be discrete, and I buried the pain so no one could find it." She paused to cut her own bite of tomato. "Then John 'fell in love' and suddenly I was perched on a pedestal belonging to a 26-year-old who didn't mind being treated like a doll, as long as she was a well-dressed doll with lots of shiny accessories."

"I wish I had known how unhappy you were. I wish you had told me."

"There was a time when you would've seen through the act. I was worried you would. I guess that's why I worked so hard to hide it from you. And why I got so upset in London that one night."

"I was over the line in London. I'm sorry. And I'm sorry for not seeing your pain anyway."

Rebecca closed her eyes and smiled. A silence fell over their table, then Richard added:

"I'm here now, Becks. I don't want you on a pedestal. I just want you."

SEVENTY-TWO

Their main course of scallops and lamb arrived a minute later, but neither Richard nor Rebecca were interested in the food. He gulped down the rest of his Old Fashioned and looked her in the eyes.

"I'm probably going to get in trouble for saying this, but I may never have another chance. You still take my breath away, Becks. Just like you did the first time I saw you. Do you remember?"

"When we met?"

Richard nodded.

"Of course. Econ class. But I didn't take your breath away. You laughed at me."

"Only because you were the most adorable creature I'd ever seen with all your pencils and papers and erasers. You were so serious with your 'this is America, speak English' bit. It was so cute."

Rebecca snorted and rolled her eyes.

"It's true," he argued. "I saw you in the hallway beforehand and prayed we would be in the same class. I was watching you that whole time. When you looked around the room as if you were expecting to recognize someone. How you bit your lip and looked nervous when you saw you were the only girl in the class, and then squared your shoulders and marched toward the seating chart – like you had given yourself a miniature pep talk and were ready to conquer the world." Richard paused and smiled. "I watched how the routine of setting out your supplies seemed to calm your nerves. You knew how to be a student . . . there was comfort in the familiarity."

Rebecca stared at Richard in amazement. *He noticed all of that? And remembers it over thirty years later?*

"I remember everything about you," Richard said before taking her hand in his and kissing the back of it.

She pulled away.

"Becks . . ."

"No." Rebecca looked down at the table and shook her head. "No."

"Look me in the eye and say it."

She lifted her eyes up from the table and looked at him through two pools of tears. "I – "

"Damn it all to hell if you two aren't a sight for sore eyes!"

Rebecca jumped, startled, and Richard spun around in his chair. *Oh my God*, he thought. He held up a hand to wave off their security details.

Walking toward them in jeans and a faded golf shirt was Howard Ratliff, a classmate from HBS. Short and stocky, Howard sported a shaved, Mr. Clean hairdo and a gray goatee. He was in the Navy before going to business school and still had the vocabulary to prove it.

"Well shit, I mean look at you two," Howard said as he arrived at their table. "Still together after all these years. I shoulda known, man," he added. "You two were like fucking Siamese twins – joined at the hip." Howard threw his head back and laughed, a loud, barrel-chested sound that filled the restaurant and drew glares from people nearby.

Hoping to avoid an even bigger scene, Richard grabbed a chair from an empty table next to them and pulled it between him and Rebecca.

"Here, Howard, have a seat. Join us for a few minutes."

"Ah hell, no, I wouldn't want to interrupt!"

What would you call what you're doing now? Rebecca thought. "No, really, join us," she said, motioning to the empty chair.

"Well, I have a policy to never say no to a pretty lady," Howard replied with a grin as he sat down.

A waiter appeared and asked the new arrival for his drink order.

"No, son, I'm good for now," he said, lifting the glass he brought with him from the bar.

197

When the waiter left, Howard returned his attention to his former classmates.

"So, what are you kids doing here, huh? Anniversary trip?"

Richard and Rebecca glanced at each other in surprise. It was rare to run across someone who didn't know who they were and the jobs they held.

"I think you've gotten the wrong impression," Rebecca replied.

"Whatcha mean?"

"We're not married," Richard said.

"Living in sin, huh? Well shit, boy, didn't think ya had it in ya!" Howard slapped his old classmate on the back so hard that Richard winced.

"No, I'm recently divorced," Rebecca replied. "From someone else. My ex-husband and I have two adult children. I live in Washington, DC."

"I've never married," Richard continued. "I live in London. Becks – I mean, Rebecca – and I are both here for the G7 summit."

"Well shit," Howard said again. Rebecca remembered that was his favorite phrase at Harvard, too. *We even started calling him Wellshit behind his back*, she recalled, working to hide her grin.

"You don't know who we are?" Richard asked.

"Well shit, of course I do," Howard said, and Rebecca stifled a laugh behind her napkin. "Richard Arrington and Rebecca Lewis. Or whatever your last name is now."

"I meant our jobs. I'm Chancellor of the Exchequer for the United Kingdom."

"And I'm Secretary of the Treasury for the United States."

Howard looked back and forth between the two finance ministers as if trying to decide whether or not they were joking.

Here it comes, Rebecca thought, squeezing her cheeks between her teeth to keep from laughing.

"Well shit," their classmate said, and even Richard cracked a smile. "That's great. Congratulations."

"Thank you," Richard replied. "You really didn't know? Our names are in the news quite often, and the alumni magazine has done several write-ups about us."

"Nah, man. I run a safari ranch in Zimbabwe now. I'm only in town to meet with some of my financial backers. Ain't got time for news and shit. Too busy taking people's money in exchange for the privilege of culling the herds."

Howard laughed at himself again, drawing more stares and glares from the other diners.

A few seconds later, a waiter returned to clear the dinner plates. Their visitor knew that was his cue to leave. Howard stood and returned his chair to the table next to them.

"Alright, I'll leave you two money people alone to talk shop. Damn good to see you both, though," he added, kissing Rebecca on the cheek before turning to shake hands with Richard. "Damn good. If you ever want to come out to the ranch, just let me know."

"Will do," Richard replied, knowing full well he'd never see Howard again.

"Well, that was interesting," Rebecca said when Howard and the waiter were out of earshot.

"Don't you mean 'well shit, that was interesting?' I saw you over there smiling behind your napkin."

Rebecca let loose the laughter she had been holding in. "That's what we called him, remember? Wellshit?"

Richard nodded. "You should laugh like that more often. Your eyes sparkle when you do."

"Please don't – "

"What? It's true. Just a friend offering an observation."

"Sure. That's what we'll go with."

Richard smiled then locked eyes with Rebecca, and everyone else in the restaurant seemed to disappear. He was soaking up as much of her as he could, and in an instant Richard's heart and mind traveled back thirty-two years to a time when he thought they would be taking anniversary trips together like Howard had guessed.

The same memories flooded Rebecca's mind and she lowered her eyes to concentrate on the napkin in her lap. *This is too much. He wants too much.* She looked back across the table and made her best effort to reign in her emotions.

"Tell me, Lord Chancellor, what are your thoughts on the proposed Rapid Response Mechanism? How can we frame economic policies to help defend democracy?"

Richard's heart sank, but he knew Rebecca was right to change the subject. If they talked about work, he would have to listen to what she was saying. After all, he wasn't just representing himself . . . he had 65 million Britons to think of. Yes, if the conversation was about work, Richard would have to pay attention to Rebecca's words. He couldn't think about the steady rise and fall of her chest, or the way her hair cascaded over her shoulders like waves of black diamonds. He couldn't get lost in eyes the color of the ocean, or feel his heart skip a beat every time she laughed.

Work, Richard reminded himself. *Work is the antidote.*

The two politicians spent the rest of their dinner talking about business, with people nearby never suspecting the depth of the connection flowing underneath the surface.

SEVENTY-THREE

While her mom and Richard were at dinner, Sarah ventured out of her room and up to the Bellerive Restaurant. The inside dining area was packed with other conference attendees, but she snagged a spot outside on the patio. The stone terrace was full of marble-top tables with umbrellas, and a row of green shrubbery decorated the wall separating the restaurant from the park and river below. The night air had started to turn cold, and Sarah made sure to sit on the side of the table closest to the tower heater.

She placed her napkin in her lap and fiddled with its edges. An introvert by nature, Sarah usually ordered room service when they went on road trips. But her window at the Fairmont overlooked the parking lot, and she wanted to take advantage of being in such a beautiful town. The hotel brochure said that the Bellerive Restaurant had a patio with a gorgeous view of the river. *It wasn't lying*, she thought as she looked out past the hedges toward the St. Lawrence. *Besides, if mom can go on a date – a freaking date! – I can eat by myself in a restaurant.*

Sarah's waiter soon arrived, and she stepped even farther out of her comfort zone by ordering a glass of red wine and the crème brûlée.

"Anything else, mademoiselle?"

"Nope, that's all."

Sarah smiled, proud of herself. *See, that wasn't so hard.*

Halfway through enjoying her drink and dessert, a man in his mid-thirties approached Sarah's table carrying a pint of beer and a plate full of poutine. Of average height with curly brown hair and glasses, he looked nerdy enough to not make Sarah nervous.

"Excuse me, miss?" the man said in a strong English accent. "Would you mind if I joined you? I do apologize, but there's nowhere else to sit. I won't interrupt your privacy, I promise. I just need a place to set my plate and glass."

Sarah glanced behind the man and saw that the patio was indeed packed. "Sure. Go ahead."

"Thank you so much. You're a life saver." The man smiled and turned his focus to his food, making good on his promise to not bother her.

His manners and friendly smile put Sarah at ease. She appreciated the fact that he didn't mind not talking. After a few minutes, Sarah was the one who broke the ice.

"How is the poutine?" she asked. "I've heard people talk about it but never tried it."

"Here," he said, holding his plate over toward her. "Have some."

"Oh no, I couldn't . . . "

"Of course you can," the man responded, spooning some of it onto her plate. "It's quite good."

Sarah put a bite in her mouth and groaned. "Mmmm. That's delicious! Thank you. I'm Sarah, by the way."

The man reached out his hand to shake hers. "I'm Tripp."

"Are you part of the British delegation?" she asked. *I wonder if he knows about the Chancellor's dinner date?*

"I am." Tripp nodded his head and looked around the patio. "I think we all belong to one country or another. But do we have to talk about work? This is my first free night in a long time. Let's discuss something else."

SEVENTY-FOUR

The second day of the conference started bright and early with a breakfast roundtable attended by all seven finance ministers. Their respective staff were in chairs placed along the outer wall of the room. Sarah saw Tripp and smiled. He nodded a greeting in return.

Rebecca, for her part, was doing everything she could to not stare at Richard the entire time. She hadn't slept a wink the night before, lying in bed rethinking every second of their date.

The dinner was fabulous, the company even better, and Richard had gone so far as to place his hand on the small of her back as they walked out of the restaurant toward her car. They had stopped on the sidewalk, and Rebecca turned to face him.

"Thank you for tonight," she told Richard. "Even though I was supposed to pay for it to make us even for the Giacomo's dinner."

Richard had inched closer to her. Close enough where she could breathe in his scent but still far enough away to not arouse suspicion from passersby.

"You're not supposed to pay people back for a birthday gift. Besides," he had said, lowering his voice, "there's no way in hell I would let you buy dinner on our first date."

Rebecca blushed. "Took us long enough, huh?"

"We're here now. That's what matters." He exhaled deeply, his breath showing in the cool night air. "I know I'm pushing you faster than you want to go," he told her, "but I really wish I could kiss you right now."

Across the breakfast table at their meeting, Richard saw Rebecca's flushed face and knew exactly what she was thinking about. He was the same way – re-thinking and re-feeling every moment from the night before. Every word; every smile. He soaked them up like a sponge and catalogued them in his mind . . . an addict who finally got another hit and was trying to extend the high as long as possible.

I have to see her again, he thought, ignoring the discussion around him. *There has to be more. This is a beginning . . . it has to be.*

SEVENTY-FIVE

The most romantic three days of Rebecca's life came to a crashing halt on the final day of the conference. After the breakfast meeting, she had one-on-ones with her counterparts from Germany and Japan. A meeting with the European Union's representative lasted an hour longer than expected, and by the time Rebecca emerged from her assigned conference room at four in the afternoon, the UK delegation was gone – and Richard along with it.

Rebecca trudged through the rest of her day with a fake smile on her face. She knew nothing would've happened with Richard – not with that many staffers and reporters around – *but I just wanted to see him again*, she thought as she rode in a motorcade to the airport along with the President and the rest of his economic advisors. *I wanted to shake Richard's hand; see his smile. Something.*

After climbing aboard Air Force One, Rebecca settled into her seat and pulled an eye mask down over her face. Although it was a short flight from Quebec to Washington, she was hoping to have a quick nap and recharge.

But sleep was not in the cards.

As soon as her eyes closed, Rebecca's thoughts turned to Richard.

It was the first of a series of dreams she had about him. Every night for a week straight, Rebecca dreamed about Richard. Almost a montage at first. A close-up of his eyes. Then his smile. Then it would be her and him together: at night walking on a bridge, or perhaps alone together in a dimly lit hallway. Once – Rebecca shivered – once in her office. *Or was it his?* The details were hazy, but there was always a desk, or a wall, or a rail . . . something for Richard to press her up against when he took her in his arms and kissed her in the way only he ever had.

Rebecca blushed at that memory, too. The night the dream was real. *Graduation night*, she thought.

"Umm . . . Mom?"

Rebecca looked up to see Jonathan staring at her across the breakfast table. Having graduated from Columbia a month earlier, he was living with Rebecca that summer while waiting on business school to start in the fall.

"Are you okay, Mom? You look flushed. Are you feeling alright?"

She nodded. "Yep, I'm fine. Must be a hot flash or something."

Hot flash my ass, Jonathan thought. Sarah had told him about their mom's dinner date in Canada, and Jonathan wasn't a fan of the idea. *She suffered enough when Dad left. She doesn't need to deal with heartbreak again.* "You've been having hot flashes a lot lately," he said, "ever since you got back from the G7."

"I'm sure it's a coincidence, honey."

Jonathan decided that now was the moment to press the issue. *She doesn't need another man in her life. She has me.*

Jonathan pushed aside his bowl of cereal and leaned forward. "Speaking of the G7 conference, you said you knew the British Chancellor in college. Right?"

"We went to business school together."

"And you were friends?"

Rebecca nodded and scrolled through her cell phone, trying to get Jonathan to drop the subject. "We were. I would say we still are. Good friends."

"How good?"

"What do you mean?"

"I mean . . . how good? Like you hung out in groups? Or friends with benefits or . . . "

Rebecca held up her hand to silence her son. "First of all, 'friends with benefits' was not a thing when I was in school. People went on real dates, not in a group, and we had real conversations using our voices instead of Snapchat. To 'swipe' something meant to steal it, not to accept or reject for a hookup."

"Okay, Mom, I get it. You're old. But you're not answering me."

"Drop the attitude, young man. Now."

Jonathan sighed and sat back in his chair. After a few minutes, he ventured another question. "So . . . was he a friend who was a boy or was he a boyfriend?"

A slight smile creased his mom's face. "A friend who was a boy."

"Nothing ever happened?"

"No."

Rebecca had grown so accustomed to telling the lie that at times she forgot it wasn't the truth. *You call that nothing?* she asked herself, her mind flashing back first to Canada, and then even further. To nights spent sharing each other's deepest secrets. Long runs along the banks of the Charles River. Intimate, too-close dances at holiday galas. And the one night – graduation night – when she and Richard could be who they wanted to be for a brief moment in time.

"Mom?"

Jonathan's voice jarred Rebecca's thoughts.

"Hmm?"

"I said that sometimes it seems like there was more. I mean, Sarah said he couldn't keep his eyes off you in Canada."

Rebecca shook her head. "I doubt he was staring the entire time. We hadn't seen each other in years, so anything your sister thought she saw was just the by-product of two friends reuniting."

Jonathan nodded. "Good. Friends are good."

SEVENTY-SIX

At 10:00am the next morning, Rebecca's cell phone buzzed.

GOOD MORNING, MADAM SECRETARY!

Buzz buzz.

HOW'D YOU SLEEP?
WHAT ARE YOU AND YOUR KIDS DOING FOR THE AUGUST RECESS?

Rebecca smiled as she read the messages. She was starting to expect her daily calls or texts from Richard. A part of her knew she shouldn't – expectations lead to hopes and hopes lead to heartache – but she couldn't help getting a little excited as the clock struck 10:00. Richard was consistent with it every morning since they got back from Canada, and it had become the favorite part of her day.

GOOD MORNING TO YOU! NO PLANS RIGHT NOW FOR AUGUST. MAYBE JUST BEING TOURISTS IN DC WHEN EVERYBODY ELSE LEAVES TOWN.

Rebecca was looking forward to a few weeks of quiet. With Congress out of session and much of the government in vacation mode, Rebecca would have a chance to explore her new home.

Buzz. Buzz Buzz. Buzz.

WHY DON'T YOU COME VISIT?
WE'LL GO TO MY FAMILY'S ESTATE IN THE COUNTRY.
IT'S QUIET. PRIVATE. LOTS OF GOOD FOOD AND WINE AND RELAXING.

PLUS, GUS WILL BE THERE.

Rebecca smiled. *How could I say no to Gus?*

LET ME CHECK WITH MY KIDS.

****

Two months later, Rebecca, Sarah, and Jonathan touched down at Heathrow Airport in London. A middle-aged man named Charlie met them at baggage claim and introduced himself as the Estate Manager at Rosewood.

"I've been with the Arrington family my whole life," he said, loading their bags into a black Range Rover with a small, gold logo on the door. "And my parents before me. The current Lord Dublinshire is great . . . but you already know that! His dad, may he rest in peace, was of a different sort altogether. But the granddad was a true gentleman. And the grandmum? Oooh boy she was fun!"

Rebecca and her kids looked at each other and laughed, bemused by their driver's accent and gossip.

"What's that logo on the door?" Sarah asked as the group of four drove out of the airport and onto the M25 motorway. "The gold thing?"

"Ah, the coat of arms, miss. The Arringtons are one of the oldest families in the country. One of the few remaining inherited titles. His Lordship was in the House of Lords for a short time before he left to run for an elected seat.

"It'll take a little while to get to Rosewood," Charlie continued. "But you'll love it. Most beautiful place on Earth."

While Rebecca and Sarah looked out the car windows and took in the scenery, Jonathan stared at his cell phone. He scrolled through Instagram and tried to ignore the other passengers' happy conversation.

At twenty-four years old, Jonathan graduated from Columbia that spring and was starting business school at

Harvard in the fall. Built like Rebecca's dad rather than his own father, Jonathan was six feet tall with blue eyes and brown hair. He was a point guard in basketball in high school, and he followed in his father's footsteps to enroll at the University of Georgia for his freshman year. He had wanted to see what a Southern college experience was all about, but quickly found himself a fish out of water. He transferred to Columbia for his final three years.

Jonathan could tell that something was going on between his mom and this British dude, Richard. *I don't like it*, he thought, huffing in disapproval. The only reason Jonathan came on the trip was to figure out what was going on and protect his mother. *After the hell Dad put her through, I'm not going to let anyone else hurt her.*

SEVENTY-SEVEN

An hour and a half later, Charlie turned their SUV off a small-town road and onto a long, winding driveway.

"We're on the estate now," he said. "Another mile or so before we reach the big house."

The three American passengers looked out their windows. Acres upon acres of grass and trees stretched out around them. Halfway down the driveway, Charlie pulled to a stop at a security gate.

"Didn't use to have this. But ever since Lord Dublinshire became Chancellor, we've had to make some changes." Their driver rolled down his window and spoke to the guard. "I've got His Lordship's guests with me, Billy. Here for the week."

Billy looked in the car, nodded his head, and waved them through.

Just past the gate, the asphalt drive turned into brown sand and gravel. A wide path led them in a straight line toward the main house. After passing through a batch of trees, Rosewood came into view.

"Holy shit," Jonathan said.

Rebecca nodded her head in agreement. She looked up the estate before their visit, but pictures didn't do it justice. The enormous main house was more like a palace, built in a half-H shape with Corinthian pilasters decorating the front. Originally made of brick, the exterior had been covered with mathematical tiles hundreds of years earlier. A beautiful, formal French garden surrounded the home, and several additional buildings dotted the landscape nearby.

As the Lewis-Bailey clan got out of the car, Rosewood's front door swung open and Richard came striding out. His chocolate lab, Gus, trotted alongside him. Wearing blue jeans and a sweater, with the sleeves pushed up to his elbows, Lord Dublinshire looked every bit the country gentleman. Sarah barely recognized him not in a suit, but Rebecca walked

211

forward and gave him a hug. Then she bent down and rubbed Gus' ears.

Jonathan raised his eyebrows and looked back and forth between his mom and sister. Sarah shrugged her shoulders in response. "Give him a chance," she whispered.

"Kids, come say hello." Rebecca waved them forward with her arm.

"Welcome to Rosewood," Richard said with a smile. "I cannot tell you how happy Gus and I are to have you here. Come in. I'll give you a tour."

Rebecca stepped inside the house and her jaw dropped. She spun in a slow circle, taking in the grand hall. The large, open atrium was almost the length of a football field and was two stories tall, with an ornate balustrade protecting the upstairs walkway. Both floors were decorated with massive paintings of what Rebecca assumed were Richard's family members. Arched doorways in the far corners of the first floor led to other areas of the home, but the *pièce de resistance* was the staircase. Framed by the same balustrade that ran along the second-floor corridor, the oversized stairs stretched out along the entire back third of the room. Rebecca guessed that each step could hold at least six people side-by-side.

"Wow," she said. Rebecca looked over at Richard and saw him watching her. "This is beautiful," she told him.

"If I had a house like this, I would never leave!" Sarah exclaimed.

Richard smiled. "It is nice, but my work is in London."

"You must come here all the time, though. Right?" Sarah asked. "Like every weekend you can?"

"Not really. I went away to school when I was a kid, and I only came back on breaks. I used to drive out once a month to have lunch with my mum, but ever since she passed I don't even do that."

"You have this huge, gorgeous house and nobody lives here?" asked Jonathan.

"Some of the staff live on property." Richard shrugged his shoulders. "I don't know. It's a big house. Gets kind of lonely, I guess, when you don't have anyone to share it with. Aside from this fella, of course." He patted Gus on the head. "He loves it out here. I had him trained by our game warden when he was a puppy, so he chases after all the rabbits on the estate."

"Have you ever taken him on a real hunt?" asked Jonathan.

"No, he's gun shy. Isn't that right, big fella? Yeah, you like to think you're tough, but in reality you're a big baby." Gus looked up at his owner with what appeared to be a smile, and everyone laughed. "Damn dog is too smart for his own good."

"This house, though," Jonathan said, "don't tell me you didn't throw some epic parties here during college."

"Epic parties? Yes. But mostly in London." Richard paused. "Once, when I was a boy, my parents went on a trip. I don't remember where. My grandfather had passed away and my grandmother lived in the big house with us. She said the dowager house was too drafty. But anyway, my parents were away and the nanny was sick, so my grandmother was watching us.

"Abuela was Spanish. And feisty. Not at all a proper English noblewoman," Richard said. "As soon as the household staff retired for the night, Abuela told us to get our mattresses from our beds. We slid and surfed and raced down this staircase for hours." He laughed. "To this day, I can't think of a time when I had that much fun."

"Not even on the obstacle course with Mom?" Sarah asked.

Rebecca's eyes grew wide and she shot a look at Richard. *How does she know about that?* she questioned silently.

He shrugged his shoulders and grinned.

"Not even on the obstacle course," Richard replied. "Although that was close. I was a bit too drunk and definitely too distracted that night."

"What are you talking about?" Jonathan asked.

"When Richard and I were in business school, we attended a big fancy dance called the HBS LiveAid. Afterward, a group of us were walking around town – "

"In our dinner clothes," Richard added.

"Yes, in tuxedos and ball gowns, and we came across an obstacle course. Being young and drunk and stupid, we decided it would be fun to run the course in our evening wear."

Jonathan shook his head. "No way. You?" he asked, looking at his mom. "There's no way you crawled under a net in a ball gown."

"It's true. I did."

Richard put his arm around Rebecca's shoulders and smiled. "Your mum was quite the adventurous lady back in the day."

Rebecca's cheeks blushed, a fact that didn't go unnoticed by her children. Shaking loose from Richard's embrace, she said: "what's next on the tour?"

"Well, if you go to the top of the stairs there, I believe you'll find some mattresses."

Sarah's eyes lit up. "For real? Come on, Jonathan."

When the kids were out of earshot and busy selecting mattresses, Richard stepped closer to Rebecca, this time sliding his arm around her waist.

"She's you," he said. "That spirit, that smile. She's exactly how you were at that age."

Rebecca sighed. "I know. I love it, and yet – "

"Yet what?"

"It scares me."

"Why?"

Rebecca opened her mouth to respond but was interrupted by Jonathan calling her name.

"Lookout below!"

214

Her son jumped head-first onto a twin sized mattress and careened down the long wooden staircase at full speed.

Richard and Rebecca jumped out of the way and laughed as the young man came to a skidding stop halfway down the hall.

"Watch out!" Sarah said from the top of the stairs. "My turn!"

SEVENTY-EIGHT

Later that night, after dinner and a tour of the rest of the house, Lord Dublinshire and his three guests went to their respective bedrooms. Richard had promised himself that he was going to behave, even though this was the first time he and Rebecca had ever slept in the same house. Standing in the upstairs corridor, he placed his hands on her shoulders and gave her a gentle kiss on the cheek. "Goodnight, Becks. I'll see you in the morning."

Richard wasn't even back to his room before his cell phone started ringing.

"It's late, Tripp. Go to bed."

"I'm sorry to bother you," his chief of staff replied, "but I have a few quick things we need to go over so I can leave you alone tomorrow."

Richard groaned. "Fine."

"How's it going, by the way?"

"Good. Really good. It's nice to have people in the house again."

"The American Treasury Secretary, right?"

"And her two kids. They're both adults." Richard put the phone on speaker so he could send a picture of them. Rebecca, Sarah, and Jonathan were all standing at the bottom of the grand hall staircase, holding up mattresses and grinning from ear to ear.

"Mattress surfing? Excellent! My little girl would be so jealous." Tripp paused and zoomed in on the picture. "Wait. The younger woman. Who is that?"

"Rebecca's daughter."

"I met her in Canada. I went to the rooftop bar and couldn't find an open table, so I sat down next to her."

"Nice," Richard replied with a yawn. "Go ahead and run through the work items, though. I'm exhausted."

SEVENTY-NINE

The jet-lagged American visitors slept in the next day, so Richard took Gus on a run. It was late morning by the time he returned and showered, and Rebecca was sitting outside on a small patio that overlooked the garden. There were four chaise lounge chairs lined up in a row, and each had its own small table beside it. The area was meant for sunbathing, but the weather was unseasonably cool that day. Rebecca had wrapped a blanket around her shoulders to stay warm. Richard poured two cups of coffee and walked outside to join her.

"Good morning, Madam Secretary," he said, handing her a mug as he sat down. "Be careful, it's hot."

"Mmm, thank you."

"How'd you sleep?"

"Great," Rebecca said. "Like a log. The blackout curtains are clutch."

Richard looked back at the house. "I think my sister had those put in. She and her husband used to come out here a lot when their boys were younger."

"How old are they now?"

"Twenty-six and twenty-four. Same age as yours." Richard paused. "That reminds me. What did you mean last night when you said you're scared that Sarah is so much like you?"

Rebecca put her coffee mug down on the table and sat up in her chair. She folded her legs underneath her, crisscross, and let out a deep breath.

"She's me. One hundred percent. She looks like me, acts like me, thinks like me. The only thing different is our accents, since she grew up in New York. I love it – us being so similar. I don't have to worry as much about her because she processes things the same way I do. Now Jonathan," she said, waving her hand, "is his father made over. That's a story for another day." Rebecca paused and looked out over

217

the gardens. "It scares me because I'm afraid Sarah will make the same mistake I did. Listen to her head and not her heart. Choose what's easy and convenient instead of fighting for what she really wants."

Richard stood up from his chair and joined Rebecca on hers. "What did you really want?" he asked. He knew the answer, at least he thought he did, but he needed to hear her say it. "What did you want, Becks?"

"You."

Richard reached out and pulled Rebecca toward him, breathing in waves of the scent that was uniquely hers. Sliding his fingers through her silky black hair, he leaned down and kissed her.

****

Rebecca felt Richard's lips pressed against hers, soft and gentle and then stronger and more passionate. She knew she should pull away; knew she should tell Richard to stop. But she didn't want to. *For once in your life, let him love you.*

Rebecca wrapped her arms around his neck and kissed him back – her passion matching, if not surpassing, his. She kissed Richard with the love she felt during business school. The frustration she felt during her marriage. The loneliness since her divorce. All of the feelings that Rebecca kept pent-up for the past thirty-four years came pouring out on the back patio of Richard's home in the English countryside.

As the kiss deepened, Rebecca's thoughts faded. She lost herself in the strength of Richard's embrace. He stood from the chair and pulled her up with him, their bodies pressed flush against each other. Without breaking their kiss, Richard walked them backward, step by step until Rebecca felt the wall of the house against her back.

Oh my God, she thought in a brief gasp for air. "I dreamt of this."

"What?" Richard asked, breathing hard.

Oh shit, I didn't mean to say that out loud. "Nothing," she whispered.

"No, what did you say?"

"I said I dreamt of this. You. Me. Pressed up against a wall . . ."

Richard smiled. "Oh really?" He brushed Rebecca's hair away from her eyes. "What else did you dream about, beautiful?"

"I . . . umm . . ."

"Mom!"

The sound of Sarah's voice broke through the morning air.

"Mom – where are you?"

Richard let out a frustrated sigh and stepped back from Rebecca, walking over to his chair and picking up his coffee. "She's over here," he called out in response.

Sarah rounded the corner to find her mother and Lord Dublinshire standing three feet apart, each holding a coffee mug and showing no signs of what happened between them.

"It's the White House," Sarah said. "The President wants to speak with you."

EIGHTY

That afternoon, Sarah and Jonathan decided to drive into the nearby town and see what they could find. Their mother stayed behind, blaming it on work calls she needed to return.

As soon as the estate's Range Rover pulled out of view on the gravel drive, Richard took Rebecca's hand in his. "Come on. I have something I want to show you."

With Gus leading the way, the pair walked around the outside of the house and past the patio. Rebecca shivered as she remembered that morning's embrace. Richard kept going, though, past the gardens and a small gate into the more wooded grounds behind the main house.

"Don't go too far, buddy," Richard said when Gus took off after a small animal. "Probably a rabbit. They're all over the place."

He led Rebecca through high grass and over fallen trees, always careful to sidestep holes or push hanging branches out of the way. After a few minutes, they arrived at their destination. The area was overgrown, but Rebecca could tell that something used to be there. A small stone wall in the shape of an L jutted up from the ground, and the remains of a crumbled chimney stood a few feet away.

"Centuries ago, this was the game warden's cottage," Richard explained. "By the time my sister and I were kids, there wasn't much left. It was our secret play place, though. No nannies allowed."

Rebecca smiled and sat down on the wall. "I like it. It's hard to picture you bounding about the woods, though."

"I'm a city boy at heart, but I have my moments. And this spot . . . this spot is special. I always came out here after a fight with my dad or a bad term at school. I came here on the day my parents told me I couldn't marry you."

Rebecca reached up and grabbed his hand, pulling him down to sit next to her. Richard put his arm around her shoulder. He used his free hand to lift her chin, leaned down, and kissed her.

"Richard – "

"Stop thinking," he whispered. "Stop thinking for one second and just feel."

Rebecca leaned into his embrace and kissed him back, reaching up to run her hands through his hair. A moment later, though, she pulled away.

"No, this is reckless. We can't lose control like this."

Richard realized that he wasn't going to kiss his way through the situation. He got up off the wall and stood facing a nearby pasture, his hands on his hips. "I've never liked that feeling," he said. "Being out of control. It's why I prepare so much for meetings. Why I don't drink to excess anymore. There's one exception, though." Richard turned to look at her. "I lose complete control when I'm around you, Becks. My brain shuts off and my heart – and other body parts – skip into overdrive. But I don't mind. I may not have control, but you do. If there's one person in the world who I trust with my heart, it's you. Because you've had it for the last thirty-four years."

Rebecca closed her eyes and a single tear rolled down each cheek.

"We're adults," Richard pressed. "We're in charge. I don't have to answer to my parents anymore – they're dead. You're divorced. Let's finally be together."

"Which one of us gives up their job, hmm?"

"Who says we have to give up our jobs? We can be long distance until we either lose an election or get tired of being that far apart. But together long distance is better than not together at all."

"The media would hound us relentlessly."

"Fuck the media. Fuck everything."

Rebecca couldn't help but smile. "I love you, Richard. I'm not afraid to say it now. But we're changing the world for the better. We can't throw that away. We can't be that selfish."

Richard stepped forward and took both of her hands in his. "Sometimes I wonder if we met too soon, when we were too young for it to go anywhere; sometimes I wish we'd been around each other in the middle years when we were figuring more things out in our respective lives; and some days – today, for example – I dare to wonder if we have actually, unintentionally, done something quite incredible . . . and found each other again."

Rebecca sighed. "My God, that's beautiful."

He took a step closer, but she narrowed her eyes and smirked. "Who wrote it?"

"What?"

"I know you, Richard Arrington. You're not that poetic. Where'd you read it – a Hallmark card?"

Richard closed his eyes, then laughed. "You always did see right through me. But no, I didn't read it in a greeting card. A friend of mine from university wrote it in a love letter to his girlfriend. I saw it on his desk before he sent it."

"And what – held on to the quote for forty years in case you ever needed it?"

"Fits our situation pretty damn well, don't you think?"

"It does."

Richard again stepped toward his old friend, this time wrapping his arms around her waist. "Does that mean you'll give us another go?"

"We never gave us a first go."

"True. It's not too late, Becks."

She let out a deep breath. "We don't tell anyone? We just talk and FaceTime and sneak in visits here and there?"

Richard smiled bigger than he ever had in his life. "However you want it to be, my darling. My beautiful, darling Rebecca."

He bent over and kissed her. This time, Rebecca didn't hesitate. Didn't question. She leaned forward and melted into his arms. For the first time in her life, Rebecca felt like she was complete.

EIGHTY-ONE

Sarah and Jonathan could tell that something happened at Rosewood between their mom and Richard, but they didn't have time to ask her about it before Jonathan left for Harvard Business School. And Rebecca kept things quiet enough that, by the middle of September, her children figured whatever was going on with Richard had faded away.

In reality, though, Richard and Rebecca's relationship was stronger than ever. She started calling him during her early morning runs, which gave them almost an hour to talk. Richard blocked the time on his work calendar as 'Do Not Disturb'.

"You must be in ridiculously good shape," he told Rebecca one morning. It was six-thirty her time, and she was barely breathing hard.

Rebecca laughed. "I wish. I'm walking right now, not running."

"When did that change?"

"A week or two ago. I'm fifty-six. My joints don't put up with me like they used to."

"Tell me about it," Richard replied. "I have to ice my knees every time I play tennis." He paused, then said: "I'm so sorry to do this, but I have to go. The only person allowed to interrupt me during this time is the prime minister, and he just called."

"Of course, absolutely. We'll talk again tomorrow."

****

Richard ended the call with Rebecca and stood up from his office chair. Putting on his suit jacket, he walked down a flight of stairs and out the back door onto his patio. Richard passed through the L-shaped garden that his home shared with his boss and neighbor, and he nodded a greeting to the security officer stationed at the door to Number 10.

"He's expecting me," Richard said. The guard spoke into his earpiece for a moment before moving aside and letting Richard walk by.

The Chancellor of the Exchequer stepped through the back entrance to Number 10 Downing Street. The prime minister wanted to talk to him in person, and the best way to do that without alerting the press was to walk through their respective back yards.

Richard climbed the stairs to the third floor. The prime minister's executive assistant waved Richard through, and he stepped inside an office to find his boss looking out the window holding a glass of vodka in his hand.

"Starting a little early today, are we?" Richard joked.

"Sit down, Arrington," the PM replied.

Richard stopped smiling and did as he was told. He had known the Prime Minister for his entire adult life, and Richard had never seen him like this. "What's going on, Jack?"

"No sense beating about the bush. I've been diagnosed with Alzheimer's Disease. It's early stages right now, but doctors expect it to progress rapidly. I've spoken with the Queen. We both agreed: I'll stay on through the end of the month, and then you'll be the next prime minister."

EIGHTY-TWO

Three weeks later, Richard trudged up the staircase of 10 Downing Street late on a Thursday night. It was only his fourth full day as Prime Minister, but his feet were heavy, his eyes drooped low, and his stomach rumbled from hunger. *Bugger, I haven't eaten all day.* He knew the job would be difficult, but this was a level of busy and exhausted that was impossible to prepare for.

His cell phone started vibrating in his pocket.

Can they not leave me alone for one fucking second?

"What do you want?" he snapped when he answered the phone.

"Umm, Richard?"

He recognized the young female voice but couldn't place who it was.

"This is Sarah. Sarah Bailey."

Richard let out a frustrated sigh. "Hi Sarah. I apologize for my tone. It's been a long day."

"Oh, no, I'm sorry for calling you out of the blue. I know you're super busy right now with your new job. I'll call your assistant tomorrow and make an appointment."

"No, no. Not necessary. You're family. Family doesn't need an appointment."

"Okay, well, I won't keep you long. I just wanted to call and invite you to come visit. Since you hosted us, I thought we could host you."

Richard shook his head as he opened the pantry door and searched for something to eat. "I can't right now, Sarah. I'm neck deep in the transition. Not to mention the press coverage if I decided to go on holiday to America right now."

"Surely you could slip in unnoticed for a few days?" she asked. "We have a house in upstate New York. Mom is spending the next two weeks there, working remotely. Come visit."

"I wish I could, honey. But your mum understands. I talked to her this morning. She's going to come over here for Christmas when everything slows down and everyone is away for the winter break."

"It can't wait until Christmas."

Richard stopped scrounging for food. "What do you mean, it can't wait?"

"Just come over here, okay?"

"What's wrong?" Richard asked. His face turned ghost white and his heart was pounding.

"I . . . she . . . she made me promise not to tell anyone."

"Including me?"

"Especially you."

"Sarah . . . tell me."

"Just come, okay? I don't know what's going on between you two, but if you value your relationship with my mom, if you still love her at all, come. As soon as you can."

EIGHTY-THREE

No matter what his title or station in life, and no matter how many times he had been there before, Richard still got knots in his stomach every time his car passed through the gates of Buckingham Palace. The five-story building with 775 rooms was as famous as it was beautiful – the London home of Britain's monarchs dating back to Queen Victoria.

Richard felt like an imposter today, even though he knew how absurd it was for the sitting prime minister to feel that way.

Get a grip, he told himself, taking a deep breath and straightening his tie. *You're telling her about a trip, not a coup.*

Even though he didn't technically need the Queen's permission, Richard felt that he owed it to Her Majesty – his boss – to tell her the truth.

Richard drummed his fingers against his legs as he waited to be shown into the Audience Room. He would meet with the Queen every Wednesday afternoon as part of his duties as Prime Minister, but today's audience was special. *Because I asked to see her*, he thought.

A few minutes later, a man in uniform ushered Richard into the medium-sized, tastefully appointed room where Her Majesty held most of her one-on-one meetings.

The Queen held out her hand, upon which he placed a light kiss. "Your Majesty," said Richard, bowing his head.

"A request for an emergency audience your first week in office," she replied. "On a Friday morning, no less. You're lucky the weather was poor in Norfolk today . . . I was supposed to have traveled to Sandringham last night."

"Yes ma'am. Thank you very much for seeing me."

"Well, who died? Who is getting sacked?"

"No one, ma'am. I needed to inform you that I must go to New York for a few days on personal business."

"I hardly think a trip to York is worthy of an audience," said the Queen.

"New York, ma'am. In the United States."

"Whatever for?"

Richard sighed. "I'm not 100% sure. My best friend's daughter called me last night and said I need to go over there. All she would say was that it can't wait, and I need to go."

The Queen was growing more and more frustrated by the second. "Prime Minister, you will find in this job that personal needs must be set aside. You are in service to your country. Your life does not belong to you."

"Yes ma'am, I understand that. I know the timing could not be worse. But she isn't just my best friend. She's the woman I'm seeing . . . the woman I love. The woman I've always loved."

Her Majesty raised her eyebrows in surprise. "I didn't know you were in a relationship."

"Yes ma'am."

"With an American?"

"Yes ma'am."

She nodded. "I've always viewed the role of the Crown to be one of advisement, not control. I will not prevent your travel, but I will advise to use your own funds. Leave now and return before the weekend is over. And have your speech prepared for when it all goes wrong."

Richard let out a nervous laugh at the last part. "Yes ma'am. Thank you, ma'am."

The Queen pressed a button on the table beside her, and the same uniformed servant appeared. Richard knew that was his signal to leave.

"Best of luck to you, Lord Dublinshire," she said. "Love is a hard thing to find, especially in lives like ours."

EIGHTY-FOUR

Following the Queen's advice, Richard chartered the first private plane he could find out of London's RAF Northolt Jet Center. The military airport was often used by Her Majesty and other VIPs seeking complete privacy in their travels. Due to the secrecy of his trip and the element of surprise involved, Richard managed to convince all but one member of his security team to stay in London.

Eight hours later, at 3:00pm Eastern Standard Time, Richard stepped off the plane at Hudson Valley Regional Airport in New York. Gus trotted behind him, followed closely by the protection officer. Sarah was waiting for them in her blue 4Runner.

"Hop in," she said as she climbed into the driver's seat. "Our house is about twenty minutes away."

South of the airport, where Wappinger Creek flowed into the larger Hudson River, Sarah pulled off Old Troy Road and onto her family's large estate. Purchased at the height of her mom's career at Goldman Sachs, the five-bedroom house in Wappingers Falls was Rebecca's refuge from the demands of high finance.

As their SUV pulled to a stop on the gravel driveway, Richard looked out the window and admired the L-shaped, Craftsman style home in front of him. He stepped out of the car and looked beyond the house to the river below. *Amazing. Absolutely gorgeous.*

A man who Richard didn't recognize opened the front door. Richard's heart plummeted for half a second before he noticed the earpiece and coiled communications wire on the other man's neck. *Secret Service*, Richard realized.

His own protection officer stepped forward and shook hands with his counterpart. Looking around, Richard noticed several other security personnel patrolling the area.

"This way," Sarah said. "Mom is on the back patio. She still doesn't know you're coming."

Richard's admiration for Rebecca's house only grew as he walked inside. Dark wood floors and high vaulted ceilings filled the upstate retreat. One bedroom was on the main floor, with another four upstairs. All of them were positioned to have a view of the river. Glancing out one of the windows, Richard saw a separate guest house that had been converted to a command center for the Secret Service.

Sarah opened the door to a wraparound porch that overlooked a pool, yard, and the river. She stepped back and motioned for Richard to walk outside. Gus ran past him and took off toward the water, but he knew the dog wouldn't go far. Richard heard a creaking noise and turned to see Rebecca rocking back and forth in a wooden chair. Richard's heart leapt at the sight of her. Walking closer, he gasped.

"Oh my God, Becks. What happened?"

****

Rebecca jumped at the sound of Richard's voice. Turning in her chair, she saw that she wasn't hearing things. He was there, in front of her, looking as gorgeous as ever in khaki slacks and a green checked button-down.

"What the hell are you doing here?" she blurted out.

"Sarah called me. She said if I ever loved you at all, I needed to come as fast as I could." Richard knelt down in front of her chair and took Rebecca's hands in his. "Baby, you're ice cold."

She shook her head. "It's just my hands. The rest of me is warm."

"Why don't you go inside and sit by the fire?"

"I like the fresh air. The doctor said it's good for me."

Rebecca watched as Richard examined her head to toe. Starting at her thinning hair, down over her sunken cheekbones and pale skin, and finishing with a scan of her thin body that was covered by a blanket. She had lost close to twenty pounds since the last time she saw Richard – two months ago at Rosewood.

230

He let go over Rebecca's hands only long enough to drag another rocking chair over next to her, then grabbed hold of them once again.

"What's going on, Rebecca?"

She could see the worry on his face and hear the fear in his voice. *He never calls me by my full name.* She took a deep breath. "I have cancer."

EIGHTY-FIVE

Richard felt like he had been punched in the stomach. He leaned forward and wrapped his arms around Rebecca's shoulders, pulling her close. They sat like that for what seemed like an eternity, neither willing to let the other one go.

Gus trotted back up the porch steps and nuzzled his way between them, looking for attention. Richard loosened his grasp on Rebecca and smiled. "I guess he thinks I'm only supposed to hug him."

Rebecca leaned over to rub the dog's ears. "Well, of course," she cooed. "You should always be the center of attention, big guy."

Gus responded by raising up and licking Rebecca on the chin.

"Hey now, big brown dog," said Richard. "Don't be moving in on my lady."

Gus snorted, turned around three times, and curled up at Rebecca's feet.

Richard and Rebecca both laughed at the dog's antics. After a minute, though, their smiles faded.

"Tell me everything, Becks. I need to know it all, so I can know how we're going to fight this."

Rebecca pulled her blanket tighter around her shoulders. It was late afternoon, and the cool October temperatures were dropping with the sun.

"It started in my pancreas," she said. "I had some stomach pain and was losing weight, but I thought it was stress from my job. I wasn't hungry all that often, but, again, I thought it was the stress. And that not eating as much caused me to lose weight." She paused. "None of it was a big deal. I was sleeping fine. I wasn't super tired or anything like that. But I woke up one morning and my eyes and skin were yellow. Jaundice. It didn't take the doctors long to diagnose me after that."

"When did you find out?"

"About six weeks ago."

Richard counted backward in his mind. "You felt sick when you were at Rosewood?"

Rebecca shook her head. "Some of the symptoms had started, but again I didn't think it was anything. I didn't go to the doctor until after I got back home. I should have gone earlier – I know that now. But I've always hated doctors." She shrugged her shoulders. "After what happened with John, can you blame me?"

When Richard didn't reply, she continued: "I've always been healthy. A regular check-up seemed pointless, especially when my time was so valuable and scarce with work. Ironic, isn't it? I didn't want to take an hour to go to the doctor, and because of that I may lose thirty years. 'If we had only caught it sooner . . . ' The doctors all tell me that. It's my own fault." Rebecca shrugged again, and Richard saw her skinny shoulder bones poke up through her shirt. "I've always hated doctors."

"It's not your fault that you got sick, Becks."

She nodded. "I know. I didn't smoke or drink too much or do anything else to bring it on myself. It's not my fault that I got sick, but it is my fault that I may not get better."

Richard heard a door creak and turned to see Sarah walk outside to join them. "It's time for your medicine, Mom," she said, handing Rebecca a glass of water and a small plastic cup full of pills. "You should probably get some rest before dinner."

Rebecca swallowed the medicine in one gulp. "She thinks she's my nurse now. Do this, do that."

"I'm making sure you follow your doctor's orders," Sarah replied.

Richard could tell that this wasn't the first time the mother and daughter argued over the issue. He stood up from his chair and offered an arm to Rebecca. "C'mon. I'll help you inside."

233

****

After Rebecca drifted off to sleep, Richard and Sarah went back outside. They walked down the porch steps and over to a small fire pit at the edge of the yard. Richard lit the firewood with a match, and they settled into oversized Adirondack chairs that were positioned to catch the heat of the fire and the view of the sunset.

The beauty of the moment was lost on Richard.

"Give it to me straight, Sarah. What are we dealing with?"

The twenty-seven-year-old let out a deep breath. She looked as if she had aged six years in the last six weeks.

"Stage Four pancreatic cancer. It's spread to her stomach and liver now, too. She's part of a clinical trial for a new drug – that's why she's taking so many pills and looks so run down. We're hoping it'll work, but the doctors aren't very optimistic. I lied on the phone – she's not working remotely. She resigned three days ago. They just haven't announced it yet."

****

Richard didn't talk during dinner. He barely even looked in Rebecca's direction. She wanted to be mad at him. Wanted to yell and scream and tell him if he was going to act like that then he should leave and go back to London.

I can't be mad at him, though, she thought as she pushed her spaghetti around on her plate. *He just found out that I'm probably going to die. Not even two months after he finally convinced me we should be together. Why wouldn't he be angry?*

After dinner was over, Rebecca gave Sarah a goodnight hug and started walking toward her bedroom. She was surprised when Richard took hold of her hand to escort her there. When they reached the doorway, he leaned down and

234

placed a gentle kiss on her forehead. "Goodnight, Becks. I'll see you tomorrow."

EIGHTY-SIX

Rebecca woke up on Saturday morning to the sound of a hammer banging in the living room. She put on her robe and slippers and walked outside to see Richard and two Secret Service agents hanging garland and flowers around the fireplace.

"What on earth are y'all doing?" Rebecca asked. Despite living in New York and Washington for most of her life, she still had a slight Southern accent that popped up from time to time.

Richard turned around, hammer in hand, and smiled at her. "Good morning, beautiful." He walked over and kissed her on the lips. "We're setting up for this afternoon. There's fresh coffee in the pot," he said, nodding toward the kitchen, "and Sarah made a breakfast casserole before she headed out."

"Wait, where's Sarah?"

"She went down to New York City for a few hours. Had a couple errands to run." Richard turned to walk back to the fireplace, but Rebecca grabbed hold of his arm.

"Richard. Arrington. Put down the hammer and tell me what the hell is going on."

The Secret Service agents chuckled at her tone, and Richard smiled as well.

"Let's go in the kitchen," he said. "I'll pour you a cup of coffee and explain."

****

"I stayed up all last night thinking about it," Richard said after they sat down at the kitchen table. "About three o'clock this morning, I figured out what we're going to do. First things first, we're getting married this afternoon. And on Monday morning, I'm going to resign. I'm staying here to take care of you."

"Absolutely not."

"It's already done, darling. Jonathan is on his way from Boston, and Sarah is in Manhattan getting a dress and wedding rings."

"You can't quit your job," Rebecca argued. "I'll be fine. I'm strong, and this new treatment is going to work. I can feel it. Besides, I'll do better knowing that you're over in England fulfilling your destiny."

"What makes you think my staying is to make *you* feel better, hmm?" He took a sip of his coffee. "I hate to break it to you, Madam Secretary, but you are my destiny. You always have been."

Rebecca wanted to believe him. She wanted to give in. *No. I didn't live without him for three decades just so he could become Prime Minister and then give it all up.*

She shook her head. "You can't throw away your life in England. You're the one who told me about all of it in the first place. The title and the family and the estate. How you care what's expected of you and you can't chuck it all away because you don't feel like it."

"I was twenty-two years old," Richard replied. "My father was alive . . . everything was different. I would've given it all up for you back then, but there's nothing to give up now. The only thing stopping us is us."

"And an ocean. And our jobs. And cancer. And – "

"And nothing."

He leaned forward and locked eyes with the only woman he had ever loved. "You told me once that you want the flame that burns the longest. That you don't need the one that burns the brightest. But what you deserve . . . you deserve every light, every candle, every fire flame. Every sun, moon, and star in the sky. Because all of those things combined still wouldn't shine as brightly as you do."

Richard paused and let out a deep breath. "I've asked you this before, and you said no. So, I'm not asking anymore. Marry me, Rebecca. That's an order."

"You're crazy."

237

"Yes. Crazy in love." Richard reached out and grabbed hold of Rebecca's hand. "Listen to me, Becks. I should have fought harder for you in business school. I shouldn't have waited until graduation to say something, and I shouldn't have let you go. We were stupid to miss our chance. And we were stupid to miss it again after the G7 when you came to Rosewood. But I'll be damned if I'm going to lose you to cancer before I ever truly have you."

"If anyone finds out . . . "

"They won't."

"But if they do?" Rebecca shook her head. "You'll lose everything that you've worked so hard to gain. Being Prime Minister is all you ever wanted."

"No. *You* are all I ever wanted. I want nothing more than for your face to be the first thing I see every morning and the last thing I see every night." Richard got out of his chair and dropped to one knee beside the table. "Will you do me the immense honor of becoming my wife?"

"I thought you weren't asking anymore. I thought it was an order?"

"It's whatever you want it to be, as long as you say yes."

Rebecca closed her eyes and nodded her head, then whispered: "yes."

"Yes?"

This time she smiled. "Yes, I'll marry you."

EIGHTY-SEVEN

Jonathan made the three-and-a-half-hour drive from Harvard to the cabin in record time, and he arrived at ten-thirty that morning with his suit and Bible in hand. Although he was skeptical of Richard at first, their time in England made it clear to Jonathan that Richard cared about Rebecca and wanted to make her happy. *That's all that matters*, the young man thought.

"Your reverend has arrived!" he said with a smile as he walked inside the house.

"The reverend?" Rebecca asked.

"Yeah, Mom. Don't you remember? When Joey and Kristin got married in college and they had me get ordained to do it?"

Rebecca shook her head and laughed. "How could I forget? The bridal party wore Hawaiian shirts and hula skirts."

"We'll be a little more formal than that," Sarah declared as she walked through the front door. She had a black garment bag slung over her arm, and she hung it up on the door frame. "I called in a favor with a friend who works at Bergdorf's. He opened the women's department early for me, and I got this." Sarah pulled a knee-length coat dress from the garment bag. It was cream-colored and had a belted waist, a shawl collar, and long sleeves embellished with tiny pearls.

"Oh, honey. It's gorgeous," her mother replied.

Sarah beamed. "I thought you'd like it." She put her tote bag on the floor and pulled out a manila folder. "I also went by the storage unit and got your divorce settlement papers, so you won't have any problems with the marriage license. And now I'm going into the kitchen to start working on your cake." She smiled and clapped her hands together. "Yay! Let's get you two married!"

****

The rest of the day passed by in a blur for Richard. There was the wedding ceremony, with Sarah as Rebecca's maid of honor and Gus as his best man. Jonathan did a wonderful job officiating the wedding, and even made everyone laugh when he joked, "when God said love is patient, he didn't mean you had to wait thirty-five years." After the ceremony came the reception, a party attended by all the Secret Service personnel as well. And then came the hard part: convincing Rebecca to move to England.

"What's the point of being married if we're not together?" Richard asked her. Rebecca was sitting in her bed, propped up against several large pillows. The day had drained her energy, and while she rested Richard sat on the edge of the mattress.

"I already told you," Rebecca replied, "you're not allowed to quit your job."

"I understand that. Which means you have to move to England with me."

She started laughing and began to cough. "No jokes. Please."

"I'm not joking. You can live at Rosewood. I'll commute back and forth. We'll hire the best care in the world. Money is no object – you know that."

Rebecca sighed. "Even if I wanted to, there's no way my doctors would allow it."

"Not true. Sarah called them earlier today. They said as long as you follow protocol and take your medicine, you can do most of your checkups virtually. We'll hire a team of nurses to make sure everything is done properly."

She stared at him. "Move to England with you."

"You already married me," he replied with a smile. "What's the big deal about a change of address?"

It actually was a big deal, and Richard knew that. But he also knew that he was done sacrificing their love for the sake of others. *We're going to be together*, he told himself, willing her to agree with him. *For however long we have left, we're going to be together.*

****

Their plane landed at Deanland Airfield, near the town of Ripe, at nine o'clock on Sunday morning. Originally a Royal Air Base that was a key player in the D-Day invasion, Deanland now served as a private airstrip and was the closest one to Richard's home. *Our home*, he thought as he, Rebecca, and Gus stepped off the plane.

A cadre of three was waiting to greet the prime minister and his new wife. The only three people that Richard would trust with such sensitive information: his longtime assistant, Tricia; his chief of staff, Tripp; and the butler at Rosewood, Mr. Guinn.

Tricia and Tripp climbed in a car along with the newlyweds, while Mr. Guinn and the security agents followed behind them.

"Is everything arranged?" Richard asked.

"Yes sir," Tricia replied. "We've code-named it Operation Starlight. A team of three nurses is waiting for you at Rosewood. They talked with the American doctors and have everything we need. And the East Wing study has been converted into a bedroom so Mrs. Arrington won't have to deal with any stairs."

Richard and Rebecca both smiled at her new name. As their car rumbled down the driveway at Rosewood, Richard took hold of her hand and squeezed it. "Welcome home, Lady Dublinshire."

EIGHTY-EIGHT

Late that night, after the staff and nurses all left, Richard walked Rebecca to the East Wing of the house. He looked around the former study and nodded his head in approval. *Guinn did a good job. It looks like a real bedroom.* The filing cabinets had been replaced by a clothes dresser, the office chairs were gone, and all the medical equipment was hidden from view by a decorative screen. Best of all, a king-sized bed now sat where the desk used to be, and it was positioned so Rebecca could look out the French doors into the garden.

She climbed into the bed, lied down, and patted beside her on the comforter. "Come over here."

Richard smiled. He walked to the other side of the bed, took off his shoes, and slid under the covers to be next to Rebecca.

She turned on her side and placed her hand on his cheek. "Make love to me, Richard."

"Is that . . . I mean, can you . . . ?"

Rebecca nodded and smiled. "I can."

"I don't want to hurt you," Richard replied, his voice barely above a whisper.

She reached out and put her other hand on his face as well, pulling him closer to her. "You won't hurt me. You never could." Her eyes turned hazy, and her cheeks flushed. "Make love to me, Richard."

The scruff of his day-old beard prickled against her skin as Richard kissed her neck, her collarbone, and her chest. He gently pulled her up against him in the bed and ran his hands from her hips up her sides to her ribcage and her breasts, taking her shirt along with him.

Rebecca lifted her arms to slide out of her top and felt a rush of cold air across her bare skin. Soon Richard's hands returned to caress her shoulders and back, and the body that had been cold seconds earlier was now on fire – his touch leaving a blazing trail wherever he went.

Rebecca's skin was soft and smooth – a stark contrast to Richard's rough, masculine body. Rebecca felt his muscles ripple beneath her touch. She started slowly, at his face, and worked her way down over his broad shoulders and chiseled back.

He rolled Rebecca underneath him and braced his weight above her, careful to not injure her.

They kissed and explored each other's bodies for what seemed like a lifetime, and Rebecca supposed in a way it was a lifetime – a life's worth of waiting and wanting and loving – finally culminating as husband and wife. When Richard entered her, slowly, gently, she knew that he had been right all along. They were meant to be together.

EIGHTY-NINE

Richard went back to work the next morning. He woke up at five and was in the office by six thirty. Some of his staff had already arrived for the day, but the press didn't start milling around until at least seven thirty. By the time reporters showed up at 10 Downing Street, everything looked business as usual. Which was exactly what Richard wanted.

He continued that routine through all of November and into December: working in London during the day and spending nights and weekends at Rosewood with Rebecca. The hours were grueling, and he often survived on less than four hours sleep, but it was worth it to be with her. *My wife.* He smiled while sitting at his desk. *Rebecca Lewis is my wife.* The hardest part for Richard was not having Gus at the office with him. His beloved chocolate lab had refused to leave Rebecca's side ever since she arrived in England, and Richard figured that she needed the dog's comfort more than he did. Every morning before he left, Richard would rub behind Gus' ears and give him his instructions for the day. "Take care of her, big guy. I'm counting on you."

At home at Rosewood, Rebecca settled into her own routine. Three different nurses worked in eight-hour shifts. Her favorite one, by far, was the morning nurse: Allie. Allie was young and pleasant but also understood when Rebecca needed space and quiet. She reminded Rebecca of her daughter, and the pair quickly became friends. Allie would bring her magazines from the store and read books to her when Rebecca's eyes were tired. Rebecca's favorite activity, though, was their morning walk. At ten o'clock, when the sun was the warmest and the wind the calmest, Rebecca and Allie would open the French doors in her bedroom and walk out into the garden. Winter weather was in full swing, and when the last of Rebecca's hair fell out, she had to wear a beanie to keep her head warm. She didn't mind the cold, though. Neither did Gus. The chocolate lab always came with them,

244

frolicking in the grass and jumping into the pond at the edge of the estate.

After their walk, Rebecca ate an early lunch and began her treatments. Her diet consisted of lots of fresh fruits and vegetables, and she drank a protein shake with each meal to try to get more nutrients. Most of the time, though, whatever she ate came right back up. A combination of the cancer medication and her pain pills caused the nausea.

By the time the second nurse started her shift at three o'clock, Rebecca was exhausted. She slept most of the afternoon, waking only for dinner and to see Richard when he arrived home.

NINETY

On the second Tuesday of December, Richard got home from work to find the grand hall decorated for Christmas. Garland was wrapped around the handrails, a life-size nativity scene was in one corner, and a giant Christmas tree occupied the middle of the hallway where he and Rebecca held mattress races with her kids only a few months earlier.

As he made his way to the bedroom he shared with Rebecca, Richard saw more and more Christmas decorations. *Where on Earth did they find all of this?* he wondered. Richard pushed open the bedroom door and saw a smaller tree in the corner, decorated with lights and full of presents at the bottom. Christmas carols played from a speaker.

"Welcome home, honey," Rebecca said with a smile. She walked forward, wrapped her arms around his shoulders, and kissed him. "What do you think?"

"I think it looks like Christmas. Where did all of this come from?"

"The attics. The staff was super excited to help me set it all up."

Richard narrowed his eyes. He stepped back from Rebecca and looked her up and down. There was more color in her face than usual, and her cheeks didn't look as hollow. "What's going on, Becks? It's 11:30 at night and you're still dressed. You don't seem the least bit tired. Normally you're lying in bed when I get home."

"A girl can't decide to get dressed up?"

"Becks . . . "

She sighed and walked over to the windows. "I talked to my doctors at the end of last week," Rebecca said, refusing to look at Richard. "The treatment didn't work. It's spread to my lungs. I've got . . . he said weeks. Maybe months, if I'm lucky."

Richard ran across the room and pulled Rebecca into his arms. Tears fell from his cheeks onto her bald head. "I'm so sorry, baby."

"Stop saying you're sorry. I don't want 'sorry'. I don't want pity. I want my life back, and if I can't have that then I want what little time I have left to be happy."

Richard pulled back from the hug and looked Rebecca in the eyes. "That's what's different. You stopped treatment."

"You've seen the x-rays, Richard. The blood tests. Our time together is already limited. The doctors confirmed it on Friday. Can't we just be happy and enjoy what time we have left?"

Richard backed away and shook his head. Every muscle in his body tensed and he felt like he might explode with anger.

"I don't fucking believe this. We're finally together, and now you're giving up!"

"I want to walk through the gardens together. I want to dance together. I want to do all the wonderful things you always promised me we would."

"We will!" Richard replied. "When we beat this, when you're better, we'll do all of that."

"No, Richard. Now. While I still can. If we wait, you'll be dancing with a ghost."

NINETY-ONE

A cold, gray blanket covered the January sky and matched the mood of the small procession as they made the slow walk from Rosewood to the Arrington family plot. Richard's ancestors stretching back hundreds of years were all buried on a small hill in the back corner of the main estate. A wrought iron fence surrounded the cemetery, and many of the gravestones were worn and weather-beaten beyond recognition. The newest stone was his mother's – added a mere eight months earlier after Victoria's stroke. The day had been one of wildly mixed emotions and a conflicted heart . . . which was also how Richard would have described his entire relationship with his mother.

On this day, though, Richard's mind drifted back further: to the first time he crossed this path, his black dress shoes crunching the gravel along the way.

The year was 1971, and his grandfather had passed away after a battle with heart disease. Richard was eight, and the death of the family patriarch elevated his father to the rank of Marquess and young Richie to a Viscount. On that cold and dreary November morning, the new Viscount Arrington looked less like a child and more like a miniature adult – a grown man in a little boy's body, with a three-piece suit to match. His father, the new Marquess, walked with his right hand on Richard's shoulder the whole time, a silent signal of the child's new place in the world. It was a memory made starker by the fact that it was the only time in his life when Richard remembered his father claiming ownership of him. There was a twisted pride on the day the elder marquess buried his father, a happiness he had been waiting for his whole life that could only be achieved by the death of his parent.

Young Richie didn't understand the undercurrents at play on that day so many years ago, but he understood everything today. Every pain, every memory, every breath.

Every crunch of the gravel and every rustle of the trees was implanted in Richard's memory on the day they buried his wife.

A small crowd assembled around the gravesite: the vicar, Richard, Rebecca's children, and Tricia. As the vicar stepped forward to take his place at the head of Rebecca's casket, Richard heard the low rumble of a car approaching. He turned to see the unmistakable Royal Standard waving from the front corner of black Range Rover.

My God, he thought. *She's here.*

A small security detail exited the car ahead of Her Majesty and Prince Philip. The elderly couple, dressed in all black, were humble in their approach and could have been mistaken for family members or friends if not for their famous faces. The pair nodded to Richard and blended in amongst the other mourners.

Rebecca didn't want a big to-do for her funeral, but she acquiesced to Richard and her kids' request for a service on the Arrington estate.

After a brief eulogy by the town's vicar, Richard stepped forward and pulled several notecards from his jacket pocket. His heart was pounding, and his chest felt like it was getting tighter and tighter by the minute. *Thank God we're outside, or I'd be sweating through my suit.*

Taking a deep breath, the prime minister composed himself for the most meaningful speech of his life.

"I've made a living off speaking and speaking well, but my darling Rebecca was the one person who could leave me tongue-tied. It seems I've had both forever and not long enough to prepare for this moment of goodbye," Richard continued. "A final goodbye. But the words fail me today. So, I'll do what all good politicians do: I'll borrow the words of someone else."

He tried to manage a small smile, but it ended up being more of a quiver. His upper lip would have to be stiff another day.

"This is 'Angel'," he said, "by an anonymous poet."

"Tear drops, slow and steady, the
Pain so real and true,
God took another angel, and that
Angel, dear, was you.
Angel wings, upon the clouds, your
Body softly sleeps,
Hush now little angel, no more
Tears you have to weep.
Little prayers are sent to you, the
Short life you led;
Your family will never forget you,
So rest your little head.
I know God will look after you, now
You are truly alive,
Your spirit soars beyond the moon,
Your legacy will survive.
You're beautiful, you're endless,
Now stretch your wings and fly,
You're loved by so many, it will
Never be goodbye.
Close your pretty eyes, no more
Tears, just go and rest,
Let your soul lie peacefully, we
Know you did your best."

Richard tapped his notecards into a neat pile and pushed
them down into his inner coat pocket. Taking a deep breath,
he looked over at the coffin beside him. "You can lie in peace
now, my darling. No more pain. True to form, you beat me
there. And true to us, we're separated once more." He paused
and swallowed back his tears. "I don't know if it will be
another thirty-five years before we're together again. I hope
so, and I hope not. But I trust that thirty-five years is nothing
in the face of eternity, where you shall be mine forever."

****

After finishing his speech, Richard left Sarah and
Jonathan alone to say their final goodbyes. While they stayed
at the gravesite, he accompanied the Queen and her husband
to their car.

"Your Majesty, I cannot even begin to express how
much it means to me that you're here today."

Queen Elizabeth nodded in acknowledgment. "I never
knew your wife," she began, "but I admire her. She made a
large sacrifice in her life to allow you to become Prime
Minister. It was no small feat of strength to put aside a love
like yours in favor of the needs of her country and ours." Her
Majesty paused. "I was raised by a strong woman and fancy
myself to be one as well, so I always admire and feel a
kinship with other strong women – and the men who love
them." She stole a glance at her husband, Prince Philip, and
Richard couldn't help but smile.

"Thank you, ma'am. It's a tremendous honor for Your
Majesty and His Royal Highness to be here today. It means a
great deal. Thank you."

As Richard watched their Range Rover pull back up the
gravel drive, he wondered if he and Rebecca could have built
what they did if given the chance. *Over seventy years of
marriage. Four children. A whole gaggle of grandchildren
and great-grandchildren.* He sighed and looked at the coffin
behind him. *If only, Becks. If only.*

NINETY-TWO

One month later, Phil Davies ran down London Bridge Street toward his office at The News Building. The young, skinny reporter was late for a meeting with his boss, and he pinballed his way through the crowd trying to get to *The Times* headquarters as fast as he could. Phil reached the skyscraper and slowed to a walk, fixing his curly red hair with his hand. Named after Prince Philip, he had a sister named Diana but hated the royals, the aristocracy, and everything they stood for. Phil was on a mission to expose the corruption of upper crust England, and he finally had his first big hit.

"You're late, Davies," his boss barked when Phil knocked on the office door. Archibald Stevens had been with *The Times* for almost thirty years. Dealing with young pups like Phil was his least favorite part of the job.

"I know, I know, but I have a good excuse this time. I swear."

"This time," Stevens rolled his eyes. "I don't know why I haven't sacked you yet, Davies."

"Because I'm charming and talented?"

"More likely because you're my sister's son. Why are you late this time?" he asked. "And it better not be more conspiracy theories about the prime minister."

"Give me two minutes, okay? If you don't like the story after that, I'll never bring it up again."

The editor looked at his brash young reporter. "What's your smoking gun?"

"Huh?"

"No smoking gun, nobody cares. What's your smoking gun?"

Phil smiled. "The prime minister's dog, Gus. He stopped coming to the office four months ago."

"Arrington never goes anywhere without that dog."

"Exactly. So why was Gus suddenly spending all his time at Rosewood? I talked to a technician at the vet – the dog is healthy."

Phil's editor and uncle leaned back in his chair and crossed his arms over his chest. "Okay, kid. Start me at the beginning."

"I got curious when Gus disappeared. I had a chocolate lab growing up, so it's always a fun part of the pressers when Gus comes in and runs around. At first I was worried, right? So I called the veterinarian and some sources I have in household staff . . . all is well with the dog. He was just spending his time at the PM's estate.

"But that didn't make sense to me," Phil continued. "Arrington loves Gus. They're practically attached at the hip. So, I dug a little deeper. Started following the PM's movements more closely. From October until January, he commuted every morning and night . . . never slept at Downing Street anymore."

"Never?"

Phil shook his head. "Never. So, what happened four months ago, right? Why did he spend every night and weekend in East Sussex? Why did he refuse to travel anywhere?" Phil sat down in a chair and crossed his arms over his chest in triumph. "Either he's sick, or he decided he doesn't give a shit and his staff is running the country."

"I highly doubt the latter."

"But don't we have a right to know? Why it started and why it ended just as fast?"

Stevens nodded. "We do. Dig more. Fill in the story. Then bring it to me and we'll see where it goes."

Phil jumped up from his seat with a huge smile on his face.

"Slow down, son. Don't go anywhere, do anything, or say anything until you give the prime minister and Buckingham Palace a chance to comment. Understood? We deserve the truth on this, but not at the expense of everything else we're working on."

Phil nodded his head. "Yes sir. Understood."

NINETY-THREE

Tricia Howell's phone rang the next afternoon.

"Mrs. Howell? This is Archibald Stevens with *The Times*. I'm sitting here with one of my reporters, Phil Davies, and we have a few questions for you."

"All press inquiries are run through the Director of Communications."

"I spoke with him a minute ago," Stevens responded. "He transferred me to you."

Tricia furrowed her brow in confusion. "I'll do my best. You're probably going to get a 'no comment' on each question, though."

Five minutes later, Tricia hung up the phone, crossed the room, and knocked on the prime minister's door. She didn't wait for a reply before going inside Richard's office and shutting the door behind her. "Sir, we need to talk."

"I'm busy," Richard said as his thumbs typed on his cell phone.

"This is more important."

Richard looked up at Tricia and saw the fear on her face. "What's wrong?"

"*The Times* has the story. Not all of it, but a lot of it. The commuting, the refusal to travel, Gus staying at Rosewood." She paused. "I said 'no comment' on everything, but we should give them some kind of response before the story breaks."

"I don't have to tell them anything," Richard replied. "It's my life. My *personal* life. It didn't, doesn't, and won't affect my job performance in any way, shape, or form. Besides, all they have is speculation. I was sleeping at one house instead of another. It'll blow over. Trust me."

Tricia nodded and left the office but shook her head as soon as the door was closed. "It won't blow over," she whispered to herself. "He can't hide this forever."

****

Three days later, Richard sat at his desk surrounded by newspapers. The front page of every outlet in the country blared headlines calling him a liar, a thief, and a coward. Most of them also demanded that he resign. Richard rubbed his forehead with his hand, hoping to make his headache go away.

He heard a knock on the door and looked up to see Tricia standing in front of him.

"Don't say it," he told her.

"Don't say what?"

Richard raised his eyebrows, and she nodded in understanding.

"Well, I did tell you so, sir. But that's beside the point. Now we focus on fixing it."

The prime minister sighed and ran his hand through his hair. "There's nothing to fix. I didn't do anything wrong. I didn't misuse public funds. I always made sure my work was complete before I left for the day. Surely, I'm not the first prime minister in history to lose a spouse while in office. Or get married while in office for that matter."

"That's not the point, sir. It's not about the money, or the commuting, or Rebecca."

Richard flinched at the mention of his wife's name.

"It's about the deception," Tricia explained. "The people think you're lying to them. And the longer the questions go unanswered, the more outlandish the theories will be. I understand why you kept it quiet. I do. But it's time for the truth. Before the media invents its own truth and we're all sunk."

Richard sighed and nodded his head. "You're right. Set up the press conference."

"Yes sir. Do you want me to send in Carlos to work on your speech?"

Richard shook his head. "No. I'll be writing this one myself."

256

"I'll make a brief statement," Richard said, "and I will not be taking any questions. Nor will my staff." He paused. "I will begin with the most important information: I have neither stolen nor misappropriated any public funds. I have not lied under oath. And Her Majesty has been fully informed of the entire truth from the beginning."

Cameras clicked and clacked, and murmurs rose through the group of reporters.

"So it's all a lie?" someone shouted. "The whole story is bollocks?"

Richard opened his mouth to respond, then stopped. He let out a deep breath and ran his hand through his hair.

"*The Times*' story accused me of many things. Lying. Stealing. Cover-ups. Those things," he conceded, "are all true."

The crowd rumbled again. "C'mon, mate. Give us the truth!"

"The truth?" Richard asked. "All right. Well, settle in. Because the truth is thirty-five years in the making."

He looked down at the cobblestones in front of him, paused, and let out a deep breath. Silence filled the air, with dozens of reporters in the street and millions watching at home all waiting to hear their prime minister try to explain away the growing scandal.

"It's hard to know where to begin," Richard said, his voice full of emotion.

He sighed again, and a car alarm blared in the distance. Richard closed his eyes. When he opened them, they glistened with tears.

"I suppose I shall begin by saying that everything in *The Times* report is true. I did fly to America four months ago without disclosing the trip. Up until last month, I was commuting regularly from my private home in Sussex to London. And I have had a large increase in expenses lately –

all of which were paid out of my own personal accounts, for which I have records and receipts." He paused. "That's all true."

Richard picked at the edge of the podium with his fingernail. "I also intentionally hid those facts from the public."

The prime minister stood up straight and his voice regained strength. "What's not true are the rumors that I am ill. I'm in excellent health, as confirmed by my annual physical last week. And the speculation that I am involved in some form of illegal or immoral enterprise is unequivocally false. I informed Her Majesty of everything that was happening and, more than that, received her blessing."

Murmurs began to rise in the crowd. Phil Davies' working assumption in his article was that Arrington had gone rogue. *If the Queen was involved*, the reporters wondered, *what was going on?*

The prime minister paused and let out a deep breath. The bastion of English aristocracy looked up at the sky and back down at his feet, unsure how to continue.

"Thirty-five years ago, I enrolled at Harvard Business School. September of 1984. Back in those days, you took all your classes with the same set of people. By sheer circumstance, or perhaps providence, I was seated next to one of the few women in the school. I promptly proceeded to fall in love with her.

"A variety of circumstances," Richard continued, "my cowardice and her stubbornness among them, prevented us from being together. But for thirty-four and a half years, I loved her from afar." A slight smile creased his face. "Nearly every journalist here today has asked me at some point why I never married. I always said I hadn't met the right woman. Well, that was a lie. I had met the right woman, but she married someone else."

Richard shoved his hands in his pockets and gripped the engagement ring box as hard as he could.

258

"Four months ago, her daughter called me. Her mum, my classmate, had gotten divorced several years earlier. I knew that – we stayed in touch over the years. But anyway, her daughter called me and told me that I needed to go to their house in America. No explanation. Just 'come now.' So I did."

He paused and blinked back tears.

"She had cancer. Stage Four. She did chemo and radiation, and even joined a clinical trial for a new medication. The only fight we ever had was me trying to convince her to continue treatment here in England. Full disclosure, since you're already learning all my secrets today, my first plan was to resign and move there to care for her. She refused that offer, but I did get her moved to England and a medical team set up here. At my family's estate in East Sussex.

"The night of our graduation from Harvard," he added, "I asked her to marry me. She said no. Four months ago when I asked again, she said yes."

Richard covered his mouth with his hands, and a long silence filled the air.

"We lost her a month ago," he concluded. "She was a fighter, but the cancer was too far progressed. There wasn't anything else we could do.

"Those three months together – even with the cancer and the commuting and the secrecy – those three months were the happiest of my life. This past month, without her, well, the light has gone out of my world." Richard paused and sniffed back tears. "Even while I loved her from afar, although I couldn't be with her, I knew she was happy. That was enough. But now she's gone." Richard dropped his voice to a whisper. "She's gone."

He took a deep breath. "I said at the start that I lied, I stole, and I covered up. That remains true. I lied about some aspects of my personal activities in order to protect the privacy of my family. I stole a few precious months with the love of my life, after being separated from her for far too

259

long. And I covered it all up to keep her safe. Even though, in the end . . . in the end I couldn't keep her safe at all."

The prime minister closed his eyes and bowed his head, once again reaching into his pants pocket and grabbing hold of his grandmother's ring for strength. *Rebecca's ring*, he thought, correcting himself. One of Rebecca's final instructions to him was to take the ring off her finger when she died.

"I don't want to bury it in the ground for all eternity. I want it to stay with you. As a symbol of me and our love."

Richard squeezed the ring box, but this time he brought it out of his pocket and held it in his hands. "When I was ten years old, my grandmother gave me this ring. It was hers – my grandfather had it custom made for her when he proposed. Abuela gave it to me and told me to keep it somewhere safe until I met the right woman.

"'But how will I know she's the right one?' I asked. And Abuela replied: 'when you are together, all of the stars will align. Every star in the sky.'"

Richard flashed half a smile at the memory and held the ring box up higher for everyone to see. "I kept this ring in my nightstand for forty-six years. Rebecca wore it for three months. But it was – and always will be – her ring all along."

Richard heard the crowd begin to rustle and cameras start clicking again, with the reporters seeking to capture the moment. He stood up straight and squared his shoulders, letting out a deep breath of defiance.

"I will not resign. I will not resign because I have done nothing wrong. I have faithfully served Crown and Country whilst coming through this whole ordeal, and Her Majesty The Queen was apprised of my situation and my wife's condition from the beginning.

"Now you, the public, know the truth. I am a man as well as a minister. I eat, sleep, breathe, and even love just like the rest of you." Richard adjusted his tie. "Now, if you will excuse me, I have a country to run."

EPILOGUE

Late that night, long after the rest of the staff went home and the exhausted prime minister retired to his private quarters, Tricia Howell stood up from her desk and walked toward her boss' office. Even though she knew no one was around, she still glanced over each shoulder to make sure. Then slowly, carefully, she opened the door to Richard's office.

The room was empty, as expected, with his desk covered in a laptop, an external monitor, and scattered stacks of paper.

Tricia smiled and shook her head. *He insists he knows where everything is in all those piles, but I don't see how.* Stepping forward, she scanned the papers for the object of her late-night search. *Ah ha! Here you are*, she thought, picking up the small set of notecards that contained Richard's planned speech for the day.

Having worked for her boss since he graduated business school, Tricia knew Richard better than anyone else in the world. She knew that he preferred coffee to tea and took one cream and two sugars. That he had his suits made at Desmond Merrion on Savile Row – each costing upwards of £50,000 – and that he secretly did yoga in his bedroom every morning.

Picking up the notecards from the desk, Tricia also knew that Richard hadn't used them at all during his speech. He looked at the cards, to be sure, but his mind was pulling information from somewhere else. Tricia was positive that she was the only person to notice, and now she wanted to be the only person to know the truth.

"What did you plan on saying?" she asked aloud.

Glancing back down at the desk, Tricia saw the unmistakable royal coat of arms stamped on an envelope.

The note from Buckingham Palace, she thought. *It arrived right before he went down for the press conference.*

Looking over her shoulder once again to make sure no one was watching, Tricia picked up the envelope and pulled out a handwritten card.

Lord Dublinshire – I know your plans for today as discussed at our last audience. I write now to urge you to reconsider your offer of resignation. I cannot imagine performing my duties without Philip by my side, and you should face no penalty for seeking out Rebecca and caring for her. I have found, over the years, that my prime ministers govern best when their home life is full of love.

Elizabeth R

###

ABOUT THE AUTHOR

Danielle knew she was born to be a writer at age four when she entertained an entire emergency room with the – false – story of how she was adopted. *Every Star in the Sky* is Danielle's seventh novel. She lives in Georgia with her husband, daughter, and two dogs.

Please write a review on Amazon to let Danielle know what you thought of the book!

Find out more about Danielle and her books on her website:
www.daniellesingleton.com

Follow Danielle on Instagram: @auntdanwrites

Like Danielle's Facebook page:
www.facebook.com/singletondanielle